Whiskey & Honey

A Country Road Novel

Andrea Johnston

andrea johnston

Whiskey & Honey
(A Country Road Novel)

Cover design by Uplifting Designs, www.uplifting-designs.com

Editing by Kristina Circelli of Red Road Editing, www.kristinacircelli.com

Interior design by Stacey Blake of Champagne Book Design, www.champagnebookdesign.com

ISBN-13: 978-1979108409
Second Edition

Dedication

For my husband.
Thank you for showing me true and
unconditional love.

Whiskey & Honey

Chapter 1

Ben

I felt it deep in my bones the minute she walked through the door.

What "it" is, I'm not quite sure. When the door opened I felt a shift in the atmosphere. As if someone lit a fire that burned only in my soul. My attention caught, I was bamboozled. This girl, no more than five feet tall, managed to drown out the sounds around me without even noticing I was in the same establishment.

Handling the large wooden door of Country Road as if it weighed no more than a feather, she seemed both determined and frightened as she walked through. Tossing her hair, the color of the most violent fire, over her shoulder, straightening her back and tilting her chin up in determination, I enjoyed the view as her hips swayed in perfect tempo to the drum solo coming from the speakers and she walked across the room. The way her jeans complement every curve, she not only has my mouth feeling like the Sahara

Desert but my dick has suddenly awoken from its recent hibernation.

It isn't either of those things that have me ignoring my friends though. No, it's something about the fierce way she has made her entrance yet not made eye contact or smiled at a single person as she made her way to the bar. Even from here, without so much as speaking a word, I can tell that she is something special. A woman made up of layers and layers of intrigue. Someone who I have to know.

"Dude, are you even listening?"

"I don't think he's heard a single word any of us said since she walked in. His dick is obviously in charge tonight."

I hear those assholes; I just don't have anything to contribute to whatever debate they're having. Besides, Owen is right. Somehow my normal level-headed self seems to have left the room and my previously mentioned dick *is* in charge tonight.

All of our lives I've been the logical and straight-laced one in this group. Suddenly a sassy redhead has taken all of my logic and tossed it aside. I'm acting like a pubescent teen. The problem is, I'm quite a few years from being a teen, and even when I was, I never had this reaction to a woman.

Nope. I, Bentley James Sullivan, am the good guy. The guy who approaches life with a plan and never does a single thing without one. Hell, I even plan spontaneity. Yeah, I teeter on the edge of boring.

I take another drink of my beer as I turn to Owen. "Kiss my ass. I heard you, and for your information, Iron Man always wins."

Without a second thought I return my attention to the

beauty who has garnered all of my interest. She's made her way to a stool at the bar and is waiving her arms around as if she's the conductor of an orchestra. I can tell from the expression of the bartender, also my sister Ashton, that whoever has her this fired up should stay clear of her.

The only time her hands still is when she grabs the shot glass my sister has placed in front of her. From where I'm sitting I can see that she doesn't even shudder as she takes the shot of dark and beautiful whiskey. I don't care what anyone says, there's something fascinating about a woman who drinks whiskey. Just the thought makes me smile.

"Why don't you just go over and talk to her, Ben?"

I shoot a look at Jameson over my beer bottle as I drain it. My best friend since, well forever, he knows I'm not the "hook up in a bar" kind of guy. But, I won't deny this girl has sparked a little something. Something familiar tugs at me, but I can't place it.

"Nah, I'll pass," I say unconvincingly. I really want to go over to this girl and tell her the fucker who made her this upset isn't worth it.

I'm not psychic, but honestly what else could have her this upset?

The reality is, guys are dicks and the only person who could make a woman this upset.

Don't get me wrong, we're not all assholes, but the reality of it all is we screw up.

All the fucking time.

I sit here with three variations of the asshole to good guy makeup in front of me. The four of us have been best friends since high school, more like brothers than anything else. When I accepted a college scholarship that took me more than three hundred miles away from home, I assumed we'd grow apart, that *I* would grow apart from the four of them. I was wrong.

Owen Butler and Landon Montgomery are two of the coolest and most loyal friends a guy could ask for. We've had each other's backs through a lot of dumb shit, and not only managed to stay friends but we've never screwed each other over either.

Jameson Strauss is like a brother to me. When we were kids we were convinced we were some sort of dynamic duo considering my middle name was close to his first name. Only the reality is that my middle name is a family name and he was named after his dad's favorite whiskey. Regardless, we didn't care and thought it made us pretty bad ass.

Jameson is the best person I know and gives to others without a second thought. I would trust him with my life. Of course, he's also a bit of a slut and has probably screwed half the women in this town, but he's not a bad guy. Sure, a few have declared their undying love and begged him to do the same. For the most part he's managed to come out of each encounter unscathed and unattached.

Then there's me. The relationship guy. I've had two girlfriends in my twenty-nine years. Well, two real girl-friends. Stolen kisses on the playground and the occasional hand-holding in middle school don't count.

"Ben, why are you staring at..."

Before Owen can finish his sentence, Jameson spills his beer.

"What's your problem, J? That was a rookie move," Landon says as he starts wiping at the spilled beer with his hand.

"Sorry, I thought there was a bee or something. I just jumped."

All three of us look at Jameson like he's crazy. Unfazed by our confusion, he signals for a waitress to come over to our table with a towel.

"Hey, Beth, sorry about the mess," Jameson says, offering this poor girl a smile that is a little predatory. I can tell from her reaction to him that there's a little history there but not in a bad way.

"Beth, this is Ben. Ben, this is Beth."

"Hey there, Ben. You look familiar, have I served you before?"

"Nah, Bethy, Ben's been gone from home for a hundred years. I think the last time he was in here we had fake IDs. He probably looks familiar because he's Ashton's brother."

Bethy? Good God, he's laying it on thick.

"Oh, *Bentley*. Ashton was just telling me that you were moving back. Does she know you're here? You should go say hi to her; she's just at the bar talking to…"

"So anyway, thanks for cleaning up. Looks like you're busy. We don't want to keep you."

This poor girl, Jameson doesn't even let her finish a sentence before he's sending her off.

"Hey, Ben, why don't you just take that twenty and go grab us another round? I've got a little spill here in my lap or I'd do it myself."

I don't need to be told twice. I grab the money and head to the bar. I already know I'm screwed.

5

Chapter 2

Piper

"He's a fucking douchebag and you should have let me cut his balls off when you first found that profile."

That's my bestie for you. Ashton Sullivan is always the girl I want in my corner, especially when my dickhead of a boyfriend tells me that he was only online dating to find us the "perfect fit." Call me naïve, but at first I had no idea what he was trying to say. Fit? For what? Then I realized he meant for sex. He acted like he was doing me a favor by dating other women.

"Ash, really? You wouldn't actually cut off his penis so just stop."

"Balls. His *motherfucking balls*, Piper. And for you? Yes, I would. Tony Dominguez would be walking around town sans balls if I had my way. Now drink this water and I'll get you another shot. We've got boot camp tomorrow morning and, while I fully support your plan to get shit-faced, you need to hydrate," Ash dictates as she slides a water my way and makes her way to the end of the bar to help a customer.

I cannot believe this is my life. I'm a good person. I recycle, minimize my swearing, only drink on the weekends, and use my blinker! If using my blinker doesn't just scream, "I'm a good person!" I don't know what does. Fucking Tony Dominguez. He's screwed me up so bad I'm not only swearing but drinking on a weeknight. So what if I'm not actually working right now, that's beside the point.

My phone indicates another text message, which should be followed by the phone ringing in 3, 2, 1 … there it is. I hit the ignore button before Luke Bryan can even ask me to shake it for him. Showing my phone whose boss, I flip it the bird before I suck down the water Ashton gave me so I can have that promised shot.

A threesome. Screw him. When he told me he wanted to spice it up a little in the bedroom, I figured we'd go to the adult store – three towns over – and pick up something together. No, his idea of "spice" was dating other women to find us the "perfect fit."

I'm not a prude. I'm not. I may be a little conservative but I'm also open-minded. I just don't like to share and I also don't want to sex up a lady. Sure, I think women are great and can appreciate an attractive woman as much as the next person. It's just that, well, I just like penis. A lot.

I also liked Tony. All six-foot, sexy, and Spanish-speaking Tony Dominguez.

Last night was like any other second Tuesday of the month. I was snuggled up on the couch in my coziest pajamas getting ready to pay bills while Tony was at his weekly basketball game. Unfortunately – or fortunately depending on how you spin it – I hadn't charged my laptop so I grabbed

Tony's. Imagine my surprise when I opened the top to find him still logged in to HookingUp.com. He wasn't even trying to find a "perfect fit" on something sweet and kind dot com. Nope, hooking up. Fucker.

"Fuck off!" I mutter as I tap the ignore button on the screen as the alerts of another string of text messages begin. I already know what they say. *"It's not what you think. I love you. We can work this out. Why are you being so stubborn? You really need to get over it. Fuck this Piper. I'm sorry."* On and on again. It's been this way since about fifteen minutes after I found the website.

"Pipe, just block him, for shit's sake." A shot of whiskey and a beer chaser appear in front of me.

Ashton Sullivan has been my best friend most of my life and tends to be a little bossy when it comes to my relationships. Of course, she's usually right, and has been my go-to for all the important things in life since we bonded over our love of all things shiny and pink at the tender age of five. Ash has been my protector, my own personal cheerleader, and the strongest shoulder to lean on when life has handed me a crap sandwich.

By the time we were approaching double digits, I was suffering from a severe case of puberty. Unruly hair that was less the dark auburn it is now and more a peach-color, bargain bin glasses, and a pudgy middle section were just the highlights of my awkwardness. Then the day came that Ashton and I found the glory of hair products.

My mom also found a job with good insurance, specifically vision insurance, and new glasses added to my less unfortunate look. Both of these simple things led to more confidence, less name calling, and fewer reasons for Ashton to channel her inner bodyguard.

Then my boobs made a sudden appearance. Any confidence I acquired quickly diminished. I suddenly found myself on the receiving end of a different kind of attention. Attention I didn't understand and frankly didn't want. Seeking comfort not only from Ash but from Ben & Jerry, I began to bury my nose in books and pack on the pounds. Truthfully, considering the amount of weight I was carrying, I was spending more time with Ben & Jerry than Ashton.

When we started high school, Ashton found a new level of popularity almost immediately. This wasn't a surprise to me considering her older brother's legacy. Bentley Sullivan was four years older than us in school, a senior when we stumbled onto campus as over eager and ill-prepared freshmen. Bentley was as close to a celebrity as we had in Lexington, and when he accepted a scholarship and moved away after graduation, the popularity torch was passed on to Ashton with ease.

As her social calendar filled, it would have been easy for Ashton to cast me aside for her cooler and less awkward friends. She never did. Instead of going to parties after the football games Ash would curl up on the couch with me, a pint of ice cream, and cheesy horror movies. If I'd let her she'd have the term "hos before bros" tattooed on her body.

More alerts of text messages and my phone ringing only add to the latest crap sandwich in my life. I rest my head in my hands as I rub my temples. Why am I such an idiot? And, why haven't I blocked Tony yet? Probably because I know I'll talk to him and consider taking him back. Not because I'm a glutton for punishment, but because it's Tony Dominguez.

He's not *the* guy that my teenage dreams … okay maybe my current dreams too … were made of, but he was a close second. When he asked me out I felt special. When we hit our six-month anniversary and he told me he loved me, I thought it was a fairytale come true. I realize he's less Prince Charming and more of an ogre, but he chose me. That has to mean something, right?

I *may* also be a smidge sick of being treated like shit and feel like unleashing that on Tony. You don't have Ashton Sullivan as your best friend your entire life and some of her not rub off on you. Tony may just deserve the wrath of all the cheaters before him. Just as I have this thought Carrie Underwood comes across the speakers and a smile takes over my face. I don't think I have it in me to actually cause damage to his car, but I can fantasize about it.

I look up at Ash and wink as I take the shot glass and let the liquid goodness slide down my throat. She just shakes her head at me and walks back to the other end of the bar while she laughs.

I begin peeling the label off my beer as I have the same conversation I have had with myself every time I'm in this position. I don't need to ask the reasons my boyfriend picker is broken, I know. I've always known. Since I was five years old and fell off the swings on the playground and a handsome brown-eyed boy helped me up out of the sand.

Bentley James Sullivan.

The man of my dreams.

My best friend's brother.

Chapter 3

Ben

While I've only been in two relationships, I consider myself a catch. I'm intelligent, a great conversationalist, a gentleman, and in all honesty I'm good-looking. I keep myself fit and my beard trim. Yes, a beard. My mother would prefer me clean shaven, as did Laurel, my recent though serious ex-girlfriend. I, on the other hand, like the beard. The first thing I did when I walked out of my former place of employment was toss my razor in the garbage.

And then take it out of the garbage, rinse it off, and set it back in the cabinet. That shit was expensive. Plus, I was going from a private school teacher's salary to a much smaller town's elementary school teacher's salary. That's not even apples to oranges, that's filet mignon to canned meat. Big difference.

I grabbed Jameson's twenty and made my way toward the bar. Toward the sexy vixen I was going to charm and hopefully snag a phone number from. Worst case, I'll strike out, say hi to my sister, and grab a few beers for the guys.

In true small-town fashion, I am stopped a half-dozen times by guys and gals I grew up with, including Mrs. Nori.

"Bentley Sullivan, as I live and breathe!"

"Mrs. Nori, how are you?" I ask as I scoop her up into a hug.

"Clarice, dear. We're colleagues now."

After a few minutes of small talk and a promise to meet for coffee and get the "down low" on the students, I once again start toward the redhead. I watch as she flips off her phone, looks at my sister, takes another shot of whiskey, and slams the shot glass down on the bar with a huff. Before I can make it to the girl who has bedazzled me, I see my sister making her way to this end of the bar.

I find a space between an older couple and a guy I played little league with just as he vacates his spot. I nod to him in appreciation and acknowledgment seconds before I snap my fingers over the bar and annoyingly shout, "Can I get some service here, barkeep?"

A cocky smile takes over my face as my sweet sister turns around to tell the rude customer snapping his fingers to fuck off and instead sees me. Even with my beard, Ashton Marie knows her brother. Releasing a squeal that would give a high-strung toddler a run for his money, my little sister runs around the bar and leaps in my arms.

"Asshole!"

"Monkey nuts!"

Terms of endearment between siblings.

I set my baby sister on her feet as she jumps up and down like that same toddler. I grab her face between my hands and she finally stills. I place a quick kiss to the top of her head.

"I missed you, monkey," I whisper. I have missed her. While I came home as much as possible, the last year or so I have managed to only make those trips when Ash was out of town.

"I missed you too. When did you get in? Why didn't Mom call me? Why didn't *you* call me?"

"Whoa there, turbo. I got in a few hours ago and I assume Mom didn't call you because, well you *are* working. And me? I figured I'd just grace you with my presence instead. You're welcome."

"Screw you. You smell like whiskey and beer. How long have you been here?"

Busted.

"Not long. I'm with the guys," I say as I motion toward the other end of Country Road.

"Mmhmm, whatever. I'm so excited you're home. Mom has been driving me nuts since you called. I think we should start looking for a place together tomorrow!"

"Umm, Ash, I love you but I'm not getting a place with you."

"We'll see. Look I have to get back to work. What can I get you?"

"Umm, another Jack and a beer? I'll go down to the other end of the bar where it's less crowded."

"Okay, let me grab those for you." She returns to her side of the bar and pours my shot, which I gladly take and enjoy the burn as it makes it way down my throat. "I'll be down in a second, I have to make another round of Red-Headed Sluts for the group of business men in the back."

The minute she says "red-headed" I feel it in my jeans. Fuck I have never been this hot for someone when I haven't even seen their face. I nod in agreement as Ashton begins making the line of shots and I make my way to what I hope … well, I don't know what I hope but I have a feeling about this girl.

I'm within two steps of her when I see her look at her phone again and toss it on the bar hard enough to make it bounce.

"I think you owe that phone an apology," I say in a voice that is suddenly gravely and husky.

I watch as she straightens her back and inhales deeply. I can see a blush begin in her arms, freckles ever so slightly appearing on her sleeveless arms.

"My phone has a thick skin; I think she can handle it."

Honey, her voice is like fucking honey. Smooth, thick, and sweet. Dripping with enough sass to draw me in and enough sugar to make me stay.

I sidle up next to her and place my beer on the bar, resting my elbow on the bar as I casually adjust myself in my jeans. The moment I catch her profile I'm a goner. There's no going back from this girl.

Clearing my throat, I reach for a strand of her hair and twist it between my fingers as I smile. "You never know; she could be hiding her softness behind her sass. Maybe you just broke her poor heart."

Fuck, when did I become a chick? Seriously, I need to man up. But this girl - sassy, beautiful, and a voice that would probably have me coming in my pants if she read the phone book - she has me all screwed up.

Then she turns to me. Perfection. Eyes the color of my

favorite whiskey with an array of golden sparkles, it feels like time stands still. Her lips are heart-shaped with a natural color that looks like she just spent an hour kissing like her life depended on it. Her skin is like those creepy dolls my Nana had sitting on the guestroom bed: porcelain. Jesus, now I have fucking ovaries. What's next? A vagina. My body will swallow my dick and I'll have a vagina. Fantastic.

I tilt my head as I take her in. As I thought from across the room, something about her seems familiar. I know I've never met her because, if I had, I'd remember. This is the type of woman you never forget. The type of woman who haunts your dreams.

"So tell me, sweetness, who is the asshole that has you all wound up and taking it out on your phone?" I ask as I take a long drink of my beer. I notice her eyes follow my tongue licking the excess beer from my lips. I suddenly wish I was more like Jameson and had it in me to take this girl home. Well not *my* home obviously, but somewhere.

"What makes you think it's a guy. And please, don't call me sweetness."

Just as she finishes her sentence her phone rings and I notice the name "Tony" appear as she hits the red ignore button. I don't know what possesses me, but I grab the phone, click the camera icon and the little button to make the camera forward facing before I grab the back of her neck and take those kissable lips with my own. I manage to keep enough of my senses as our lips meet to snap a picture before I toss the poor hurt feelings phone on the bar and grab her head in my hands to deepen the kiss. Her lips open a little as she lets out a slight purr and that's all the incentive I need to plunge my tongue in her mouth, where I'm greeted by her own tongue. This must be what heaven is because I can't get enough. I can taste the mixture of my whiskey and her whiskey with every swipe of my tongue and it's intoxicating.

"OH MY GOD, BENTLEY JAMES, GET YOUR TONGUE OUT OF PIPER'S MOUTH!"

I jerk back as a wet towel hits my face. The moment I do I watch as the whiskey-colored eyes staring at me fill with tears. Suddenly the keeper of those enticing lips is scurrying off the stool and quickly makes her way across the room. I turn to look at my sister, whose hands are on her hips, eyes ablaze and lips pursed.

Shit. Piper? No way that was little Piper.

"What the hell, Ash?" I ask as I toss the towel on the bar and grab a stack of napkins to wipe the side of my face.

"What the hell? Are you fucking serious? I walk over to see if you need anything and find you with your tongue in my best friend's mouth and you ask me what the hell?"

Whoa. Piper Lawrence.

"*That* was Piper Lawrence?" I ask, completely bewildered.

"Yes, that was Piper Lawrence. Are you high? Jameson, talk to him and tell him he can't go around molesting Piper while I go check on her."

I grab my beer and finish it off in one drink while I motion to the other bartender for another and turn to Jameson, who is now sitting in the spot Piper just vacated. Fucking Piper. I can tell by the shit-eating grin on his face, Jameson knew exactly who had peaked my interest when he sent me over here.

"You dick. You knew it was Piper, didn't you?"

"Of course I did. I live here remember? So, how was it?

God, she's a hot piece of ass. Too bad she's always dating a bunch of dicks; she's probably a hot mess."

I don't know what comes over me, but Jameson's assessment of Piper sets me off. I grab him by the arm and jerk him toward me as I grit between my teeth, "Don't fucking say that about her."

He shrugs me off and puts his hands up in defense. "Whoa, buddy. Relax. Sorry. Damn, that girl did a number on you. It was a kiss, dude, not like you're in love. Plus, Ash will never let that happen. She's been protecting Piper their entire life and you know her motto, hos before bros."

We each grab our beers as they are placed on the bar in front of us, taking a long drink before another word is spoken.

"You knew who she was before I walked over here? You're an asshole. All of you. Those two schmucks in on it too?"

"Relax, Ben. You're all fired up. Like I said, I'm perfectly aware of Piper. We all are. I thought you'd come over here and try to flirt, unsuccessfully I might add. Figured you'd have a good laugh that you were picking up on your little sister's friend and that would be that. I had no idea you were going to put on some real moves and kiss her."

"I had no idea I was going to do that either. I can't believe that's Piper. She seemed familiar but I couldn't place it."

"Yeah, well a lot has changed around here since you've been gone, not just Piper's looks. The occasional twenty-four-hour visit doesn't exactly allow you time to get up to speed. I'm not sure how you didn't recognize her. Ash is always taking selfies of them."

"Honestly?" I ask, and he half nods and shrugs in

response. "I don't pay attention to Ash's pictures. I sound like a jerk, I'm sure, but I've never paid much attention."

"Well, whatever the reason, that's Piper. She's cool and fun to hang out with. Girl has shit luck with boyfriends but she's part of us and your sister is still her self-proclaimed bodyguard. Speaking of, we should probably get out of here before the she-wolf returns to give you an earful."

As I'm about to agree with Jameson and suggest we get out of here and correct his nickname of my sister, Piper's phone goes off again. Against my better judgment I pick it up and swipe the screen to see that it's that Tony guy again, but this time it's a text message. I open the text message to see "She meant nothing. Call me." This Tony must have cheated. I don't even give it a second thought, I click respond and attach the photo of us kissing with "I'm busy" before I hit send. Fuck that guy and his stupid "she meant nothing." Piper deserves better.

I motion for the bartender and hand him Piper's phone before I turn to Jameson. "Let's roll, I don't have the patience for the shit storm my sister is going to bring. I've only been home for five hours."

As we head for the door, my mind is spinning with what just happened and I wonder what the fuck I just did. I'm not sure what pathway to Hell I opened but I'm sure of one thing: a single kiss from Piper Lawrence won't be enough.

Chapter 4

Piper

"Pipe, let me in."

"No. Go away, Ash, please."

I can't do it. I cannot look at Ashton and see the disappointment in her eyes. I just made out with her brother. With *Bentley Sullivan*. That's not even the problem. The problem is that I'm not sorry. I've waited my entire life for that moment. Blame the whiskey, blame the fact that my boyfriend has been cheating on me, blame it on the fucking rain. I don't care. It was fantastic, and lord help me but I want to do it again.

The moment he started flirting with me I knew he had no idea who I was. That stung a little, but when I realized this was my only opportunity for a moment as someone other than his little sister's best friend, I took it. And fuck me if it wasn't worth every minute I'm going to spend lying to my best friend telling her it was awful.

His lips are like soft caramels I felt myself melting into.

The moment his tongue touched mine I could feel it all the way to my toes. Of course, it took an excellent detour in my panties along the way. I feel something on my foot and look down.

"What are you doing, Ashton?"

"Well, if you aren't going to let me in, I'm going to just crawl on this disgusting bathroom floor and under the stall door to get to you. It's really gross down here, I'm going to need to talk to Taylor about this. Eww, is that pee?"

I open the stall door and laugh at the ridiculousness of this moment.

"I don't think its pee; this is the women's restroom. Get up, that's gross," I say as I tug at her hands to pull her up. I see the sympathy in her eyes and realize I maybe had one too many shots tonight as I burst into tears.

Ash gathers me in her arms and is rubbing my back as she tries to reassure me that she'll deal with her asshole brother and make sure he never pulls a stunt like that again. For some reason this sets me off even more. Of course, she thinks it is because I'm upset about Tony, upset Ben just gave me the best kiss of my life, and I'm drunk. She's got one thing right – I'm drunk.

"Ash, I need to go home. I'm sorry. I'll get a cab and I'll call you in the morning."

"I understand. Let me walk you out and make sure you're okay."

We stop by the bar to grab my phone and Taylor lets us know he already called a cab for me. I attempt to open the compartment on my phone case that holds my debit card when Taylor waves me off from paying. I let Ash guide me out of the bar and say a little prayer I won't see Ben along the way. The wait for my cab is minimal and once I'm inside Ashton heads back in to work and I head home.

Bentley Sullivan. Even thinking his name makes me touch my lips. I cannot believe the direction this night took. I went to Country Road because Tony was, is, a cheating bastard and I needed my best friend and booze. I never expected to have one of my teenage fantasies come true. Then real life resurfaced and now I find myself drunk in the back of a cab driven by the man who used to be the crosswalk attendant when we were kids regaling me with stories of his own drunken nights. Fabulous.

Mr. Denning pulls up to my apartment and argues with me over the fare before I agree to keep the money and take my mom for coffee instead. I wave goodbye and make my way up the stairs, sobering up a little with each step. I unlock my door and feel my phone vibrate in my hand. Once I make it in the door, lock the door behind me, and toss off my shoes I allow myself to look at the phone. It's a text from Tony. Apparently I'm a glutton for punishment because I open the text.

Tony: What the fuck Piper!

As soon as my eyes finish reading his text I glance up to see what he's talking about. Someone sent him the picture of Ben and me kissing with a comment. Oh shit, that's funny. I grab a bottle of water from the fridge before I head to my bed and throw myself down on it. I can't stop laughing. The idea of Tony receiving that text is more than I can handle. Imagining his face when he opened the picture throws me into a bigger fit of giggles.

I click on the picture so that it fills my screen and my heart flutters. Seeing the kiss sends my lips tingling at the memory. I've kissed my share of guys, not a boat load or anything but enough, and thought they were good kisses. But, I was wrong. Those kisses, in fact all the kisses before Bentley Sullivan, were mediocre at best.

This time in response to Tony's text I power off my phone and crawl under the covers, not even bothering to change my clothes. I fall asleep to the memories of Ben's voice, his hands on my face, and his soft lips. I'll deal with the repercussions tomorrow.

Tomorrow is minutes after I fall asleep, or so it seems. I am jarred awake by a banging on my door. I glance at the clock to see it's eight in the morning. Shit, I missed boot camp. This can't have come as a surprise to Ash considering my state when she put me in the cab. I throw back the covers and slowly make my way to the front door. I open the door to the aroma of freshly brewed coffee and a greasy bag of goodness.

"You are a goddess," I say to Ash as she pushes past me and straight to my small living space. I live in a small apartment so I have very little furniture, but have managed to make it homey and mine.

"Yes, well that is always the case, but today I have to say I'm in agreement. You look like death and smell like you slept in a bed of whiskey." Offering me a smirk, she hands me a coffee and a bag that is already sporting grease stains from the piece of heaven I know waits for me. A breakfast burrito from Rosa's.

"Please tell me this is the meat lover's," I mutter as I stuff my face with the deliciousness.

"Of course. I know you and what you need after whiskey. I'll give you a minute to devour that burrito and maybe shower before we talk about my brother's attack on your poor mouth."

I guess it was wishful thinking to assume Ash would let this go. I take another bite of my burrito before rolling it back up and putting it in the bag. I set the bag in the fridge and head toward the bathroom. I recognize I haven't responded and I'm sure Ash will think it is because I'm upset about the kiss. The reality of it all is that I need to get my game face on. There is no way I can tell her it wasn't an attack. That I welcomed it and wouldn't turn down an opportunity for it to happen again. Ash is a lot of things, but I know for a fact she wouldn't be okay with me having a thing for her brother.

I turn on the water and strip off last night's clothes. As soon as the water hits my skin I feel the tingles everywhere. I stand under the hotter-than-normal water for a few minutes before slipping in my shower routine. Once I am sufficiently free of last night's ick and the lingering smell of whiskey I towel off and wipe the mirror of the steam.

Looking back at me is a tired girl who is losing herself in these loser guys she's been dating. I shake off the pitiful thoughts as quickly as I let them surface. I brush my teeth – twice. And manage to feel more human by the time I put on some lounge wear and grab my phone off my nightstand. I make my way out to the living room and plug my phone in before powering it up.

Ash is in the kitchenette washing my dishes. That girl cannot go a day without cleaning something. It's almost compulsive but beneficial to those she loves. My phone is just powered up when she flops herself on the couch next to me and my phone starts going off with every type of alert available. Text messages, voicemail, e-mail notification, and private messages. I groan as I start with text messages. Three more from Tony, two from Ash this morning, and one from an unknown number.

I delete all of Tony's without reading them. I laugh at Ash's texts and hit her with the pillow.

"Really? I'm the asswipe for missing boot camp? *You* are the bartender that got me drunk!"

We are both laughing as she grabs the remote to turn on the TV and I click on the unknown number.

Unknown: I stole your number from Ash's phone. Don't be mad. I wanted to make sure you're ok.

I don't have to know who the number belongs to; I know it's Ben. I sneak a peek to Ash and make sure she's distracted before I respond.

Me: I have a horrible hangover but I'm okay. Ash brought me Rosa's, all is well. Thanks for checking on me.

Learning from last night's crapfest of texts, I turn the sound off my phone so any response doesn't send an alert and set my phone down. Deep inside, okay not so deep just pretty much on the surface, I am giddy that he found my number. But, hos before bros and all that.

Ash and I spend the next few hours just watching television and taking the occasional cat nap. By mid-day I can feel the tension mounting and am bracing myself for the moment Ash hits me with the Ben confrontation. When she gets up to use the restroom, I grab my phone to check for texts. I see a few more from Tony – delete. Then I notice three from the unknown number, which I quickly change from "unknown" to "B," then click on the text icon.

Ben: Rosa's. Jealous. I just had a bowl of cereal and wheat toast. Not even a comparison.

2 minutes later:

Ben: I should be sorry about last night but I'm not.

Ben: Sorry about that. Pretend this never happened.

Of course he's sorry. No matter how far I've come I'm still Piper Lawrence, frizzy-haired chubby best friend of Ben's little sister. Regardless of how much time has passed and how much we've aged, he is still Bentley Sullivan and completely and utterly unattainable. But, for a brief moment, I allow myself an opportunity to imagine a life where a Bentley Sullivan wants more than a bar kiss with a Piper Lawrence. I grant myself that daydream knowing good and well it'll never happen.

"What has you looking all dreamy?"

I'm startled by Ashton's voice as she throws herself on the couch next to me and tosses me a water.

"Nothing," I say, shaking my head. "Just a one of those hot guys with a cat meme. You know hot guys don't have cats. I'm bored and could stand getting out of here, how about it?"

"Uh sure, but a quick talk? First, how are you holding up with this Tony bullshit? My offer still stands to cut off his balls."

I smile and nudge Ash with my foot. "Ha-ha, I think we should leave his balls alone. Oh my God! Do you thinking he's been having sex with the girls he finds on that site? What if ... what if he has *a disease*?" The last part comes out almost a whisper. I hadn't thought about that. Crap.

"Oh, Piper, I don't know. He's obviously a lying bastard

so we should probably get you to the clinic. Sorry, babe. I know its borderline inappropriate but I kind of told you. Remember how Tony was in high school? He was a total man-whore." I offer her a raised brow and begin to reply. "Yeah, yeah, I know," she says as she waves her hand in the air dismissively. "He's not a good guy. Remember what a dick he was to Ben?"

I do remember. I hated the way Tony was toward Ben. Even though Ashton and I were only in school a year at the same time as Ben and Tony, I knew enough from spending my free time at the Sullivan's' that the rivalry between Tony and Ben was epic. Competitive by nature, the guys were always competing for a starting position. The rivalry only intensified when Ben and his high school sweetheart, Claire, were nominated for homecoming king and queen every year. Tony hated all of the attention good-guy Ben received. I have to give Tony some credit though, while he was obviously not putting my feelings first when he was off canoodling with girls from that dating site, he never said one negative thing about Ben while were together. He knows how important the Sullivan family is to me. Plus, I think he was a little scared of Ashton and didn't want to piss her off by talking smack about her brother.

So, yes, I certainly remember. "And?" I ask. She looks at me, confused. "You said first, which implies there are more points to make."

"I hate when you get all teachery on me. Fine, *and* my brother shouldn't have kissed you like that and I'm sorry. I know how disgusting that must have been. I'll have a talk with him and make sure that never happens again. God, what a jerk. I swear, that's what he gets for hanging out with

Jameson Strauss. Talk about man-whore. That guy is disgusting and I bet his dick falls off one day."

I do love when Ashton gets riled up about Jameson. That girl has been crushing on Jameson about as long as I've crushed on Bentley. Jameson has never seen Ash as anything other than Ben's little sister and it drives her nuts. When we were in high school and Ben was gone, Ash hoped that was her chance at putting the moves on Jameson, but he rejected her at every turn. Personally, I think that Jameson hasn't given Ash the time of day because he may actually like her. Ashton is challenging and that is something Jameson doesn't experience often. No, Jameson usually has girls flinging their panties at him like he's a rock god. Which, by the way, he isn't. If there is one thing Jameson Strauss lacks, it's a singing voice. But, like she said, man-whore. I don't think there's a girl in this town Jameson hasn't spent time with.

"Umm, well…" Do I dare say anything? "So, maybe it wasn't so bad," I say rapidly as I stand up and slide my feet into a pair of flip-flops and head toward the door.

"Whoa. What now? It wasn't *so bad*? Do you mean you *liked* it? You liked kissing my brother?" The squeak in her voice stops me and I turn toward her. Her eyes are so big they look like little green saucers and her mouth is formed into some sort of grimace that is slightly laced with exasperation and very laced with horror.

"What? No, of course not. I didn't *like* kissing your brother." I see the tension leave her face and eventually her shoulders. Relief. I see relief in her previously shocked eyes. I don't dare tell Ashton that I actually loved kissing her brother. That a kiss from Bentley Sullivan set my soul on fire as easily as it triggered something in my lady parts

I've never experienced. Yeah, it's probably best I keep that to myself.

"I just mean, well, it wasn't awful. So, you know, don't make a big deal about it, okay? Let it go. It was a drunken night. I just found out about Tony and he just moved back. Hey, maybe someone saw and word will get back to Tony I moved on or something. You should be thanking your brother!"

I know Ashton Marie Sullivan better than I probably know myself. I know when she's assessing and in this moment her assessment is about to blow my nonchalant attitude out of the water. I offer her a raised brow and a slight smirk to show I'm not taking this kissing thing too serious. She smiles and heads my way.

"Thank goodness, because that shit cannot happen again. It not only grossed me out, causing me to have really bad dreams about you and my brother making babies, but it's just bad news. It was just wrong on so many levels." She dramatically shudders as she walks passed me and heads down the stairs. I love that girl, but now I can't get that visual out of my mind as I lock the door. Before I turn toward the stairs my phone vibrates.

Ben: I've thought about it. I'm not sorry. Can we meet?

How do I respond to this and not completely ruin my friendship with Ashton? I shouldn't respond. I should let it go. It's true what I said to Ashton, it was just a kiss. Bentley doesn't know the depth of my childhood crush. He probably just wants to clear the air so it's not awkward. Nothing major is brewing; this is just friends. Totally just friends. Friends meet for coffee.

Me: Come by my place tonight. 8pm
Ben: Can't wait. 8pm

Sometimes a girl has to throw caution to the wind and hope the wind doesn't blow her away.

Chapter 5

Ben

I let a smile take its place as I glance at the text again. Talking is good. We'll talk. I'll apologize for kissing her. I won't mean it but I'll apologize.

A knock at the door pulls me from my self-imposed pep talk. Before I can make it to the front door, Jameson is walking through the living room.

"Why knock if you're going to just walk in?" I ask him as I grab my wallet and put it in my back pocket.

"I knock because your mama would have my ass if I didn't. I walk in because I've been walking in that front door almost as long as you. Wait, probably longer since you've been gone for close to a decade. Where is your mom anyway? I need some Patty hugs."

I ignore his comment as I walk past him and out the door. "Shut up. Let's go, I'm starving and itching to get my hands on some of Rosa's tacos."

Other than my family and friends, food is what I've

missed most from Lexington. Sure there are incredible restaurants in the city, but the good, stick-to-your-ribs food that you get in a small town can never be outdone by a five-star restaurant with portions the size of half dollars. The minute I read Piper's text mentioning Rosa's I knew I had to have it and sent Jameson a text to pick me up.

"Explain to me why I had to drive across town, past Rosa's by the way, to pick you up when you have a perfectly good car sitting right there?" Jameson asks me as he motions to my sedan parked in front of the house.

"What if I just wanted to spend time with you?" I joke as I climb up into his monster of a truck. "J, what are you overcompensating for? This truck is fucking ridiculous."

"If by ridiculous you mean awesome, then yes it is. You're one to talk, Mr. Yuppy Sedan. What are you trying to hide? Do *you* have something to tell me? You lose yourself in the city?"

I know he's teasing, but the reality of his words hits me hard. I did lose myself, and I never realized how much until we left the bar last night. Those few hours with my friends I felt more like Bentley Sullivan than I have in a long time. Add to that the stolen moments with Piper and that kiss, well it all came at me like a meteor. I felt more alive by the time I got home than I can ever remember. Something about that girl made of a little whiskey and honey had me seeing things clearly.

I'm pulled from my thoughts when I hear Jameson clear his throat. I glance over at him, noticing he hasn't even started the truck yet. "Well? Did you? I have to say, last night you seemed more like you than you have in a long time." I let out a sigh as he starts the truck and pulls away from the curb.

"Truthfully, it was the most like me I've felt in a long time. Speaking of, I wanted you to pick me up because after we hit Rosa's, I want to stop by Sully's and check out a truck I saw on my way into town."

"Shit, what's next? Ya wanna go fishing?"

"Not today, but yeah."

Jameson shakes his head and snorts. I'm not sure if it's a snort in disgust or agreement.

"Come on, J, you know I've been drowning the last few years. Quit giving me shit, will ya? Just drive," I say as I reach to turn up the music. I let my arm hang out the window. A deep inhale and I know that my move was the right one. I feel my phone vibrate in my pocket and won't even lie that I hold a little hope that it is Piper telling me to come over earlier. Only, it's not.

Laurel: I'm not trying to be weird but I kind of miss you.

It's not weird. I miss her too, but it's not romantic. *That* is the weird part.

Me: It's not weird. I miss you too. How's my TV?

Laurel: Jerk. Its fine and enjoying all that the Hallmark channel has to offer.

Me: Please tell me that is a lie! But really, you doing okay?

Laurel: Ok, I'll tell you it's a lie. Yeah I'm good. It's just different.

Me: I get it. I'm about to grab lunch. Talk later?

Laurel: Sure. TTYL

"Okay, pussy, we're here," Jameson declares as he jumps down from his truck. I'll never understand the need to have raise your truck so much you need a damn ladder to climb in and out. Seriously, this thing is ridiculous.

"Whatever. You good with stopping by Sully's after we're done here? Don't you have a business to run?"

"Nah, I'm good. I worked it out with Owen. I am at your disposal all day. Which I'll remind you of this weekend when you are the DD and I'm kissing girls at the bar," he smugly replies as he opens the door to Rosa's.

The minute the door opens, my senses are in overload. I'm not even going pretend to know what exotic spices and ingredients Rosa has brewing in the kitchen, nor do I care as long as they end up on my plate. Before I can even get three steps in the door my stomach is rumbling in agreement. Just like last night at Country Road, I see a few familiar faces and nod in acknowledgment as I make my way to the counter.

"Ben Sullivan!" Rosa shouts as she makes her way around the short counter with her arms extended for a hug. Another thing I missed from home, the hugs.

"Rosa," I sigh as I scoop her up into a hug. Rosa and my mom have been friends all of my life, and even though her son is a self-centered dill weed, I love her. "How are you? It smells amazing in here. I've missed you."

She laughs at me and swats me on the arm, "Oh hush up. You didn't miss me, you missed my food. I know your mother must be thrilled to have you home."

"What about me, Rosa? Am I chopped liver?" Jameson exclaims as he opens his arms for a hug.

"Jameson Strauss, you are in here at least five times a week, chopped liver my left toe. Give me a hug, you big lug."

Once hugs are complete and orders placed, Jameson and I grab a spot at a corner booth. An awkward silence takes over our table.

"So things…"

"What are…"

We both say simultaneously and laugh. Jameson gestures for me to go first.

"So things with Owen are going well? Him working for you and all that?"

Jameson owns his own construction company, and when the market tanked it looked like his business would, too. Now that things are turning around, he's been able to grow his crew, including bringing on our down-on-his-luck buddy, Owen. I don't know how the two of them work together and maintain a friendship. Jameson can be a class A jerk and I'm sure one of us would be walking around with a black eye most days. More power to them, I'll take thirty ten-year-olds any day.

"Yeah, it's cool. We had a few issues in the beginning but worked through those. It helps that I put him with a different crew than I work with. He's actually on a trial run as foreman on a project. If all goes well, it'll allow me to take on more jobs with two of us leading a crew."

"That's good," I say as our order is called out from the counter. I get up to grab the tray and return to the table. Neither of us talks for a good three minutes as we begin to devour our food. You'd think by looking at us that we hadn't eaten in days. After the first three tacos I sit back a little and take a drink of my iced tea.

"So, as I was about to say before I was rudely interrupted," he says. I offer a huff of minor annoyance in response. "What are you going to do about the Piper situation?"

The million-dollar question. "What do you mean? What situation?"

"Um, I mean the big game of tonsil hockey you played last night? What else do you think I mean? Ashton must be crazy pissed off."

"First, tonsil hockey? What is this, 1978? Second, I haven't seen Ash but I imagine she's going to want to rip me a new asshole considering how she flipped out last night. You know, you could have told me it was Piper."

"Could've, should've. Whatever. I wanted you to have some fun for a change. Shit, man, I know you loved Laurel but that girl is a total buzzkill. I figured if a girl across a bar caught your attention like that, why not let you have a little fun. And you did, didn't you? Have fun?"

I did. I can't deny it. And I was very much caught by that girl. Damnit, I'm getting hard just thinking about our kiss. Her lips - so plump, like little cherries ready to be sucked. Fuck, think of old ladies and cats puking. Anything to get this rapidly growing hard-on under control.

"Dude, you're thinking about her right now, aren't you? One kiss and you're fucking whipped! I figured you'd at least wait a few months before you married up again." Jameson's hostility is not something I expected. I sit there for a few seconds as he gets up and tosses his tray in the trash, heading for the door.

I follow suit, but instead of being a childish ass I wave goodbye to Rosa and thank her for the delicious food. As I make it outside I find Jameson just standing off to the side, head thrown back facing the sun.

"What's your problem, man? You're acting like a jealous girlfriend." He is, too.

"Look, I'm sorry. It's just that I figured you'd come back to town and we'd have the crew back together. I guess

I expected us all to hangout and enjoy the rest of summer. The lake, grilling out, the usual. Oh and maybe, call me crazy, maybe meet some girls…" He stops himself from finishing the statement and begins making his way through the parking lot. I fall in step with him.

"And?" I ask. There's more and we might as well get it all out now.

"Fine. In there?" He motions toward Rosa's. "You looked like a teenage girl thinking about her first crush. How long until you're finding a way to start seeing Piper? I'm sure you'll sweet talk your sister and it'll be just like high school with me playing third wheel."

"Okay first, your vagina is showing. Second, what the fuck are you talking about? I've been home like eighteen hours and you're already marrying me off? And, to my little sister's best friend? You and I both know that will never happen unless I want to lose my balls. Ash is going to lose her damn mind about this entire thing and won't accept that I didn't know it was Piper. Besides, I just got out of a relationship and have no business getting into another. So just relax will you and stop being a jealous girlfriend."

We both start laughing, and he takes his ball cap off and rubs his hand through his hair before placing it back on his head and looking at me. "My vagina? You really are a pussy. Let's go to Sully's."

And just like that, we're back to normal. This is why I can't be the guy who hooks up at a bar. There are far too many dynamics to consider and apparently feelings for everyone in a fifty-foot radius.

Three hours after Jameson picked me up from my parent's house in his monstrosity of a truck, I have managed to secure a trade-in for my sedan with Sully. With an agreement to bring the sedan back tomorrow and promise to bring him a piece of my mom's pecan pie, Sully granted me permission to drive my new-to-me truck home. Living in a city, having a truck never made sense, but here it is the only thing that does. The truck I found is actually the same one I had in high school; well, except about twenty years newer. It seems that every hour I'm home I'm one step closer to being me again, and being me never felt so good.

I pull up to the house and see that my sister's car is in the driveway. I am so not ready for this conversation. I love my sister and she really is one of my best friends, she's just a little spirited. Well, I say she's high strung, feisty, and overly dramatic. My mother calls her spirited. I suppose there is no time like the present to face the wrath of Ashton Marie Sullivan.

With every step toward the house, I feel more and more like a man walking the plank. Something about the way Jameson reacted to my kissing Piper isn't sitting right. I recognize that my kissing her, any woman for that matter, in a bar is completely out of character for me. I can't even begin to understand my reaction to her. It was something I've never experienced and, quite frankly, if someone else had told me they had this response to a woman I'd probably demand he turn in his man card. I feel like one of those ridiculous Hallmark movies. Only, I don't see how this story will have that cheesy happy ending each of those movies does. No, I imagine I'm going to walk through this door and my sister is going to rip me a new asshole and I'll feel shitty and apologize and make promises that will suck. Promises I'll probably hate making but I'll keep because I'm the good guy.

I'm within four steps of the door when I hear Ashton's sweet voice. My sister has a magnificent singing voice and can make a grown man cry with her rendition of *Amazing Grace*. When we were growing up my parents saw Ashton's talent early on, and while I was running bases and practicing my swing, she was in voice lessons. Jameson and I used to joke when we were in high school that we were going to kidnap her one night, drive to the open auditions for one of those singing competition shows on television, and make her buy us extravagant gifts to thank us.

We joked and never followed through. Not because Ashton doesn't have the talent or doesn't deserve the recognition. To the contrary, Ashton would make it far in any competition. Not only is she talented beyond comprehension, cute - in a stubborn and annoying little sister kind of way - she is also one of the kindest and most outgoing people I know. Unfortunately, Ash also suffers from panic attacks. The idea of being in front of a crowd of more than the Thursday night karaoke regulars at Country Road sends her into a full panic attack. Not a "she's a little stressed" attack, no Ashton has these frightening attacks that paralyze her and find us rushing her to the hospital.

That's why there was only teasing of the kidnapping and plans for extravagant gifts and no golden ticket to Hollywood.

I put my hand on the handle to the screen door and take in a deep breath. Ass, hold on because I have a feeling you're about to get chewed out.

"Quit being a pansy ass. Get in here so we can do this," Ash commands before I can even take a step in the door.

"Pansy ass?"

Ash turns from the sink where she's washing vegetables from Mom's garden. As she grabs a towel to dry her hands, I am taken aback a little. My baby sister isn't a baby anymore. We may only be four years apart in age but growing up that seemed like a million. I spent half my time threatening my friends and the other guys in school with their life if they so much as looked at my baby sister. Most of the jerks listened. I'm sure a few snuck around behind my back, but for the most part I managed to keep Ash protected from the douchebags around town. After I left that job fell to Jameson and he has assured me that while she's dated, Ashton has been more focused on trying to figure out where she's going in life than who she's going with.

Ashton is full of spunk as usual but there's something else in her eyes. I know it's been a tough year for her and she's less than thrilled to be living back home with Mom and Dad but I wonder if it's something more. Thankfully, her sass outweighs the sadness.

I ignore the look she's shooting my way and open the fridge to grab a beer. I pop the cap off and take a seat at the island before another word is uttered by either of us.

"Well?" I ask.

"Well? That's what you have to say? Well?"

"How about ladies first? That better, Ash?"

"Ugh! You are so infuriating, Bentley. What was that last night?"

"What do you want me to say? Sorry? Okay, sorry."

Ashton stops her foot in frustration and tosses her

hands up in the air. I smile and take another drink of my beer.

"You should have one of these," I say, motioning toward my bottle.

"I couldn't agree more, but I have to work in an hour," she replies, taking the seat next to me.

I nudge her a little with my knee and she lays her head on my shoulder.

"Please don't hook up with Piper, Ben. She's been screwed over so much and I don't want to see her hurt."

"Gee thanks, sister of mine. So much confidence in me I see."

"I'm sorry. It's not you. You're the best guy in the world and if you weren't my brother you are the exact guy Pipe should be with. It's just…"

She pauses and turns toward me. I follow suit and look at her. Are those tears?

"Ash, what's wrong? Are you crying?"

"What? No. Okay, maybe. I don't know. It's just that Piper is my best friend and you're my brother. If you hooked up and it didn't work out, I'd be in the middle. I don't want to lose my friend and I don't want to have to hate you and say awful things about you in the name of sisterhood. So just do me a solid and don't hook up. Please?"

"First, don't cry. It's not that serious, okay?"

She nods.

"Second, I don't plan on hooking up with anyone. You know Laurel and I just broke up. Besides that, I just moved back to town and am living with Mom and Dad. I'm in no position to start something up with anyone, Piper or not."

Ashton smiles at me and it looks as if a thousand-pound

weight has been lifted from her shoulders. As her brother I am happy to be the one to relieve some of that stress. As the man who experienced the best kiss of his life less than twenty-four hours ago, I feel defeated.

"You promise? You won't start something up with Piper? Last night was just a mistake?" she asks me hopefully.

"I promise. I will not start anything with Piper. But can I ask you something?"

A little reassurance from me seems to be all she needed because the usual pep is back in Ashton's step as she hops off the stool and back toward the sink to her vegetables.

"Sure, shoot."

"When did Piper get so hot?"

I can't help it. I'm the big brother, it's my job to piss her off.

Ashton turns to me with a mischievous smile on her face. "Piper has always been hot. Boys are just dumb and it isn't until they're men that they appreciate what's always been there."

Touché.

Chapter 6

Piper

What in the world was I thinking inviting Bentley Sullivan to my apartment? More importantly, why did he accept? He obviously lost his mind when he moved away. It's the only answer. No, he was abducted by aliens who replaced his brain with someone else's. Yes, that's it. That's what makes sense.

It does.

Don't question rational thinking.

Okay, fine. Perhaps he wasn't abducted by aliens. And, perhaps, he hasn't lost his mind. He was obviously drunk and didn't know what he was doing last night. There is no actual reason that makes sense as to why he would so openly flirt with me and then kiss me.

A kiss that I swear I can still feel.

A kiss that seemed full of promises and questions equally.

A kiss I have dreamed of most of my life.

A kiss that made me forget stupid Tony and his stupid ideas of relationships.

I've been a bundle of nerves all day. Ash was trying hard to avoid the topic and it only made my anxiety worse. Besides the anxiety, it cast this weird vibe over our day and made me uncomfortable around the only person in my life who has never made me feel awkward. After breakfast and a little retail therapy she drove me back to my place.

As I turned to open the door, I couldn't take it anymore.

"*Are you mad at me?*" *I asked.*

"*What? No. Why would you say that? I've never been mad at you a day in my life.*"

"*Not true. You didn't talk to me for two hours when I declared my undying love for Joe Jonas.*"

"*Hmm. That is true. You knew I was going to marry him and you still called dibs. Uncool, sister friend. Uncool.*"

"*Yeah well, he proved us both wrong, didn't he? No ring on either of our fingers.*"

"*Eh, it's cool. He couldn't handle either one of us anyway.*"

"*I just want to make sure we're okay. That thing last night with your brother. It was just a random bar thing. No biggie.*"

Oh yeah. I'm a liar. Big fat dirty liar.

"*I know. I just … I don't want to see you get hurt again. Ben and Laurel just broke up. You and Tony just broke up. Plus, while my brother is a great guy he does hang out with the douche crew so, you know, birds of a feather and all that. He may pick up on their nasty habits and you don't need that.*"

"*Oh please, Ben is definitely one of the good guys. But you're right. I don't need to start anything with anyone. Its best we just forget about it. I probably won't even see him around much.*"

It may be best if we all forget last night happened, but there is no way, in this lifetime, I'll ever forget. I'm just glad I had a breakdown and ran for the sanctuary of the women's restroom instead of declaring my undying love to Ben. I can't even imagine the humility that would have followed that kind of proclamation.

I glance at the clock and notice I still have about an hour before Ben said he'd be here. Again, what was I thinking? I wasn't. Obviously.

I pick my phone up and realize I never turned it back on after the tenth text from Tony while we were shopping. I hit the power button and set the phone back down as I head to the shower. I'm not primping or making an effort. Nope, I just cleaned my place and need to freshen up. Totally not anything special or anything to do with Bentley Sullivan.

Nope. Nothing. Nada.

I take my time in the shower. I mean, I'm here I might as well shave and deep condition my hair. It's absolutely all about efficiency. Nothing to do with Ben.

I almost believe myself.

A little pep talk in the shower calms me down enough to think rationally about tonight. This is my best friend's brother. Practically *my* brother growing up. We were both drinking, he didn't know it was me, I was sad. All a big misunderstanding.

I'm going to keep tonight casual. No candles burning, no music, no effort. I grab a pair of my soft-as-butter leggings, a loose-fitting top, and my favorite fuzzy socks. Really sealing the casual, no-effort look is my messy bun with toweled-dried hair and only a little mascara and some gloss for makeup.

I have managed to use up thirty minutes. Perfect. I light a candle on the mantle - strictly for the scent, not the ambience, obviously. I'm still not putting music on or putting forth any effort. Two out of three shower plans is better than none.

I have a few minutes to spare so a little glass of courage or, as regular people not about to discuss a life-altering kiss with their best friend's brother call it, Chardonnay.

Just as I'm about to check my phone there's a knock at my door. Of course he's early.

I take a sip of my wine as I open the door. Only instead of Ben, it's Tony. Great.

Tony slithers in the door before I can stop him.

"Hey, I didn't invite you in," I say, still standing with my hand on the door handle and the door open.

"Come on, babe, when have you ever needed to invite me in?"

"Don't *babe* me. We broke up. Please leave."

He's made his way to the fridge and already opened a beer before I finish my sentence. He really is handsome. *And a cheating jerk, Piper.* Don't forget that. I'm still standing at the door but have released the handle as he places his beer on the counter and begins walking toward me.

"Piper, you didn't mean it. Let's make up."

I know that look. It's the same look he's used on me the last few weeks when he's been late for dates, cancelled at the last minute, or didn't do either and just didn't show up. I assume now that he was out looking for the "spice." Asshole.

"Tony, I did mean it. We are finished and I would like for you to leave," I say while crossing my arms over my chest. I know that this is technically a defensive position, but suddenly I feel vulnerable and need the hug, even from myself.

"I'm not leaving until we work this out, Piper. Come on, I'm sorry you got pissed but I thought it would be fun for us. I didn't know you were going to get all Miss Priss with me."

Is he kidding me? Miss Priss.

"I'm willing to forget your little stunt last night with whoever that asshole was. I know you were just trying to get back at me. We'll call it even. Now, let's watch a movie and start the making up."

"I don't think so. The lady asked you to leave."

Oh, shit.

"Who the fuck are you?"

Oh, you know who he is. This is not going to end well.

"Tony, you know damn well who I am. Now, I believe I heard Piper ask you to leave. Why don't you do us all a favor and just go," Ben says as he makes his way directly behind me and places his hand on my shoulder.

I can feel the heat from his hand through my top and a shiver makes its way down my spine. I uncross my hands and stand up straight. Just knowing Ben is here and has my back has me feeling more confident. Before I can demand he leave, I see the recognition register on Tony's face.

"Sullivan. Of course you're the one to come to her rescue. Wait."

Here it comes. Recognition begins to turn to rage. If steam could actually come out of a human's ears, Tony's would be a smoke stack.

"That was you in the picture. What the fuck, Piper? Him? That's how you're going to get back at me? Of course it is. You really are a little slut, aren't you?"

"Whoa there, pal…"

What a dick.

I turn toward Ben. "I've got this."

His smile says that he'll give me this moment even if he really wants to punch Tony in his stupid arrogant face.

"Look, first I am not a slut. You, on the other hand, may be. I wasn't the one out cheating, you were, so before you start throwing words around, take a look in the mirror." Kudos to me, I managed to get all of that out even though in my head I was confident and sassy. In real time, it was a single sentence without a breath.

I feel Ben lean down just to my ear. "Breathe, Piper."

I offer a little nod and continue.

"What I do and," I motion toward Ben, "who I do it with is none of your concern. You lied, you cheated, and you hurt me. I'm done. You need to leave. Please, for once, Tony, just do what I ask."

The tension in this room is thick. I can feel the anger building behind me as Ben places his hand on my shoulder again. I can see the conflict in Tony's expression. He's torn between doing what I ask and fulfilling his life-long pissing contest with Ben.

"Fine, I'll go," he reluctantly concedes as Ben and I move out of the doorway. Our movement almost as if we are one. Before he makes it over the threshold, Tony turns to us, "It's not over, Piper. I decide when we're done and I haven't decided yet."

Before Tony can make it more than three steps, Ben closes the door and turns the top lock. I release the breath I was holding as he spoke those final words.

"You okay?" he asks me as he turns toward me. My

entry way is just that, for entry. It's not meant to hold a conversation. I feel like the space is smaller than normal with Ben's large frame filling the space.

"Yeah, sorry about that," I quietly reply as I thank my lucky stars I'm still holding my wine and finish off the glass in one drink.

"Hey." Ben takes a step toward me and places both hands on each of my arms. His gesture is undeniably comforting and equally confusing because it makes me feel something I shouldn't.

I look up at him. I swear time stops as I look into his gorgeous chocolate-colored eyes. It's only when he reaches for my face and wipes a tear from my cheek that I realize I'm crying. Ben pulls me into a hug and I unleash a bounty of tears. My level of self-pity is epic. Goodness this man smells good. What is that? Mint? Pine? Leather? All three.

I pull away and wipe the tears still streaking my face with my free hand.

"Sorry."

"No apology necessary, Piper. You didn't do anything wrong. I see Dominguez is still a class A jackass."

I offer a snicker in response.

"How about more wine? Go sit down, I'll get it," he says, taking my glass and guiding me toward the couch.

I offer a nod in response as Ben takes my glass from my hand and makes his way to the kitchen, then stops to look at the beer Tony left on the counter. I hear a simple grunt of annoyance as he sets the bottle in the sink and turns to the refrigerator. After filling my glass and handing it to me, he opens a beer of his own. We each take a drink and look at each other.

And laugh.

Not chuckles or giggles. No, this is all-out belly laughing.

A few minutes of much-needed laughing and I finally speak.

"Why are we laughing?"

"I don't know, but it feels pretty damn good."

"Agreed. And, you're right."

He raises his brow at me and I smile and turn toward the living room and the couch. I scoot into a corner and bring my knees to my chest as I take a small sip of my wine.

"Tony is still a jackass. Ugh, I'm so embarrassed that I was even dating that guy."

Ben joins me on the couch. Not too close, but also not on the other end where most people would sit.

"Hmm, I'm not touching that comment, but maybe let's just be glad you ended it. I will say, I didn't like his parting comment. Has he ever been violent?"

"Tony? No. He'd have to take a step away from the mirror, talking about himself, or online dating to do that. I think he was just flaunting like a peacock once he realized who you were. Thanks, by the way."

"For?"

"For showing up when you did. Of course, if you hadn't sent that text last night he may not have been over here trying to stake his claim. So maybe I shouldn't be thanking you."

"Nah, I'm pretty sure you should be thanking me. Not just for showing up, mind you, but for sending that text last night."

Damn him and his smirk.

"If Dominguez was stupid enough to cheat on you then

I think a kick to his ego knowing you moved on … or pseudo moved on … is only a fraction of what he deserves."

I can't really disagree with that logic.

"Hmmm … Bentley Sullivan, have you always been so wise?"

"Of course I have. So, tell me, Piper, what have you been up to all these years?"

Well that's a loaded question. Instead of replying with the details, I skirt over the emotional bullshit of the last few years and instead hit the highlights. After about an hour or so we've managed to summarize, very sparingly I might add, the last few years of our lives. I'm finishing up a story of my first year teaching kindergarten, which, by the way, included not one but two marriage proposals from five-year-olds. Before I can ask about his plans now that he's back home Ben stands and takes my glass from the table.

"More wine?"

"I better not. Two glasses is already past my weekday max."

"You do know we don't have work tomorrow, right? Come on and live a little."

"Fine, but if I'm hungover again tomorrow, you're bringing me Rosa's instead of your sister."

"Deal."

I offer him a closed smile in response. We've managed to skirt the topic of last night and I know in my gut we have to get it out of the way. It would really help my cause if Ben hadn't strolled in here like a hero and saved me from stupid Tony. And if he didn't smell so damn good. And if he didn't make me laugh. And if his smile didn't send shivers down my spine.

Yeah, all of that would *really* help.

I glance toward the kitchen where he's pouring my wine. Goodness, he sure knows how to wear a pair of jeans. It would help a girl out if he didn't fill out a pair of jeans like they were designed just for him. Damn he's distracting.

Yep, we need to have this conversation so he can go.

Since I'm throwing my rules out the window tonight, I might as well go all out. I drag myself off the couch and make my way into the kitchen. Ben turns to see me and offers me that smile again. Settle down, ovaries, it's Ben, not a Calvin Klein model.

"I would have brought you the wine, Piper."

And there go the ovaries. Something about the way he says my name … like chocolate slowly pouring over a hot pan of brownies. Rich, creamy, and sinful.

"I … uh … wow, it's hot in here. Is it hot in here? I should turn on a fan. Are you hot?"

I sound like an idiot. It's not hot at all. Ben must agree by the sound of the chuckle and shake of his head as he hands me my wine.

"Nah, it's not hot. Probably just the wine."

"You're right. I was going to just grab us a little snack. Are you hungry?"

"I'm a guy. I can eat at any time. What were you thinking?"

"Sweet or savory?" Oh good lord, what kind of come hither voice was that? I set my wine down and grab a bottle of cold water from the refrigerator. This wine is obviously going to my head.

"Both? I always like a little sweet after I savor."

My eyes go wide as I start choking on my water.

"Oh my word, you did not just say that! Bentley James! That was the corniest thing I have ever heard and I work with five-year-olds!"

"Oh, busting out the middle name. What can I say? I'm a bit rusty in the flirting department."

"Yeah well, no flirting here, buddy. Go sit and I'll put together a few snacks," I say as I push him out of the kitchen.

I need space. I need time without his smell in my senses. Without him being within arms' distance. I know I can't act on my attraction to him, but damn if I really want to.

Chapter 7

Ben

I need to change my name to Pinocchio. I'm a liar; it *is* hot as hell in here, but it's not from the wine. No, the sexual tension between us is out of this world.

By the time I made it halfway up the stairs to her apartment, I could hear the voices. The tone in her voice was strained and almost had a quiver to it. I could feel in my bones that she was not only angry, but nervous. The first thing I noticed when I approached the open door was her pert ass in those damn pants. More like a second skin than pants, they showed me what I dreamed about last night was reality.

Then I heard the male voice and something about the way he said her name made the hairs on the back of my neck stand up. It wasn't as if he was threatening, no it was more of a manipulative and patronizing tone than anything else. I instantly felt protective and slightly territorial. Okay, more than slightly.

I know starting something up with anyone, let alone my sister's best friend, is the last thing I need to be doing, it doesn't mean I want someone else to have her. That kiss last night sparked something in me that I didn't know existed. I'm not a possessive guy, but I swear I want to beat the shit out of any guy who thinks about putting his hands on her and that's only after one kiss. I can't imagine what spending time with her would do for my suddenly discovered caveman reaction.

After Dominguez left, I only meant to stay long enough to apologize for last night and promise nothing like that would happen again. Then she cried and we laughed. Suddenly, the tension was gone. I enjoyed talking to her and now find myself trying to come up with a reason to stay longer.

I lay my head back on the couch and take in a long breath. I can hear her mumbling to herself in the kitchen. She has to be feeling what I am. Or, maybe she isn't. Maybe I'm reading all of this wrong and I'm about to make a complete ass of myself.

What kind of moron lets someone like Piper go? No, what kind of asshole throws her away? I shake my head in disbelief; it's unimaginable to me.

"You doing okay there, cowboy?"

That voice, it sends my pulse running. I turn my head to look at Piper as she sets a tray on the table and cocks her head toward me. Damn, she's beautiful.

"Huh?"

Wow, Ben, you have a way with words.

She smiles at me and shakes her own head. I sit up and look at the tray she's set down. As promised she's set out a little bit of savory and a little bit of sweet. I reach over and grab a piece of bread and dip it in the bowl of creamy goodness and reach for my beer. Time to peel off the Band-Aid.

"Thanks, that's good stuff. What is it?"

"Just some dip I had in the fridge. So, umm, I was thinking."

"About?" I ask as I reach for more dip. This shit really is good.

"Last night. Obviously we were drunk and it was a misunderstanding. We should just pretend it didn't happen and be done with it."

And here I thought I was going to have to be the bad guy. That kind of stings.

"I wasn't, it wasn't, and no."

"What?" Piper questions as she furrows her perfect brows in a way that manages to make her look more adorable than she did flustered in the kitchen.

"I wasn't drunk, it wasn't a misunderstanding, and I don't want to pretend it didn't happen."

"Oh. Uh, well, uh…"

I grab a napkin from the table and wipe my hands before turning toward her.

"Look, this is a really awkward conversation," I say as I run a hand through my hair. "I like you, Piper. Not just because you're my sister's best friend and I've known you forever, but because you're smart, funny, a little sassy, and I like talking to you. Plus, you know, gorgeous."

I take a quick breath before she can reply.

"That being said, it can't happen again. I just ended a long relationship and am starting all over. I'm living in my childhood bedroom for Pete's sake. I'm in no position to start something up. Plus, I promised Ash I wouldn't and I don't break promises to my sister. So, I just wanted to say that if this were a different time and we didn't have Ash to consider, I wouldn't be sitting here eating dip and talking about kindergarten marriage proposals."

"You, you wouldn't?" she asks with big saucer sized eyes.

"No, Piper, I wouldn't. But, that doesn't matter. I'd like to be your friend though. And, *your friend*, not just Ash's big brother. What do you say to that?"

She's still staring at me with wide eyes and now her mouth is gaping. I smile and shake my head and stand. She seems to gather herself and stands to follow me as I head to the door.

"So, friends?" I ask as I open the door.

"What? Oh, yeah, of course. Friends. Absolutely. And, co-workers," she replies and offers me a smile. It's another closed mouth smile. The smile that doesn't reach her eyes. The smile that tells me she's thinking again.

"Right, co-workers. We still have a few weeks until school starts but I'm sure I'll see you around. You're going to the lake with us next weekend, right?"

The mention of the lake must be a neutralizer because she offers me a full smile. The smile that calls my dick to attention and the smile that makes me curse my sister just a little.

"Actually, Ben, I think the question is are *you* going to the lake with *us* next weekend. We go every year for Ash's birthday, you just haven't been around to join us."

"Ouch. You're right, I've kind of sucked the last few years. Yes, Piper, I'll be at the lake next weekend with *you* all. But don't forget, if you have a headache tomorrow from that third glass of wine, I'll bring you Rosa's."

"I'll be fine, but thanks," she says as I step out on to the landing. Before she can say goodbye I turn toward her.

"And, I'm sorry for making your situation with Dominguez worse with that text. He's a dick though, Piper. Please promise me if he gives you any more trouble you'll call me." I look directly in her dancing whiskey-colored eyes. I want her to feel my sincerity in the apology and seriousness that I will deal with Tony if he so much as says one negative word to her.

"It's okay, he deserved to feel like shit. Well, as much as he capable of anyway. Tony won't be any trouble, he's really harmless. And, even though he's a horrible boyfriend, he's not a bad guy."

"Just call me if you need anything, okay?"

She nods. "Goodnight, Ben."

"Night, Piper," I say as she closes the door and I turn toward the steps. I hesitate before I start down until I hear the lock click.

As I drive home, I contemplate a stop at Country Road to have a drink and decide against it. My mind is full of Piper and the last thing I need is for Ash to ask where I've been. I know we haven't done anything wrong and no lines were crossed but I still feel protective of my time with Piper.

I hate that a part of me feels like I'm betraying my years with Laurel, that I'm not giving our relationship the respect it deserves. I absolutely loved Laurel; I still do. But this pull I have to Piper and the immediate sense of familiarity and connection is something we didn't have. Considering I've had two serious relationships and didn't experience anything remotely close to what I have felt in the last twenty-four hours, I'm feeling a little dazed.

Once I'm parked in front of the house, I take a few minutes to just sit and take it in. This house, this street, this town, they all represent the person I was and have me questioning the person I am and who I want to be.

Leaving home at eighteen, I was convinced I had all the answers. Like many driven teenagers, my future seemed laid out with a perfect plan of a successful career, wife, kids, and weekend fishing trips. The reality of it all is life can't be planned. The man who believes the ideals of a boy hold his future is a fool.

I reach for my phone and notice the light blinking that I have a message. A quick swipe has me smiling instantly.

Piper: Thanks again for coming to my rescue.

Me: It's what a knight in shining armor does.

Piper: Good grief.

She manages to make me smile even by text. I get out of the truck and make my way up the drive when my phone pings again.

Piper: Weatherman just said a storm is coming, better make sure the armor doesn't rust cowboy.

Me: Cowboy?

Piper: Best Halloween of all time.

Me: Well if your best Halloween memory is when you were 8, we have a problem.

Piper: Night Ben.

Me: Night, Princess Piper.

I chuckle to myself at the memory of Piper dressed as a princess and demanding we all call her Princess Piper. She was a force to be reckoned with when she was little. Bossy, silly, and always wanting to dress Jameson and me up like peasants or something equally boring. Then something happened when she hit those awkward years. I guess part of that had to do with the age difference. Somehow at eight and eleven it didn't feel like much of an age difference. By the time I was thirteen the difference seemed like light years and Ashton and Piper were more annoying than fun to hang out with.

I open the back door and am slightly startled by the shadow at the table also known as my dad sneaking his late-night bowl of ice cream. As long as I can remember, my dad has snuck down to the kitchen for a bowl of ice cream. Obviously if I know about it, it's likely my mom does, too. I think that's one of their secrets to a happy marriage – her pretending she doesn't know and him still calling it sneaking.

"Hey, Pop," I say as make my way to the cupboard to make my own bowl.

"Don't tell your mother you saw me down here."

I laugh and take a seat at the table with him.

"Dad, I'm pretty sure it's not sneaking anymore. You've been coming down here at this time my entire life."

"It didn't used to be sneaking, but now it really is. Your mother is on some sort of kick about my diet and is driving me nuts. I've been hiding these small containers of ice cream in frozen broccoli bags. You know your mother would never look in a bag of broccoli."

That's true. Mom has some random fear of broccoli. I've never understood it but she calls them creepy little trees and refuses to cook them.

"Well played, Pop."

"Where were you tonight? Out with the guys again?"

"Nah, I'm going to check out my classroom tomorrow so no late night for me."

Dad finishes his last bite of ice cream and starts to stand. I stop midway with the bite of ice cream on my spoon with a look of confusion as I watch him sit back down.

"How are you doing about all of this change? I know you're a bit, uh, how should I put this?"

I set the spoon down and sit back in my chair, crossing my arms defensively.

"Oh, Ben, don't go getting all shut off from me. I just want to make sure all this change is okay. I know you like to live life with a plan and this all came on sudden."

Wow, getting called out by your dad at twenty-nine is as shitty as it is at seventeen. I put my arms down and release the tension in my shoulders. I don't know why my instinct was to become defensive. I know my dad means well and he's right, I prefer a life plan and not having one is a little out of character for me.

"Come on, I'm not that bad. Yeah this is a lot of change but you know that I have always wanted to come home and teach. I loved, no, I love Laurel, but we aren't forever. I think we've both known that for a while and just needed this change to push us both along. I'm happy to be home, happy to be teaching at Peabody, and I really am happy at the prospect of finding my own place," I tease as I take a spoonful of my ice cream and pop it in my mouth.

"Well, son, I will say that at this point in our lives your mother and I didn't plan on having either you or your sister home, let alone both. So, ya know, if you need help finding a place let me know."

"I don't think I want to even have this conversation if

it's going where I think it is. So, maybe we just say good-night?" I ask as I grab his bowl and mine and head to the sink. The idea of where my dad was going with that state-ment has suddenly made this delicious ice cream turn to acid in my stomach.

Dad approaches me and places a hand on my shoulder, "You're a man, Ben, and I don't think we need to have this conversation. Goodnight, son."

Damn, I need to get settled in this job and start actively looking for a place. I shudder at what I may walk into one afternoon. Visibly shiver. Let Ash walk in on that shit. A smirk takes over my face as I contemplate if that's a possibil-ity. Setting it up so Ash does walk in on that. Oh dang, she'd shit herself.

I finish cleaning up the kitchen and hit the light as I begin up the stairs to my room. I stop for a minute at the pictures displayed on the walk up the stairway. Moments of time that my mom has deemed "the" moments of our lives. These aren't silly posed school photos; no, these are mo-ments from our lives displayed for everyone to see.

The first I stop and look at is a picture of Ashton's first birthday. She's pretty in pink with her ruffled skirt, sparkly crown, and cowgirl boots on sitting before a big cake. The look in her eyes is the same one she has every time she's thinking up a prank, mischievous and innocent at the same time. I am, of course, nearby in the photo. I have the most annoyed look on my face and you can just see my hand sneaking up from the side to steal a piece of her cake.

The closer I get to the top, the older we get in the pho-tos. The last few stop me in my tracks as I realize I'm not in them. These are pictures of Ash, Piper, and even Jameson.

The last few years I've been gone, they've been here and to-gether. Life moved on without me. What Piper said at her place is true. I'm going with *them* to the lake next week. I'm the outsider in this group.

As I come to this realization I focus on the last photo. It's a picture of the girls in a selfie. I can tell that it's pretty recent and from the background can tell it's at the lake. The smile on Piper's face is sweet and real. Those whiskey-col-ored eyes of hers are sparkling. She looks truly happy and invigorating. My eyes fall to Ashton in the picture. Equally as happy, my big brother heart is full of love for my sister. I will never intentionally do anything to hurt her.

I finish my trek to my bedroom and once inside I kick off my boots, which are immediately followed by my belt and my shirt. I lay down on my bed and vow to stay friends with Piper and not pursue anything. As I make this vow, I begin repeating my new personal mantra, "friends and co-workers," and know every single time I say it, I mean it.

Mostly.

I'm ninety-seven percent sure I won't pursue anything. Someone may want to talk to that three percent.

Chapter 8

Piper

To say that I slept last night would be a lie. I don't know what possessed me to text Ben after he left my apartment. So stupid. I lay awake all night wondering if there was a way I could claim momentary insanity. Or drunkenness. Something, really anything, to give me an excuse for being flirty and reaching out unnecessarily.

I glance at the clock and am not surprised it's just a little after sunrise. I drag myself out of bed and go straight to my dresser and grab my running bra and shorts. I need to run this feeling out of me and, hopefully, run out this attraction I have to my best friend's brother.

A quick stop by the bathroom before I put my sneakers on shows the signs of just how little sleep I had last night. I strap my phone onto my arm and grab my earbuds. I take off at a slow pace and contemplate the position I've put myself in. I've had a crush on Bentley Sullivan most of my life. A completely one-sided crush. The day he left for college was a sad and empowering day. I no longer had to watch him fawn all over Claire and wish I was the pretty, popular, kind, smart, funny girl he was holding hands with in the halls or on the Sullivans' couch.

I cannot believe how easily I can find my way back to that place of insecurity and self-doubt. This only confirms what my mother has said to me since I was a little girl: no matter how far and fast you run, the past always catches up. Of course, my mother was talking about men and her poor choices when it came to said men. Regardless of her intent, this saying holds true to my opinions of myself, and how no matter how hard I have worked, they manage to reappear from time to time.

I pick up the pace as I start making my way out of my neighborhood and toward the edge of town. I pass Peabody Elementary and smile. With only about two weeks until the new school year starts, I cannot wait to get back into a routine and meet my new students. I've finally found my stride in timing with the music on my run playlist and find all of the tension leaving my body. With each breath a piece of the tension falls away and I breathe a little easier.

An hour after leaving my apartment I find myself under the warm spray of the shower. I have a clearer head and am committed to moving past this kiss nonsense and the little butterflies in my tummy response I had to hanging out with Ben last night. I need to focus on the upcoming school year and nothing else.

I finish getting myself ready and shoot a text off to Ashton that I'm heading to my classroom to start preparing it for the new year. She doesn't respond, and when I look at the clock I realize that's because she's probably still asleep.

It is, after all, when most people that have day jobs are only getting up to start their day.

After a few hours in the classroom I stop to take a look around. I really love every moment I have in this room. Watching little minds come alive as they start discovering that education is an honor and a privilege. Of course, teaching the kids of some of the people I grew up with is sometimes less of an honor. I look over the list of my incoming students with notes and see that once again the Karma Gods are plotting against me.

Jacob Thorne
Age 5
Parents:
Michael Thorne and Felicity Remington-Thorne

Fantastic. I throw myself in my chair and lean back rubbing my temples. Felicity Remington hyphen Thorne. Note the hyphen for future reference and need for her to have the longest name in the universe. I knew this day would come but I pretended that somehow the little spawn of the she-devil would be a genius and skip kindergarten and go straight into first grade. No such luck.

A glorious cup of goodness lands on my desk and startles me out of my chair.

"Hey, sister from another mister."

"Ashton, you scared the shit out of me!"

"Oh you must really need this if you're cussing in the classroom."

"Whatever," I say as I reach for the cup of coffee and sit back down in my chair.

"Whatcha got there, doll face? Your class list? Gimme," she demands, holding out her hand. I hand the list to her and watch as she looks it over and her eyes land on little Thorne in My Side.

"Ah, Felicity. God she's such a bitch. I bet her little kid is rotten, too. Your year is about to suck."

"Wow, thanks, Ash. I have another few weeks until I have to deal with this, let's not discuss it. What are you even doing here?"

"I was bored. Stupid Ben is stomping around the house grunting and mumbling some sort of mantra or some shit. I don't know. He was bugging me. I wanted to go look at apartments again and figured you could stand getting out of here."

Here we go again. "I'll go with you, but you know I'm not moving in with you, right? We've talked about this."

She rolls her eyes at me like she's one of my students and hops off the desk she had perched herself on.

"Whatevs. Come on."

My turn to roll my eyes and pull myself up from my chair. Ashton grabs my hand and starts dragging me for the door as I manage to snag my purse off the counter before closing the door.

"Okay, geez. I may need my arm, ya know. What's your hurry anyway?"

"What? Oh, sorry. No hurry I just want to get out of this

building. You know it creeps me out."

I laugh. One of Ash's odd phobias is small children. She hates helping me with anything that has to do with my kids.

"You are so strange sometimes," I reply as we walk out of the building and toward her car.

"Fear of small children is a real phobia; you shouldn't mock me. That has to be some sort of law or something."

"Pretty sure it isn't but fine, I'll stop for now," I concede as I buckle myself into the car and prepare for another afternoon of Ashton loving every apartment she can't afford and me reminding her of her budget. We play this game every other weekend and, while it drives me nuts half the time, it makes her feel like living with her parents isn't forever.

Four hours, six apartments, and half a pizza later I'm finally home and on my couch. As expected it was six "I love this place! It's perfect!" from Ashton and six "budget buster" replies from me. I love my best friend, I really do, but her idea of a budget versus what the rest of the world considers a budget is vastly different.

The long day I've had hits me like a ton of bricks and I look over at the television that is a blank dark screen. The remote is just out of arm's reach and I have to talk myself into grabbing it. I flip on a marathon of Dateline and snuggle into my comfy fuzzy blanket and close my eyes.

I've spent the last week cutting, pasting, organizing, and hanging up everything to make the kindergartners feel welcome and less overwhelmed. I look around my room and it's coming along great. Thankfully I have another few days to finish it up before our weekend at the lake.

Normally Ashton and I will hang out a few times throughout the week or I'll go in to Country Road at least once or twice, but I've been spending time with Netflix this week. I'm not avoiding anyone or intentionally keeping myself busy. Nope, I needed to clean out my closet, deep condition my hair, and alphabetize my canned goods.

There is always a silver lining to everything and, this week, that silver lining is not seeing Tony. Come to think of it, I haven't heard from him either. That in itself is strange. I've never known him to give up on anything without a fight. Not a parking space, not a pick-up basketball game, and surely not a girlfriend breaking up with him.

I finish setting up the reading corner, choosing to stick with a classic Dr. Seuss theme this year, before deciding to call it a day. I grab my things and turn the lights off as I make my way out of the school to my car. I love the history of this school. When our grandparents attended this school, it was actually the middle and high school. Gradually, as the town grew the school changed along with it and is one of two elementary schools. I glance toward the playground and smile at the memories I have.

Lost in thought, I almost don't see the flowers laying on top of my windshield. I look around and don't see anyone who may responsible. No card, no surprise. I pull the roses from the windshield and it is less than ten seconds before my sinuses start filling and the pressure in my head makes itself known. Obviously the person who so lovingly thought of me didn't know that I am allergic to roses. I walk the bouquet to the trash can on the sidewalk before returning to my car and taking the hand sanitizer from its home in the center console.

I slather on enough of the stuff to compete with an actual bath. My efforts are for not because the sneezing begins in sets of four with no end in sight. Damn flowers.

I'm in the middle of a set of sneezes when a knock on my window startles me.

I slowly peer up at the knock and see Ben with a concerned look on his face. I hold my finger up to signal for him to wait as I finish out the current set of sneezes. Once I finish, I turn my key and roll down the window.

"Hey, are you okay?"

"Yeah, just allergies. I'm fine, thanks," I croak out. My voice sounds like I swallowed a jar of razorblades and I can feel my eyes watering uncontrollably. Sexy.

"Okay, if you're sure." He doesn't sound convinced.

"I'm sure. I should go."

"Wait, umm … what are you doing now?"

I want to tell him I'm currently trying to breathe and that I probably look like a raccoon with my mascara running down my face. I want to say that he's making my stomach do flip flops standing here with his forearms leaning on my car and his dark, chocolate eyes looking at me with concern. Of course, he still hasn't shaved so he has that perpetual scruff happening, too. Jerk. I look down as his hand touches my forearm and look up to see him looking at me confused.

"Huh? Oh, nothing. Why what's up?"

"You sure you're okay? Do you want me to take you to the doctor or something?"

"What? No, don't be silly. I'm fine. Just the sneezing and all, I'm a little slow. Why'd you want to know what I'm doing?"

"If you're sure. I wanted to see if you could help me figure out what to get Ashton for her birthday. We're having family dinner tonight to celebrate and I haven't picked anything up yet. I'm kind of at a loss at this point."

"I-" That's all I can say before I sneeze again. "Sorry. Ugh, stupid roses."

"Why did you have roses? You're allergic."

"You know that I'm allergic to roses?"

"Of course. Remember that time my dad filled the house with roses for my mom's birthday? You were sicker than a dog and my parents felt so bad."

I start laughing because I do remember. Paul had wanted to surprise Patty for their fifteenth anniversary and filled the house with fifteen dozen roses. Like every other weekend I was spending the night and the minute I walked in the house I started sneezing. It got so bad they thought they'd have to call an ambulance. Instead they called my mom, who explained my allergy and came and picked me up. I was so embarrassed because Bentley and Jameson had been there to see me in all of my snotty glory.

"I forgot about that; it was awful. I can't help you though, I really need to get home and shower. That's all that will really help me get this pollen off of me. Plus, I will be at dinner tonight and I need to still pick up my gift before. I'm sorry, Ben."

"Shit. I really need help, Piper. Please. What if I go pick up your gift for her and then pick you up? That'll save you time while you get ready and then you can help me out. What do you say?"

I say he really needs to shave and not look so damn handsome leaning in my window looking helpless. I also say this is a bad idea.

"Okay."

I say a lot of things. To myself, obviously. I'll likely regret this but nobody ever said I was the smartest girl. He offers me a smile that sends the flutters in my belly to make their way downtown. Slow down there, lady bits, get a grip. I find the claim ticket in my purse for the engraved compact I picked out for Ash and hand it to him. The moment his fingers touch mine my breath catches and I swear I see his eyes go wide.

"Uh, yeah, so thanks for getting that for me. I'll see you what, like an hour?"

"Forty-five minutes okay? We don't want to be too late or Ash will never let us live it down. It is her day, after all."

We both laugh and I agree to forty-five minutes. Although I'm pushing it by sitting here, I can't help but allow myself a few seconds of watching Ben walk away. The way the shorts ride low on his hips and his leg muscles flex as he walks, I'm going to need to make that a cold shower. Just as I put my car in gear he turns back toward me and smirks.

So busted. I offer a shy little wave and he shakes his head at me.

I have less than forty minutes before he'll be here to pick me up. I have no time to waste and work double time to get ready. Thankfully the evenings are still warm and the Sullivans always grill out for Ashton's birthday. It's her requirement, along with strawberry shortcake for dessert. And presents. Really her only requirement is presents. For someone who gets stage fright and doesn't do well in crowds, Ashton loves being the center of attention.

Once I've showered and chosen a simple summer dress, I reach for my signature cowboy boots. Glancing at the clock, I note I either have time for makeup or my hair. Hair wins out and I am just finishing when there is a knock on my door. I grab the card I have for Ash, open the door, and momentarily lose my ability to breathe.

Standing before me dressed casually in a pair of shorts and collared navy-blue shirt showing off his very toned and tan arms, wearing a pair of aviator sunglasses with his hands in his pockets ... is the man who has starred in more of my dreams in the past week than I care to admit. Wow, that shirt hugs him just right. I bet if I reached out I'd feel the ripple of his abs through the fabric. If I just put my hand out ... no, no, Piper, no naughty thoughts. Just appreciate his perfectness and move right along.

I double blink and am pulled from my thoughts as he clears his throat and removes his sunglasses to hang off the front of his shirt.

"Wow, Piper. You look beautiful."

I roll my eyes in response as I grab the gift bag from him.

"Don't sound so surprised, Ben. I'm not an awkward teenager anymore. I thought you already had that part figured out." I step out and turn to lock the front door. I take and release a deep breath as I finish and move past him to begin my descent down the stairs. I hear his footsteps behind me as I make my way to his truck.

I attempt to open the truck's door, but it's locked. I can hear Ben's footsteps as I stand there with my arms crossed in a childish and stubborn stance. This is a bad idea. The minute I opened that door and saw him standing there I should have said I couldn't help him. I should have not answered the door. Thank goodness I can blame the heat on my sweaty palms and inability to sit still. As the truck signals that Ben has unlocked the door, I put my hand on the handle, but before I can open it he places his hand on mine.

"I'm not surprised, Princess. That was a moment of my breath being taken away. Don't be so defensive; accept a compliment, would ya?"

I turn to him and see nothing but sincerity and maybe a little frustration in his eyes.

"You're right," I say as I offer him an apologetic smile. "Thank you, Cowboy. Now, are you going to let me open this door so we can figure out what to get your sister for her birthday?"

He laughs and shakes his head at me. Not another word is exchanged as he opens the door for me and then makes his way around to his side. Once he's in and pulled away I realize we haven't even talked about what he's thinking of for a gift.

"So we should probably figure out what you want to get her before we start this little adventure."

"Oh, I already got her gift."

"What? I thought that's why you were picking me up."

"It was, but then I remembered I already had something for her. My bad." He motions to a bag identical to the one I have in my lap.

"How do you forget you already have a gift? Why didn't you let me know we weren't going shopping? I could have used the extra time to do more with myself." I begin straightening the skirt of my dress and messing with my hair.

"You look perfect so no more time was necessary. Plus,

I want you to see something and give me your opinion."

I just stare at him while I process this entire gift thing. Did he really forget he had a gift or was he messing with me? My frustration mounts as his nonchalant attitude takes over the cab of the truck.

"So let me get this straight. You just *happened* to find the perfect gift while picking up mine?" He shrugs in response. "Whatever, this is ridiculous. Where are you taking me?" No answer. "Can we just go to your parents' house? I'll help Patty with dinner."

He reaches over and grabs my hand. Tingles. Every damn time he touches me the tingles begin in my toes and make their way up my legs, stopping for a little visit in the lady parts, who by the way are really aware of how close I'm sitting to Bentley, before stopping in my tummy. I look down to where his hand is and then up quickly to his face. He's looking forward toward the road as if he doesn't feel the same connection I do. Of course he doesn't. I look back down at our hands and pull mine from his and place it in my lap.

Ben pulls his hand from where it was just holding mine and puts it on the wheel to replace the one he's now resting on the window. The mood in this truck just went from banter-filled to awkward.

Clearing his throat, he turns his attention to the road. "Relax, I'm not kidnapping you or anything." I start to reply but he cuts me off. "You sounded panicked for a second. I found a place I'm considering and I want your opinion."

"Not you, too," I sigh. "What is it with you and your sister? If you found a place, great. You have to live in it, not me." That may have been a tad bit snarky and reflected a smidge too much frustration. I'm less frustrated with going to look at an apartment than I am that his simple touch put me on edge.

Ben doesn't even respond; he just begins singing along to the radio. I concede I have lost this battle. I am officially the Sullivan Apartment Hunting Chaperone.

Chapter 9

Ben

Deep cleansing and calming breaths are perfect for regulating your heartbeat. They are also detrimental to their purpose if it means you take in the scent of Piper Lawrence. I realize I sound like some sort of lovelorn teenager, but the minute I saw her open the door I couldn't breathe. That dress not only hugs her in all the right places, it also puts her tits on full display. The most glorious set I've seen outside of a magazine. Her long hair just barely grazing their tops had my attention right away. I managed to get my act together and move my attention to her face. I swear my heart stopped. How is it possible for one woman to be so absolutely perfect?

Then she spoke. That sweet and sultry voice, full of sass to cover the insecurities I see in her eyes, sets my soul on fire. I was thankful she walked ahead of me down the stairs allowing enough time for a few cleansing and calming breaths. That was, until I caught sight of her ass in that dress.

I spend more time thinking of kittens and reciting baseball stats when Piper is around. Each statistic is an attempt to rid myself of the raging hard-on she gives me.

I do find how uneasy I seem to make her very interesting. I see how much she tries to fight the attraction and her reaction to it. The sassier and infuriated she gets only entices me more. Whether she's sassing me because I already purchased a gift for my sister or because I hold her hand, seeing her unsettled in her seat puts a smile on my face. It means she feels something. As confusing as it is and complicated as it makes things, I want her to feel everything too.

"Where are we going, Ben? There aren't any apartments out this way."

"I never said apartment. Stop being so impatient, enjoy the ride."

A roll of her eyes and she promptly turns her back to me, looking out the window. Sass, so much sass.

I'm not sure what prompted me to want to bring Piper out here with me. When I was looking at rental ads earlier in the week, I had every intention of finding a little apartment to call my own. Then, as luck would have it, there was a listing for a house. Not just a house but a traditional farm house on acreage.

After giving in to my curiosity, I drove out here the other day and it was love at first sight. Well, as much love as you can have for a house that looks like its dying. I'm not even kidding, it looks dead. A dead house.

During my walk of the property, I happened up on the cherry on the house sundae - the land backs up to a stream. A rambling, ready-to-drop-my-fishing-pole-in-it stream. I knew in that moment that this was my house. I've thought of nothing except this house since but can't seem to shake this need for someone else to react the same way. Some sort of confirmation that my reaction isn't abnormal and maybe, just maybe, find it as fantastic as I do.

My eyes wander from the road and over to Piper. I can tell that her tension has eased a little. I also notice that the hem of her dress has raised a little and I see just enough leg to make me let out an audible groan. Piper looks at me, and while her posture shows she's releasing the tension, the look in her eyes is anything but relaxed. Another eye roll and she adjusts her dress to cover the exposed part of her leg and begins to braid her hair.

I approach the turn to the long drive and cautiously make the turn, avoiding the previously standing mail box that now lays partially in the drive. I suppose the list of things I'll have to replace at this house is going to quite lengthy if that mail box is an indicator.

As we make our way down the long drive that is lined with a few trees, I feel Piper sit up straighter and roll the window down all the way. The way she is peering out the window is like a puppy catching the wind in his face. Although I see beyond the unkempt land and home, I'm not sure what Piper sees but I hear her gasp as I bring the truck to a stop in front of the house.

"Ben," she whispers. Unbuckling herself, she opens the door and hops out of the truck. I follow suit and walk around the truck to stand next to her.

"What do you think? Too much for a bachelor?"

She doesn't respond so I look at her. Her mouth is open in awe and her eyes are shimmering with the slightest hint of tears.

"Piper, what's wrong?"

She waves her hands at me, takes a long breath, and releases it as she wipes her eyes.

"Sorry. Ben, it's wonderful. This house. It's..."

She doesn't finish her sentence and instead begins walking toward the steps that lead to a wraparound porch and the front door. Stopping at the base of the steps, she turns to me and I can still see the slightest hint of tears.

"Can we go inside? Will the owners mind?"

"Nah, that's why we're here. Come on," I reply as I grab her hand. This time she doesn't pull away but instead squeezes my hand.

I point out a few spots that are questionable and we step around them. Savoring the feeling of her hand in mine, I lead her into the house. Standing in the foyer, I look over at Piper. Her eyes wide as saucers and her mouth open enough that she'll catch a fly given the opportunity, she's uncharacteristically quiet.

I was here yesterday so I'm familiar with the layout and turn toward the living room, giving her a little tug as I do. She closes her mouth and silently follows my lead. I move so that that we are in front of the large window that looks out past the porch we just stepped across and down the drive.

"It's a four bedroom and two bath on four acres. Obviously it needs a lot of love and care but I'm thinking I'd be a fool if I didn't scoop it up. What do you think?"

Piper lets go of my hand and starts walking around the room and eventually back out and toward what is the kitchen. I let her go ahead and follow her. She seems familiar with the layout, which would be strange if it wasn't a typical farmhouse. Most of these homes have a similar floor pattern, but

I'm surprised Piper would have such a familiarity. Growing up she was either at our house or the apartment she shared with her mom.

Once I make it to the kitchen, I lean in the doorway. When I was here yesterday, I immediately thought of family dinners that could be prepared in here and of the imaginary smiling faces of kids sitting at the long table, and I knew there was no doubt I wanted this house. Watching Piper make her way around the room, I allow myself a nanosecond of those smiling faces belonging to a woman like Piper.

As Piper runs her hand across the counter and over the front of the large sink, I feel a tug and need to break the moment. It feels too intense and like there is something more to this house with Piper here.

"Cat got your tongue, Princess?"

"What? Oh, I'm sorry. It's wonderful, Ben. Breathtaking."

"Oh good. My gut said the same thing but I needed a second opinion before I put in an offer. It's going to take a lot of work, but in the end I think it'll be worth it."

"This kitchen. It's a dream kitchen, Ben. I have a Pinterest board dedicated to dream kitchens and this is what they all look like. You have to get this house. It's too perfect to let go."

"I agree. Of course, this doesn't get me out of my parents' house any faster but it is a great investment."

I look down at my watch and see that we're going to be late if we don't leave now. "We should go; Ash will have a meltdown if we're late."

Silently, Piper tilts her head in contemplation and, instead of walking out of the kitchen, she walks to the back door and places her hand to the piece of stained glass that sits in the center of the door. It's a simple design that projects little prisms all over the room, almost like a kaleidoscope. After a few heartbeats with her hand on the glass she turns and offers me a small closed-mouth smile before heading toward the front door.

Once outside, she begins walking toward the back of the house. Again, I follow. Piper stops to stand in the knee-high dead grass with the sun shining bright; she's never looked more beautiful or serene. I walk up behind her and place my hands on her shoulders. She doesn't move, but I feel her take a deep breath and I swear I also hear a sniffle.

"Just beyond that tree line is a stream. It's not much, but it'll be great for a little after-work fishing, that's for sure."

Only nodding in response I hear it again, a sniffle. This time, instead of ignoring the sound I turn her toward me. Those tears that were lingering are now freely falling. What is going on? I place my finger to her chin to catch one as it falls.

"What is it? What's wrong, Piper?" I can't hide my concern or confusion in my voice.

"It's nothing, I'm being silly," she says, gently shaking her head. I won't be swayed.

"It isn't nothing, Princess. Why are you crying?"

"The house. This land. It's all … it's all so familiar."

"What do you mean, familiar? Have you been here before?"

She shakes her head no and another tear falls on my hand that is now tipping her face up. I look into those gorgeous eyes. The lightest brown with gold flakes, they never cease to take my breath away. For a brief moment time stands still. I want to kiss her.

"You'll think I'm crazy."

"I won't think you're crazy, but you're kind of freaking me out here." She offers me a tentative smile.

"Sorry, I don't mean to. Ever since I was a little girl, I've had a recurring dream. It's silly really. These dreams have always come and gone but they never change. There's a long drive, a beautiful house." She pauses and another tear drops.

I wipe the stray tear from her cheek as she puts her hand on mine and lowers my hand from her face but doesn't let go of my hand.

"You used to dream of my house? This house?" I ask, and she nods.

"It's just a coincidence. I don't know why I'm crying," she says, releasing my hand and wiping the remaining tears from her face.

"Hey," I say and she looks up at me. "Are you sure you're okay?"

"Yeah, I'm sure. I just felt overwhelmed. I guess it's a good thing you didn't leave me more time to get ready or I'd be Rocky Raccoon with my makeup a hot mess," she jokes.

"You could never look a hot mess, Princess. We really should get going."

She agrees and we fall in pace side by side back to the truck. Once we're both in I start the truck and look at Piper. She's staring out the window, but the tears seem to have stopped.

It's silent for a few minutes as I drive toward my parents' house. Thankfully, the tension from the earlier silent treatment is gone.

"Thank you for taking me there, Ben. I can't believe that house actually exists. That's so crazy. What are the chances?"

"It's a pretty run-of-the-mill farmhouse, Pipe. You probably saw one when you were little and it stuck with you."

"No, Ben. I mean it was *the* house. The porch, foyer, and kitchen, all of it. Even that little stained glass window in the kitchen. All of that was from my dreams."

The look on her face as she tells me this is one I want to memorize. She is equal parts excited, mesmerized, and a little scared. I imagine it's similar to the look I have each time I touch her.

"The stained glass?" I ask.

She nods in response.

"Huh, that's pretty cool."

"Yeah, pretty cool. Completely weird and a little on the creepy side but cool, Ben." Giggles and a smile take over her face as she reaches toward the radio and turns up the volume, ultimately regulating the moment.

We make it to my parents' house with less than four minutes to spare. As we make our way up the to the kitchen door – nobody uses the front door here – the door flies open with the birthday girl shouting.

"Where the hell … Why are you guys together? Oh presents! Gimme!"

I shake my head and lift my gift bag up as Piper does the same and they are snatched from our hands. "Why are they the same? Did you get me the same thing? Ben, did you keep the receipt?"

I walk in and scoop my mom up in a big hug and offer a kiss to her cheek. I turn to Dad and he hands me a beer. "Ash, if they are the same, why would you take mine back and not Piper's?"

"Because, you big oaf, she's my bestie. Yours goes back,"

she says, sitting down at the kitchen table. Before she can begin pulling the pink paper stuff the shop girl put in the bag, my dad takes the gifts from her.

"You know the rules, Ashton Marie. No gifts until after we eat. Piper, can I get you something to drink? A glass of wine?"

"Thanks, Paul. Actually, I'll just take some water for now. I had to take allergy meds and need to drink more water."

That reminds me, I never asked her about the roses. "Hey, Piper, who left you the roses? You never said."

She shakes her head and takes a drink of water. Ashton, still pouting from Dad taking her gifts, looks between the two of us. I know that look so I put finger up to stop her before the inquisition starts.

"Piper and I were both at the school today when I found her in the middle of an allergy attack." My mom turns to me with an arched brow as she sets the final tray of food on the counter.

Before Ashton can offer commentary, my dad looks at Piper, confused. "What idiot gave you roses? You're allergic." Piper smiles in response.

"That's what Ben said too. Obviously it wasn't a Sullivan as you all seem to be up to speed on my allergies." We all laugh before my mom declares it dinnertime. Dad and I let the ladies put their plates together and head out to the patio before we start on our own.

"So, you spent the day with Piper?"

Here we go. "No, Dad. Piper and I are both teachers at the same school. I saw her like I said and made sure she was okay. Don't make this something it's not."

I finish putting my burger together and grab my beer to join the ladies outside when he starts laughing.

"What's so funny?"

"You. I think you almost believe that line of shit you just fed me, son. The only time you have ever been defensive is when you're caught in a lie. I can probably count on one hand each time. I believe this conversation just started me on hand two."

"I'm not lying. Piper and I are friends. And co-workers. Look, I was thinking of getting Ash a second gift and figured who better to help than her best friend. So yeah, I asked Piper to help me. Come on, Dad, you know Ash is a royal pain when it comes to her gifts and if I screwed this up I'd never hear the end of it."

"Royal pain is being kind to your sister. She's the most selfless person I know except on her birthday. If we let her, she'd have it declared a national holiday."

This time, we both laugh and join the women outside. Dinner goes along as normal with no more comments about me and Piper. Of course, since it is Ashton's birthday most of the conversation is geared to her liking.

Once we've cleaned up dinner and let the meal settle Ashton declares it shortcake time. A quick rendition of the birthday song and she quickly transitions us to gift time. First up is the gift card for a day at the spa for Ashton and Piper from our parents. Squeals and high fives abound as they declare it the best gift ever. Which is funny because it is the same gift they have both been getting from my parents since they were sixteen.

Next is Piper's gift. I admit I took a peak when the clerk first handed me the bag. Ashton is instantly crying as she opens the box the silver compact sits in. She flips it over and begins reading the inscription aloud, "Friends by chance. Sisters by choice."

"Oh, Pipes! It's perfect. You bitch, now I'm crying!"

Everyone laughs as the girls hug and sniffle together. Next up is my gift. I hold my breath a little as she pulls a box similar to that of Piper's gift. This one, instead, is long and rectangular. My mom looks at me with a twinkle in her eye and I know more tears are coming.

Ashton pulls the locket from the box and she lets out a gasp. With glistening eyes, she looks at me. "Open it," I tell her. I watch her as she does and the tears freely fall.

"Ben," she whispers and comes flying at me.

"I love you, Monkey."

"Thank you, I love you too. I'm so happy you're home."

"Well, let me see what has you all teary-eyed, Ash," Mom says, crying and holding her hand out for Ashton to hand her the locket.

Ashton shows Mom and Dad the pictures I had put in the locket. The left side is me holding Ash when she's a baby and the right is a picture of us on Halloween. It was the year I was dressed as the Cowboy and Ashton was dressed as a very well-endowed Dolly Parton.

Mom smiles and looks at me. "Oh, Bentley James. Is that why you were in the old photo albums? It's perfect."

I smile in acknowledgement while she dabs her eyes with a tissue. I glance at Piper and she raises an eyebrow at me. Busted. She knows that I had a pretty spectacular gift for Ash and didn't need her help after all. I shrug in response and she just smiles and shakes her head at me. My dad clears his throat and I glance at him as he shakes his head and smiles. Yeah, he's not buying what I tried selling him earlier.

"Thank you for the gifts, everyone. I appreciate them all." Ashton stands and begins putting the locket on and gathering the leftover paper from the gifts in a pile. "It's been real, parentals, but we've got a party to get to. Are you two ready?"

I look at Piper as she looks at me, equally confused. "Party?" we ask in unison.

"Yeah, party. Did you think we were going to sit around here all night and play Monopoly or some shit? It's my birthday, we're going out." After her proclamation Ashton heads to the front door.

I glance at Piper and she just shrugs to tell me she had no idea this was happening, but regardless we're going out to celebrate Ashton. Dad grabs his keys. "I'll drop you kids off so you can just take cabs home."

Ashton thanks Dad and I stand back as she and Piper make their way out the door. Piper walking in front of me just demands that I look at her ass. Again.

I have a feeling this is going to be a long night.

Chapter 10

Piper

I'm impressed by Ben's birthday gift for Ashton. Those pictures were perfect and the locket itself is perfect for her. When he said he had a gift for her I assumed it was an iTunes gift card or a book. Then again, I shouldn't be surprised he went out of his way to get her the perfect present. He's that guy.

I watch Ashton subconsciously finger the locket on the chain as she rambles on and on about, well I don't really know. I'm a horrible friend because instead of listening to her, I'm more interested in watching the way Ben moves his arms while talking to his dad in the front seat. I can't help but imagine what those arms would be like holding him over me as he kisses me. His hands really are quite big, have I ever noticed that before? His fingers, I bet they can create magic.

"Hello!" Fingers snap in front of my face, pulling me from my less-than-innocent thoughts. "Are you even listening to me?"

"What? Oh sorry, I was just thinking about how much I love you and how much fun we're going to have." Liar, pants on fire.

"Well, of course we are! Are you going to dance with me? I feel like dancing tonight. Plus, you've got on your dancing boots!"

Ben laughs and turns around from the front seat. He looks at me with eyes full of questions and mischief. I roll my eyes at him and turn toward Ash. "First, stop shouting, we are all right here. Second, I'm pretty sure I don't dance. Like ever. And last, I always have my boots on. Look, we're here."

Chuckles from the front seat won't sway me from my "no dancing" rule. I'm laughing to myself and shaking my head as we head inside Country Road. I will never understand why Ashton would want to spend her nights off at her place of employment, but here we are. Of course, this thought on my part may be the fact that my place of employment smells like glue and crayons. Regardless, I don't understand.

Ash links arms with me and attempts to get me to skip with her to the door. "Ashton, you did just turn twenty-five. Maybe you should give up the skipping."

"Pish posh. I'm twenty-five not eighty-five! Come on, girlfriend, let's boogie!"

It has been two hours since we arrived for the "Ashton turns twenty-five extravaganza" and so far so good. Ashton is having a blast and there has been zero drama, aka no Tony sightings. I've enjoyed watching Ash float around laughing and dancing. I've also managed to dodge her demands for me to join her on the dance floor.

"Whew, it's hot in here. Are you having fun, Pipe?" Ashton shouts at me as she flops into the booth next to me. She literally flops, almost laying down as she does it. Giggles and snorts abound as I slide a water toward her. "Drink up, Ash, you need to have some water."

She doesn't even argue and takes a few hearty drinks. The guys are all up at the bar right now taking shots. Well, all except Ben. I noticed he's taken the same path as me and hasn't been drinking. I have been stealing glances in his direction far too often.

"Shit. I knew it was too good to be true," Ashton hisses.

I follow her sight line and notice my night of fun is about to end.

"Hey, sweetheart. Ashton." Addressing Ashton must have killed Tony.

"Dickhead and dickhead's friends. Could you leave, please? You're ruining my good time." I laugh as Ashton attempts to dismiss Tony and his friends.

"Nice to see you too, Ashton. But no. Last I checked you don't actually own this place. Plus, I want to see my girl. How about a dance, Piper?"

I glance toward the bar and see that Ben has caught sight of our newly arrived guests. He turns to walk toward us and Jameson stops him. They exchange a few words and now all the guys are headed our way. This can't be good.

"Tony, hey. What's up?" Jameson asks, offering his hand to Tony.

"Hey, man. Not much, just seeing if my girl is up for a dance."

I hear a low rumbling of a growl come from Ben as

Ashton hops up from her seat. "No can do, dickhead. She's already got a full dance card. Ben, weren't you just about to take Piper for a spin on the dance floor?"

My eyes go wide as I look up through my lashes. "Ash, hush. Ton…"

"You bet I was," Ben says as he extends his hand to me and I take it. "Shall we? Excuse us, guys."

Holding my hand, Ben leads me to the dance floor as a slower song comes through the speakers. My heart can probably be heard over the music, it's beating so loud. My palms are sweating and my breathing is questionable. It's possible I'm having a heart attack. At twenty-five.

As he pulls me to him with ease, I find my body melting into Ben, my nerves easing, and the tension leaving my body. Just as I'm starting to relax, his right hand comes around to grip my lower back and I let out a little gasp and he laughs. My eyes shoot up to his to find him smirking and his eyes hazy with more than humor. Lust? It's not something I'm really privy to but if I were to put a label on it, lust would be the one.

"Relax, Princess."

"Sorry, I am not much of a dancer and I feel like everyone is watching us. It's nerve-wracking."

"Well, they are all watching us, but I think that is a good thing. If they are over there they can't talk to us. I don't know about you but being sober around that group is exhausting. I'm ready to call it a night and them a cab."

I couldn't agree more and laugh at his comment. "I thought it was just me. I love your sister but the more she drinks the higher her pitch goes."

We manage to relax. Okay, I manage to relax for the rest

of the song. And the next two. I don't know who decided to play all of these slow songs but I'm not complaining. Three songs in this man's arms is nothing to avoid. With each song I find myself closer and closer to his body. At this point, we are practically one person.

As the final song ends, I begin to pull away. Ben clears his throat to say something but is interrupted. "Well done, you two. Captain asshole and his friends left. I guess he figured out Piper wasn't interested. Thanks for taking one for the team, Ben." Ashton has managed to separate us and is standing between us as the music switches over to something faster.

I offer Ashton a small smile, the kind that is forced and not sincere. I feel disappointed that our moment has passed but that's exactly what has happened.

"I think I'm going to call it a night, Ash."

"No! What? Why? Come onnnnn…Pipes, stay. Please!"

"I'm just exhausted and since I didn't exactly know we were doing something tonight I didn't plan on being out late. I have so much to do and besides we leave in like forty hours for the lake. You stay and have fun. I'll talk to you tomorrow." I grab her and hug her before I turn toward Ben. "Thanks for the dance. I appreciate the intervention from Tony. I guess I'll see you later."

Before either of them can respond I return to the table and grab my things. There are usually a few cabs outside Country Road and I manage to grab one immediately. Once I'm safely inside the car, I am overwhelmed with exhaustion. My anxiety has been through the roof since I found those damn roses on my car. If I thought for a second I was going to convince myself they weren't from Tony, I was mistaken.

As I'm leaning my head back and massaging my temples, wishing it was a real massage, my phone alerts a text. Actually a few in succession.

Ashton: Did ou mae hm!

Ben: Just wanted to see if you made it home safe.

Ben: I think Ash is trying to text you. I'm going to help her.

Ashton: Did you make it home safe?

I smile to myself as the cab pulls up in front of my apartment. I thank the cab driver and pay before exiting. Once I'm safely in my apartment I pull up the text messages, choosing to respond to Ashton before Ben.

Me: I'm home. Have fun and happy b-day. Love you.

Me: I'm home. Thanks for helping her.

Ashton: Luv u 2

Ben: Of course. Sleep well, Princess.

Me: Night, Cowboy.

Ben: I enjoyed having you in my arms.

Is Bentley Sullivan flirting with me? Surely he isn't.

Ben: Hope for another soon.

Ben: Yes, I'm flirting. Now I have to get the birthday girl some water. Night.

I only allow myself a smile in response to the last text message. Once I have my boots off, I head to my bedroom. Sleep beckons me and my pillow is lonely.

I need to have a conversation with Ben this weekend; the flirting needs to stop.

Sadly.

The best part of our weekend at the lake is the three full days we are out of communication from the outside world. Aside from the land line in Jameson's cabin we have no phone service. I also use the term cabin loosely. Really, it's a large bedroom with a bathroom (yay) and a kitchenette where we happily brew coffee (double yay). The worst part of our weekend, well there are actually two, the first is that at the lake we sleep in tents and the second is that it means we are at the end of summer and I go back to work. I love what I do but come on, it's summer.

Up before the birds, I'm enjoying a cup of coffee while I wait for Ashton to pick me up. After Ben's flirtatious text messages the other night, I have hardly slept. I'm overwhelmed with feelings I shouldn't have. Something about being in his presence puts me at ease. The way his voice settles over me is both comforting and panty melting. How can one man's voice send goosebumps all over my body in sexual desire and comfort me like a familiar blanket?

My phone goes off with a text from Ashton telling me she's downstairs. I grab my duffel and pillow before locking up and heading downstairs. I stop suddenly at the bottom step when I look up and see Ben standing next to his truck. He begins walking toward me but I'm stuck in place.

"Morning, Princess. Let me take your stuff."

I silently hand him my bag. "I'll keep my pillow, thanks."

I follow him to the truck, and as I approach I see Ashton in the front seat.

"Hey, girl, Ben offered to drive. I agreed as long as I have control over the radio. Who knows what kind of crap music he discovered during his city years. Probably something awful."

I shake my head at her assessment. I've been in this truck and can confirm that Ben's music preferences are no different than hers or mine.

"Ashton, how much coffee have you had this morning? You're awfully chipper."

"Uh, I don't know. Enough. I'm just excited. Three days of laying in the sun, drinking with my friends, and not a care in the world. You know this is my favorite weekend of the year. Plus, my big brother is here this year. Finally, someone to deal with Jameson and his dramatics. And, hopefully keep Tony from bugging you again."

"Ugh, do not say his name. He's like some evil spirit and if you say his name too many times, he'll appear. And I, for one, don't want to deal with him."

"Good point. He isn't stupid enough to show up at the lake this year. I mean, we all know he's an idiot but surely he has enough sense to avoid any more scenes."

I wish I could agree with her but if there's one thing Tony likes, it is being the center of attention. Plus, he's not on bad terms with the guys. Except Ben, that is.

"I'm looking forward to the lack of cell service and his inability to keep texting and calling me. I swear, Ash, if you thought that dance the other night was going to somehow keep him from me then you were mistaken. All that did was make him more determined."

I catch Ben's eye in the rearview mirror and offer him a shrug, telling him that it's out of anyone's control at this point. His response is a shake of his head followed by a sigh of frustration.

"Piper, I told you if he kept bothering you to tell me. Maybe he needs to be confronted. Your niceties don't seem to be working."

"Ben, I appreciate it but really he's harmless. I think it's less about me and more about the fact that I broke up with him. Other than tears of humiliation I haven't even cried over it. Obviously he isn't the love of my life or anything. Plus, since he thinks you are interested in me he's just going to be like he was in high school and try to win. This time, instead of the role of starting pitcher, I just happen to be the trophy."

Ashton laughs until she's bent over smacking her leg like it's some sort of tambourine. Ben looks at her and I look at him, both of us confused at what she's laughing at.

"What's so funny?"

"You. Ben being interested, that's gross. Tony's an idiot. You're like a little sister to him. Now, everyone hush, you're killing the coffee buzz I have going."

I shake my head at her comment and cuddle into my pillow; car rides always are a one-way ticket to a nap. Before I doze off I offer up a silent request to the man upstairs. *Please make this weekend drama free and encourage Ben to leave the flirtations at home. Amen.*

Chapter 11

Ben

Caffeine buzz my ass. Just like when we were kids, both girls are fast asleep before we are more than a few miles outside of town. I'm going to enjoy the silence while the girls sleep; Ashton is a lot louder than I remember.

I sent an email to the realtor this morning and put in an offer on the dream house. Piper's dream house. I can't see there being much of a bidding war for a house that is barely standing so I'm pretty confident I will be a home owner when we get back to town on Sunday.

The look on Piper's face as she stood in that knee-high grass has been consuming my dreams the last few nights. Those dreams are likely to find their spot in the archives and be replaced by the version of Piper today. Watching her walk down those stairs about did me in. Short, cut-off denim shorts show off her amazing legs and the loose-fitting tank she has on compliments her in ways that have me thinking thoughts I shouldn't have. Her long hair is in some haphazard bun that makes me want to tug it loose, allowing her hair cascade down like a waterfall.

Obviously I didn't forget to pack my vagina. Good lord, I need to get a grip or it's going to be a very long weekend.

An hour after we left Piper's house we pass the sign that indicates we'll be at the lake in a few minutes. I nudge Ash awake and instantly regret it. I forgot how violent she can be when she's woken up and my arm pays the price. The ruckus of my near-death experience at the hands of my sister wakes Piper up and the moment I glance at her stretching I regret my peek in the mirror. Her tank barely lifts but it's enough to show me a sliver of her bare belly. I wonder if it's too late to suggest the girls wear wet suits this weekend.

"Finally! I thought we'd never get here!" Ashton frustratingly exclaims as I pull up next to Jameson's truck. I shake my head at my sister's dramatics. She's acting as if her nap was hours long instead of minutes.

"Ben, you should really talk to J about that monstrosity of a truck. What is he compensating for? Small dickitis?" Ashton asks as she hops out of the truck and heads to the back and starts pulling bags out.

I laugh and meet her at the tailgate along with Piper.

"Yeah, I'm not having that conversation with him but knock yourself out."

"What conversation?" Jameson asks as he walks up from around the cabin to help us.

"The one where Ben tells you that your little dick is showing with your need to drive that truck," Ashton says as she stomps off. It's a stomp for sure. I don't know why she has so much hostility toward Jameson but I just shrug and pull the cooler out before closing the tailgate.

"What's up her ass? I almost regret putting the tents up, should've made her do that herself."

I look at Piper and she shakes her head and smiles before turning to Jameson. "Don't mind her, she was sleeping before we got here. You know what a pill she can be when she wakes up against her will."

That seems to pacify Jameson as we head toward the cabin with all of the bags and food. The girls start emptying the bags and boxes of food while Jameson takes me on a tour of the property.

"I can't believe you bought land out here. It's pretty cool, man."

"Yeah well, it's not much but it's mine. If it wasn't such a drive for work, I'd live here, that's for sure."

Once we walk over to where Jameson has set up the tents, the girls have made their way over to where we stand. Ashton seems to have relaxed a little and is more herself. We're all in agreement that food is the number one priority. A quick loss in a game of Rock Paper Scissors finds Jameson and I tasked with cooking breakfast while the girls ice the beers for later.

Contemplating simply pouring cereal in a bowl and declaring breakfast served so the girls won't have high expectations from our cooking skills, we reluctantly prepare a feast of a breakfast.

Once we've all finished eating and the mess is cleared, I change into some workout gear and start out on a hike around the lake. I've never considered myself a loner, but being back in the thick of things with this group has made solitude and quiet something I yearn for.

When I return to Camp Shenanigans, as it has been

deemed, I notice that Owen's truck is parked next to mine. In the distance I hear laughs and splashes coming from the water. I lost my shirt early in my hike as the sun beat down on me making it feel more like a blanket. I pull the shirt from my waistband and wipe my head as I grab and down a cold water. Tossing the bottle in the recycling bin, I turn toward the cabin. Before I have an opportunity to open the door, it comes flying open and a bikini-wearing Piper slams right into my chest with an audible *oomph*.

"Whoa there, where's the fire?" I ask while I reluctantly peel her from my body.

"Ss … sorry. I was just using the restroom and didn't see you there. So uh, yeah how was your hike?"

I smile, noticing she hasn't looked at me yet. Not true, she seems to be quite interested in the waistband of my shorts, but she hasn't looked up at my face.

"The hike was good. Hot, but good."

"Wow, it is crazy hot today. I should get down to the water; you should join us, ya know, after you, umm, change or whatever. I mean you don't need to change if you didn't want to so yeah I should go okay bye," she rattles off in a rambling sentence and takes off in what can only be described as a stumbling hustle toward the water.

Laughing to myself, I go inside where it is slightly cooler and embrace the temperature change. Once I've changed into my trunks I grab a protein bar from my bag and another water before I head down to the lake. The closer I get, the louder the hoots and hollers get. I missed these kinds of weekends since I've been gone and the realization hits me again. I am the outsider in this group. Funny how Ashton seems to have moved into my place with my friends. It makes me happy to know they embraced and protected her while I was gone even if I do have a twinge of jealousy.

As I take a seat next to Jameson I notice that the girls are in the middle of an intense game of chicken. "Wow, that looks pretty serious. They do know it's a game of chicken, right?"

"Yeah, it's how they decided to determine who is on dish duty tonight. You know Ash, she'll do anything to get out of dishes so she's determined to win," he says as he takes a long drink from his beer.

"Beer already? Is it even noon yet?" I ask and recognize how old I sound.

"Relax, bud, we're on vacation. There aren't any clocks here. Besides, it's five o'clock somewhere, right?" he asks as he finishes off that beer and hands one to me that I waive off.

"I guess. I'll stick with water for now. Hydrate and all that."

We sit here, in the blazing sun, watching our friends battle it out to avoid dish duty. Once Ashton and Owen secure the win, they perform some sort of awkward victory dance that includes poking fun at their opponents, Piper and Landon. Eventually, we all settle in for an afternoon of swimming and, for everyone but me, drinking. I notice as the day wears on that my sister avoids direct conversation with Jameson. They've never been very close but they have always been civil. I assumed since they hang out as a group that they had bridged whatever gap existed between them. Apparently I was wrong.

Much to Ashton's dislike, Piper declares it dinner time, which sends Owen and Ashton to the cabin to begin preparing. Feeling the need to impute a little big brother advice, or really just figure out what is going on with her and Jameson, I offer to take Owen's place in the kitchen. He willingly takes me up on it and suddenly it's just the Sullivans in the kitchen.

I take the lead and start seasoning steaks as Ashton shucks the corn. A few minutes into the process I decide to bring up the subject of Jameson.

"So what's the deal with you and J? You pissed at him or something?"

"What? No. Why would you say that?"

"I don't know, maybe because you never speak to him. You were pretty bitchy when we got here this morning, too."

"You know I don't like to be shaken awake, I apologized for that. And for your information, I do speak to Jameson. I just don't speak slut so he probably doesn't hear me and thus doesn't respond," she declares as she walks out of the cabin with the corn.

Just as I'm about to join her with the steaks, Landon walks in the cabin.

"Hey, man, those look good. How's it going?" he asks me, pulling up a seat at the table.

"All is well. How's it going with you? How's the HVAC business?"

"It's good. My dad and I haven't killed each other yet so that's always a bonus."

I laugh with him and cannot imagine being business partners with my dad. I love him and we're close, but business partners? No thanks.

"Yeah, I don't think I could do it. I thought you'd bring a date this weekend."

"Nah, we've all tried that. Bringing someone outside the group for this last weekend of summer never goes well. The girls we've brought have never really meshed with your sister and Piper. Girls are catty, man. I just don't get it. Last year Tony came with Piper and that was cool."

I don't respond to that last comment. I pick up the tray of steaks to head out to the grill when Landon asks me the million-dollar question. "How about you? You plan on hooking up with Piper again?"

I set the tray of steaks down and put my hands on the back of the chair, leaning in a little with a shrug. "We didn't hook up. It was," I pause searching for the correct word," spontaneous. Something that ended once I found out who she was."

Landon laughs. "Yeah, man, you keep telling yourself that."

'What's that supposed to mean?"

Shaking his head, he stands and smiles. "Ben, come on. I see the way you look at Piper when you think nobody is looking. Yeah, I get it, she's fucking hot in a bikini, but it's more than that. We all appreciate what she's displaying, but you? You look at her like, hell, man, I don't know, like something."

I don't respond. I stand there watching as he enters the bathroom, letting his words settle before taking the steaks to the grill. Yeah, she's something all right.

A few hours after my conversation with Landon, his words are still ringing in my head. I know Piper and I have a connection that neither of us can deny but that's all it can ever be. I will never do anything to come between her friendship with Ashton and I really don't want my sister pissed at me. While I'm convincing myself of this fact the same sister declares it bedtime and, along with Piper, heads to the tent they're sharing. Landon and Owen follow shortly after, leaving Jameson and me alone with a fire and the crickets.

"So what's the deal with you and my sister?"

Jameson must be taken by surprise at my question because he wastes a good portion of his beer by spraying it toward the fire.

"Where'd that come from? Nothing, man. She's a royal pain in my ass as always but we're cool."

"She seems really pissed at you all the time. I figured maybe something happened."

"Nah, she's always like that. It's worse when I have a date around. That's why we don't bring them anymore. The last time I had a girl here for our last weekend Ashton kept saying things like 'slut' and 'hoochie' poorly disguised as coughs. Poor Candi had to be consoled all night. It was really a tough job."

"Yeah, I'm sure you were really put out with that job. If you say everything's cool, then I guess it is."

As I respond I hear a zipper from a tent and see Piper walking toward the water. Jameson must follow my gaze.

"She does that every night when we're out here. Says it is the only time she can think."

I watch her as she makes it to the water's edge and starts skipping rocks. Even from this distance and in the dark I am mesmerized by her. Never taking my eyes from her, I feel Jameson's hand on my shoulder as he stands.

"Quit fighting what is so obvious to us all. Go to her, Ben, see what happens. I'm hitting the sack."

I don't move right away. I battle myself and know I should go to my tent too. I should get up, put this fire out, and go to sleep. I don't. Instead, I find myself walking toward the woman who consumes my dreams and is easily making her way into my heart.

Chapter 12

Piper

This is always my favorite part of our weekends at the lake. Of course, I love being with my friends. It's just that it can be overwhelming. Jameson, Landon, and Owen are a lot of testosterone while Ashton is her own little party of crazy. Add to that already rowdy bunch one Bentley Sullivan, and it's a little too much.

Ashton and I always share a tent, well except last year when I brought Tony with us. We had only been dating a few weeks but I was smitten. My excuse in breaking the "no date at the lake" rule was that we all knew Tony and so it was less like a date and more like just another friend. Unfortunately, with him here I didn't get my nights at the water. He didn't understand why I'd want alone time when I could be with him.

Waiting until Ashton is asleep, I quietly walk toward the water. This time of night, the only light that guides me is that of the moon and it's perfect. I know this land well enough to know it's safe. This is one of my top five favorite places in our area and it centers me when I need it. Having Ben here is throwing me off and I need this time more than ever.

I pick up a rock and attempt a skip and then another. Only instead of skipping these are tosses. Frustrated tosses. I hate that I brought Tony here to this place that means so much to me. I had always promised myself I wouldn't blindly share with just anyone the places and things that matter the most to me.

How did I ever think I was in love with him? I wasn't. I acknowledge that now. I cared about him, but if I loved him like I should have, would I care so little about the breakup? We were together just shy of a year and I can't even pretend to be sad he's not in my life anymore. Truthfully, I think I was happy to have someone like him choose me. I believed him when he said he cared and I trusted him with the things that matter the most to me – my friends, my family, and my heart.

It feels empowering to finally admit to myself that I was searching. I've always loved the idea of love, something I get from my mother. As I've gotten older I realize that my dad leaving her alone to raise a baby did a number on my mom. She's spent most of my life, and hers, searching for her Prince Charming. Regardless of how many frogs she's had to kiss, Tessa Lawrence believes her one true love exists.

When I was little she would tell me stories of princes and white knights saving the lonely princess. Even at a young age I knew the princess was her and that the men on white horses she described weren't the men she actually dated. My mom settled. As an adult I see now that she took attention from whoever was giving it, not necessarily from the men she deserved. Dread hits me like this rock I'm skipping. It's possible I've turned into my mother.

I pick up another rock and, after successfully completing the triple skip and admiring the ripples in the water, I sit down on the shore. Pulling my chin to my knees, I think of all the vows to myself I've made over the years. I'm always trying to better myself and not fall into patterns of my past or those of my mother.

Deep in thought, I don't hear Bentley walk up behind me, nor do I hear him sit down beside me. I'm slightly startled when he begins talking.

"You had a good spin on that rock, Princess. Some awesome guy must have taught you how to skip."

That comment makes me laugh because, in fact, an awesome guy did teach me to skip rocks. The guy sitting next to me to be precise.

"I have no idea what you're talking about. Some weirdo tried to teach me to skip rocks when I was a kid but he wasn't very good."

Ben returns the laugh and nudges me with his shoulder. On instinct I lay my head on his shoulder as we both stare out at the lake. The moon is beautiful and the stars are shimmering in the sky like mini beacons. It's breathtaking.

"Are you okay? You've been quiet all night," he asks me.

I don't answer right away. The honest truth is I *have* been quiet. I'm trying to process why every time this man is near me my heart races like it's making a run for a gold medal. I breathe in the scent that I've grown accustomed to. The one that makes the hairs on the back of my neck stand up, sends chills up my spine, and even manages to send tingles between my legs. The scent of the man who has now put his arm around me and pulled me to his side.

"I'm okay, just having a moment," I finally reply.

"J said you come down here a lot. It's really peaceful. I can see why you like it."

I push a stray hair that has fallen in my eye, and as I put my hand back down I realize I have nowhere to put it but on Ben's leg. I feel him stiffen as I do and I don't mean his posture. A slight smile takes over my face when I realize that he feels it, too. Somehow, in this crazy world, the one person I share a true connection with, the one person who can make me equally frustrated and happy at the same time, is the person I'm not supposed to feel something for.

We sit like that for a few minutes. I'm nestled into his side with my head on his shoulder and hand on his leg. I feel my eyes becoming heavier and before I can tell Ben that I am going to head to bed a noise startles me, causing me to jump almost directly onto his lap.

"Whoa, it was just a frog."

"Well, it sounded bigger than a frog." The defensiveness evident in my reply, I begin to move from his lap, but he puts his hands on my waist.

"Hey, it's not a big deal. I was just teasing."

I shift my weight so I can begin moving when I hear a rumble from the back of his throat that stops me. Through gritted teeth he looks me in the eye. "Piper, if you don't want what we already agreed can't happen again to happen, please stop moving in my lap."

My eyes go wide as I look down and then quickly up. I've never been more grateful for the darkness as I am now. Surely my face a color close to that of my hair.

"Oh, uh. Sorry?"

"Is that a question, Princess?"

Oh, his voice. Down, girlie bits. "No, no. I'm sorry. So I'm going to get up now. If you now want to, I don't know, think of zombies or something."

He chuckles as he releases my waist and I stand, brushing off the non-existent dirt from my shorts. Following suit, Ben stands. As I turn to talk away he grabs my hand.

"This is really hard, Piper. I didn't think it would be, but it is."

I won't even pretend to play dumb.

"Ben…" I don't manage much more than his name before he releases my hand and places a hand on either side of my face, fingertips in my hair, and thumbs on my cheek. My gaze drifts to his lips as my hands reach his wrists. I want him to kiss me. I *need* him to kiss me. He's closing the distance between us and can feel his breath mingling with mine.

"Tell me no, Piper. Tell me to stop."

"Ben."

"That's not no."

Before I can respond his lips are on mine. His lips are gentle at first, as if he thinks I'll break. I won't. I can't with him. I feel that in my soul.

On instinct, I begin lowering my hands to rest on his hips and my body fits perfectly against him. That must be the invitation he needs because the kiss intensifies as he licks my lower lip. I release a pent-up purr as I open for him. The moment our tongues meet I see stars dancing. The tension in my body releases as a euphoric feeling begins its takeover. From my toes to my ears, I feel my skin tingle and my heart race. It's an exhilarating ride of feelings. A series of extreme highs that should scare me. Highs that only seem to ground me and have me gripping his shirt like a life line. I feel his left hand on my waist as he holds me to him, keeping me upright. I'm thankful for that move because without it, I think I would fall.

Or, maybe I'm already falling. The moment I have that thought, I feel the tension return and Ben begin to pull back from me. He doesn't immediately break the kiss. He seems to be savoring it and simply reversing it back to where it began with the gentleness returning. Resting his forehead to mine, we both breathe each other in and I feel like I'm about to cry. What is it with this man and my need to cry?

"Ben," I say as my hands return to either wrist and I take a small step back.

"Don't, Piper. Please, don't say anything."

As much as I don't want to, I completely step back from Ben and put distance between us.

"We agreed, Ben. This is a bad idea."

"No, Piper. We actually didn't agree that this is a bad idea. We agreed that Ashton is important to both of us and we won't do anything to hurt her. But what about us, Piper? There's something between us. We both know it; why should we suffer?"

It seems like an eternity as I stand here, letting his words process. Suffer. That word seems extreme. And accurate. Sighing in frustration, I retreat even farther. Not only in space but within my heart.

Distance.

I need distance and yet with each step I take, he follows.

"You're right."

That statement stills him.

"Ashton is important to me. She is the best friend I've ever had, Ben. I won't do anything that may jeopardize that."

Ben seems to also be processing. The difference between him and me is that when I process I am serious and quiet. When Bentley Sullivan processes, he smiles and tries to hold hands.

I attempt to tug my hand back but he doesn't let me as I continue.

"Tell me, Ben, what happens after we hook up? We'll go on a few dates? Maybe hang out? Sure, that sounds great. Then you'll realize I'm boring and not worth the effort. Regardless of what happens, it is bound to get awkward."

The smile is gone.

"And when Ashton feels like she has to choose? What then? No. I won't do it and you shouldn't ask me to."

Congratulations to me, I said all of that without crying. High five, self.

Now it's Ben's turn to sigh in frustration as he drops my hand.

Finally.

"Why do you do that?"

"Do what?"

"Why do you put yourself down?"

Before I can respond he has taken both of my hands and attempts to tug me toward him. This time I'm ready. Taking my hands back, I wrap them around myself while taking a small step back.

"Piper," he begins while stepping toward me. I put my hand up to stop him. "Fine, I'll stand over here. Why do you put yourself down all the time? I can tell you one thing,

Piper, I would never be bored with you."

I snort in disbelief.

"Don't." The frustration is evident in a single word. "I wouldn't. I've already told you how great I think you are. Shit, I'm putting myself out there, Piper. I'm telling you I want you. That I want to pursue this connection we have."

A stand-off of sorts happens. Seconds pass while we just stand there, staring at each other without speaking. There is no way to respond to him without making this situation worse. I should walk away and end this conversation. Just as the thought occurs to me Ben takes a small tentative step toward me and continues his frustrated speech.

"Tell me why when you walk in a room, without me even seeing you, the hairs on the back of my neck stand up. Why is it that the minute you speak I lose all ability to think rationally? Your voice, Piper. God what your voice does to me. When you speak each syllable slips over me like the slowest pour of honey. I would listen to you read the phone book if you wanted." My breath hitches as he takes another step. "Baby, I want to know why every single time I look in your eyes, so beautiful and kind, that I see so much more than I ever thought was possible."

A final step and he's directly in front of me again. My defenses down with each word he speaks. Tears freely flowing as he places those damn hands on my face again. Sighing in resignation. Each movement is precise and cautious, leaving me more conflicted.

The little angel on my shoulder is telling him not to kiss me while the little devil on my other shoulder is encouraging the opposite.

"I'm not going to kiss you again, Piper. I've laid it all out on the line. I've told you how I feel. The next move is yours. No matter what you decide, I'll still be your friend. I won't like it but I'll do it."

With that declaration he drops his hands and walks away from me.

Left alone watching his back as he retreats to his tent, I am left with nothing but my thoughts and emotions. Regardless of how beautiful his words are or how he makes me feel, I'm not willing to take the risk of hurting Ashton nor our friendship.

I begrudgingly return to the tent I share with my best friend. As I settle in to my sleeping bag, Ashton rolls over and smiles at me.

"Did you get your alone time?" she asks me between yawns.

"Yeah, I did. Go back to sleep, it's late."

"K. Night, love you."

"Love you, too."

And, that is why Bentley Sullivan and I will only ever be friends.

The problem with heart-to-heart conversations under the moonlight is the morning after. Unlike romance movies or novels, I didn't have some epiphany of how Ben and I could pursue our feelings and not hurt Ashton. Just the opposite, actually. I tossed and turned all night, and when I did manage a few minutes of sleep, my dreams were consumed by flashes of the moments we've had together. And that damn frog. I'm still not convinced it was just a frog.

After finally emerging from our tent, I join the rest of the group for breakfast in the cabin. Grateful no life-changing decisions need to be made today, I savor my coffee. Only once I've made it halfway through my second cup do I notice that Ben isn't at the table.

Fine, I noticed when I sat down but it's only just processing.

"Where's Ben?"

"Nothwer ike," Landon answers as eggs fall from his mouth. I raise an eyebrow at him and he swallows before offering me a smile. "Another hike, sorry."

I return his smile as I grab another piece of bacon.

"Piper, are you going to be boring again? Do you plan on just sitting around drinking water and reading?" Ashton teases as she nudges my shoulder with her own.

"Hush up. I had fun yesterday and had a few beers. I actually feel like today may be a perfect day for day drinking."

"Yes!" Ashton shouts as she offers me her hand for a high five, which I give her. "Tell me more about these day drinking plans? Are we starting with red beers after breakfast? Bloody Marys? Man-whore, do you have any champagne? Mimosas may be what the doctor ordered!"

"Ashton," I say with a warning in my voice.

"What?" Ashton unconvincingly questions. I just shake my head and stand to put my cup in the sink.

"I assume you are speaking to me?" Arms crossed as he leans back in his chair, Jameson acts as if Ashton calling him a man-whore, or any other name, doesn't bother him, but his eyes tell a different story.

"Obviously, I don't see another man-whore around here."

With the exception of Jameson and Ashton, we all laugh as Owen and Landon start to argue that perhaps they, too, should be considered for the title. Seeing who will blink first, Jameson and Ashton stare at one another, brows raised and lips pursed. The tension is both ridiculous and unnecessary.

"Good grief. Ash, please stop calling Jameson names. This *is* his place. And, J?" Jameson turns to look at me. "You blinked first, you lost. I'm going for a run, see you all in a bit."

Leaving the cabin, I can still hear Owen and Landon campaigning for the elusive title. Thank goodness for those two and their banter. If there is one thing their argument is sure to do, it's to ease the tension between Ash and Jameson. Tension that is giving me a headache, and tension that is bound to implode when we all least expect it.

After an internal battle over a run versus nap, the run wins out. There is no way Ashton will let me out of a day of drinking and shenanigans. I'm going to enjoy the day and my friends without letting last night's conversation with Ben interfere with any of it.

Four hours after the stare down in the kitchen, we are all enjoying the sun, water, and coolers full of drinks. The guys have tossed some food on the grill and left Ashton and me to our own devices for a while. It's a much-needed moment of quiet.

"Ash, can I ask you something?"

Ashton raises her head from where she's laying on her towel and looks at me over her sunglasses. "Obviously. What's up? Don't look so serious, you'll kill the moment."

I laugh at her. "Sorry, it's not serious. I don't think so anyway. What's your deal with Jameson? Did you guys hook up and you never told me?"

Putting her sunglasses back in place, Ashton buries her head and mumbles a response I can't quite make out. "Stop mumbling."

"Ugh," she sighs as she sits up and looks at me. "Nothing ever happened. I just … I don't know. He drives me nuts. He both infuriates and saddens me at the same time. He makes my insides flip. It reminds me of that time I bungee jumped. Then he'll say something and I want to kick him in the nuts and never speak to him again."

Interesting.

"Do you like him, Ash?"

"That's a dumb question, Piper. We're friends. We've been friends most of our life; he *is* my brother's best friend. Of course I like him. He's just annoying and set on screwing every ho-bag in the county." Ending her short monologue with a huff, she lays down again.

"Would you ever date him?" I don't know why I ask this, but I do, and part of me hopes she says yes.

"Yeah, no. Jameson and I, well we aren't like that. Plus, he's Ben's best friend. That's a violation of some sibling best friend code or something. Besides, my brother would lose his shit if I went to him and said I wanted to ride Jameson's pony."

I offer her a little laugh. "Pretty sure you should never refer to a man's penis as a pony. Do you really think Ben would care?" He'd be a hypocrite if he did.

Shrugging, she starts to settle back on her towel. "It doesn't matter; I'd never do that. No good could come from hook-ups among friends. One breakup and the entire group would be chaos and I just think it would put my brother in an awkward position."

"I guess it could be weird."

"Weird? Piper, it would be more than weird. I'm Ben's sister. If something happened, and that's a huge if by the way, and it ended not only would Ben have to choose sides but he'd probably always choose mine. He'd lose his best friend and that's not worth a pony ride."

"Stop with the pony reference. I just think there's a reason Jameson gets you in knots and maybe you should think about that."

No reply given says volumes. The guys return with food and another great day at the lake continues. No drama, no chaos, and no serious conversations with Ben or Ashton. Another game of chicken between the guys this time gives Ashton and me enough time for quick showers before dinner.

Before I join the group at the bonfire, I excuse myself into the cabin for a few minutes to myself. I'm washing dishes when those little hairs on my neck raise. I don't need him to speak to know Ben is behind me. He doesn't touch me but I feel him as if his hands were on me.

"You doing okay? You're a little quiet tonight."

Rinsing the dish in my hand, I place it in the drainer before grabbing the next or offering him an answer. After what feels like minutes but is only seconds I resign myself to answer.

"I'm great. It's been a fun day. I am ready to get home though."

"Piper," he says, but I don't let him finish as I rinse and place one very clean plate to dry and grab a towel turning to him.

"Ben, please don't. I really had a good day and don't want to talk about this anymore. Can we please just be friends? We have less than a week before school starts. We'll see each other every day and it'd be great if we were in a good place."

A small smile appears and he nods. "Okay. So, *friend,* can you please tell me why we start work on a Thursday? This really seems ass backwards."

I laugh and know then and there that everything will be okay.

Chapter 13

Piper

The first day of the school year finds me pulling on my oldest pair of cowboy boots. Tall, almost to my knee, they are bright and colorful with a floral design that the kids always love. One of my mentors from college told me that he discovered early on if he presented himself to the kids with something of interest they almost always eased into the new school year with less anxiety. Or, at the very least less tears at drop-off. I noticed then that he always wore a wild bow tie.

On my first day of teaching, I didn't wear the boots. It was the most chaotic day of my life. Nothing could have prepared me for the level of hysterics presented in the form of eighteen humans under four feet tall. The next day, I dug my boots out of the back of my closet and said a little prayer they worked. As the children filed in the classroom that day, full of trepidation, one little girl saw my boots. She pointed and whispered to her mom who looked at me and smiled. I approached the little girl and dropped so that I was eye level.

"Simone, right?"

Hiding behind her mother's leg, she nodded.

"I saw you looking at my boots, would you like to see them up close?" Another nod. With a nudge from her mom she approached me almost as if she wasn't sure I was real. Mesmerized by the intricate design, she ran her tiny finger over the design. As she did, other children in the class noticed our interaction and joined. The day wasn't perfect, but it was significantly better than the first day and only managed to get better as the week went on.

I went home that night and sent an e-mail to my mentor and thanked him for the idea. He sent back an e-mail that told me the idea was less for the children and more for the teacher. Sometimes we, too, need a way to take the focus off of what is happening and on to something else. So very true.

I arrive at the school about thirty minutes before the authorized drop-off time and spot Ben's truck immediately. Contemplating parking near his truck, I instead choose a spot on the opposite side of the lot.

Once I've made it to my classroom and checked the class fish tank, we can't start off the first day of school with a fish funeral after all, I take a few deep breaths when there's a knock at my door.

"Miss Lawrence."

"Mr. Sullivan."

"You look pretty. I bet all of the boys in your class have a crush on you by the end of the day."

Laughing, I walk over to my desk and take a drink of my coffee.

"What about you? The glasses are a nice touch, by the

way. I'm sure not only will the second grade girls will have a crush on their new teacher, but the moms, too."

Before he can reply, voices in the hallway signal that the conversation is over and the new year is starting.

"Well, I better get back to my class. Have a good first day, Piper."

"You, too."

Nodding and turning to walk out the door, I give myself just one second to check out the jeans Ben is wearing. That's completely fine. We're friends and even friends can appreciate what their friends are wearing.

Before I can fully appreciate the view, Ben turns and winks at me before turning down the hall. Damnit. Busted again.

As my new flock of students begins filtering in, I am greeted with familiarity by a few of the parents and even a few of the children who have siblings I've taught before. Then the sweetest little face catches my eye and my teacher heart swells. An adorable little boy tentatively walks in holding the hand of an older woman, grandmother perhaps. I watch as his big blue eyes dance around the room. His blond hair, refusing to be tamed, a little long in the front, gives him a bit of an Owen Wilson look. When I notice his eyes are lined red as if he's been crying I decide to introduce myself before any sort of meltdown begins.

I introduce myself to the woman who tells me her name is Mrs. Honeycutt. Not recognizing the name from my student list, I drop down to a squat so I'm level with the young man who appears to be on the verge of a new set of tears.

"Hi there. What's your name?"

I hear a sniffle of a response, "Jacob."

Great, the kid who has my heart full of compassion and me wondering how long until I can have babies of my own is Jacob Thorne. Child of uber bitch, Felicity Remington hyphen Thorne.

"Well, Jacob, I'm Miss Lawrence. It's very nice to meet you," I say, offering him my hand. He shyly shakes it and looks up at Mrs. Honeycutt for reassurance.

"Jacob, it's a pleasure to meet you. We're going to have a wonderful time here in kindergarten. Would you like to come with me and find your seat? Your name is written on a tag so we'll need to look at them all until we find yours. How about it?"

Once again looking at Mrs. Honeycutt, who adoringly looks at this sweet boy, he turns to take my extended hand. We locate his seat, which is next to Patty Wilmington. Patty is an outgoing and talkative child who I've known since she was born and have no doubt will be a perfect seat mate for a shy little boy like Jacob. Leaving Jacob to be Patty's sounding board, I return to Mrs. Honeycutt.

"I think he'll be just fine."

She looks at me and smiles. "Yes, I suppose he will. I think this is more difficult for me than it is for him. I suppose you see this reaction from parents all the time."

"I do, yes. But if you don't mind me asking, what is your relationship to Jacob?"

"Oh, I'm his nanny. I came to work for the Thornes shortly after Jacob was born. He was a colicky baby and with a toddler underfoot his mother needed help. He's quite special to me and I'm a little heartbroken to see him growing up. Silly, I know."

"It's not silly. He seems like a sweet boy. I promise to

look after him. May I ask where his parents are?" Not that I really want to see his mother but I should at least ask.

"His father is away on business. Mr. Thorne travels a lot for his company and is only home a few days a month. Mrs. Remington-Thorne is with Jacob's sister, Clementine. She's a second grader at this school."

That means Felicity is with Ben right now.

"I see. I don't recall having Clementine in my class before."

"No, Mrs. Remington-Thorne had her in a private school until this year. We have only just moved to Lexington full time. Mrs. Remington-Thorne grew up here. Perhaps you know her."

Oh, I know her. "Oh, perhaps. I should get this day started. Again, Mrs. Honeycutt, I think Jacob will be just fine."

The morning has minimal tears from most of the class and only one meltdown. Of course the meltdown was of epic proportions and perhaps some bodily fluids were lost. Still, I made it through the day and, as expected, Jacob Thorne was fine and Mrs. Honeycutt was grateful. No Felicity sightings and for that I'm grateful.

As I'm turning off the lights and heading down the hall-way, Ben walks out of his class.

"Miss Lawrence, how was the first day?"

"Pretty good, yours?"

"It was good. I have a great group of kids. Hey, guess whose daughter is in my class?"

"Felicity Remington, yeah I heard."

"Hyphen Thorne. Don't forget the hyphen," he says, shaking his head and laughing.

"Oh yes, we mustn't. I have her son, Jacob, in my class. Adorable kid. Sweet as pie and kind-hearted. How's the sister?"

"Clementine? She's her mother's daughter. I had a few flashbacks to childhood with her today."

"I don't envy you. I'm not looking forward to dealing with Felicity this year."

"She was a bit tough on you growing up, wasn't she?"

We stop at his truck at that question. "Tough? She made my life a living hell, Ben. We grew up during a time that girls like her were referred to as 'Mean Girls.' In reality she was just a bitch and found some sick satisfaction in making me miserable. I'd rather go the rest of my life without having to deal with her. I'm grateful the nanny seems to be the primary point of contact for little Jacob."

"Where's your car?" he asks me, looking around. I point him toward the other end of the lot.

"Were you running late this morning? That's a crap parking spot."

I turn to start walking away. "Not late, just getting in a few extra steps. See ya later, Ben."

I'm opening my car door when I hear something behind me.

"Hey, baby."

"Tony, what are you doing here? And I'm not your baby."

I toss my bag in the passenger seat and before I can take my seat Tony puts his hand on the door, slightly closing it and preventing me from opening it further to take my seat behind the wheel.

"You didn't call me after I left you flowers. I figured you were still mad."

I grunt in disbelief at his statement.

"I'll take that as a yes. Look, Piper. I'm sorry. I know I screwed up and you're angry but come on." He's almost pleading as he removes one hand from the door and places it on my waist to turn me toward him. He really is handsome.

No, Piper, he's a cheater.

"Please, Piper. Give me a chance to make it right."

The moment he finishes his sentence I hear a sound of an engine and my eyes look over Tony's shoulder to see Ben leaning against his steering wheel looking at us. Gone is his teacher attire and instead he's in a well-worn T-shirt and a ball cap. The scruff on his face just right, his eyes saying more than words ever could, and my heart skips a beat. I feel a sense of guilt for how intimate this must look and take a slight step back from Tony as he turns to see Ben.

"Sullivan, do you need something?"

"You okay, Princess?"

Words not forming, I simply nod in response.

"See you at dinner?"

Another nod, which he returns before turning his attention to Tony. The look on his face is enough for Tony to release his hand from my waist. That must satisfy Ben because he drives away.

"Dinner? Are you seeing him, Piper?"

"Not that it's any of your business, but no. We're having family dinner at the Sullivans'. Look, thank you for the flowers. That was, well, the thought was nice, but please don't do things like that. Tony, you're not a bad guy. Hmm, actually that's not true. You don't *have* to be a bad guy. Just remember that with the next girl. I've got to go."

"So, that's it? You're over me that easily. I love you, Piper.

That has to mean something."

I take a deep breath and look up at Tony and see sincerity in his eyes as I sit down behind the wheel and roll down my window. "Tony, you don't love me. You loved the idea of me. And, honestly, I don't think I loved you either. At least I wasn't in love with you. I'd like it if we could still be friends though."

"But I did, do love you."

"Tony, what's my favorite flower?"

"Roses. All chicks love roses."

"No, Tony they don't. I, for one, am severely allergic to roses. We were together almost a year and you didn't know that. We had fun and I don't regret our time together but we need to just call it a day. There's someone out there for you but it's just not me. Now I have to get going." As he steps away from the door, obviously absorbing what I've just said, I roll up my window and drive away, leaving him standing in the parking lot.

As I drive to my apartment I find myself feeling lighter and relieved. Once I make it inside, the first thing to go are my boots. Adorable and serving a purpose, they aren't the most kindergarten-friendly piece of footwear I own. Changing into a pair of leggings, I make myself a light snack and pull out my planner. I look at the seating chart I made prior to meeting the kids and make a few notes when my phone signals a text message.

Ben: Everything ok?
Me: Yeah, I'm fine.
Ben: Is he with you?
Me: What? No! Why would you even ask that?
Ben: He looked pretty cozy with you in his arms so I

assumed you were getting back together.

I can't help it, that little hint of jealousy brings a smile to my face before reality reminds me, friends only.

Me: Well, FRIEND, we aren't. I don't think Tony will be leaving me any more roses or looking to reconcile. I'll see you at dinner.

He doesn't respond and I'm not surprised. Perhaps the all caps were a bit shouty. Until I have the option for italics in a text it's the only way I can think of to remind him of the "friends only" agreement.

Dinner with the Sullivans is never boring. I've been coming to family dinner every Thursday as long as I can remember. A few years ago Jameson started joining us. That's just like Patty and Paul, to take in their kid's friends who are maybe a little light in the family department.

I'm in the kitchen helping Patty while everyone else is outside. I love spending these quiet moments with Patty. My mom is great and I love her but she's never been much of a cook. Patty was the one who taught me to cook at a young age and it's still something that we share.

"How's your mom, Piper?"

"She's good. She and Michael get back from their cruise next week. She said she's going to stay in Chicago with him for about a week before coming home."

"My goodness, that's one heck of a vacation. She must miss you terribly."

"I doubt it, she's called me non-stop and sent me a post card from every port. She seems happy, though, and that's all I can ask for. Michael is nice and seems to really care about her. Of course, we'll see when they get back. I don't know how you spend that much time together and then go back to long-distance dating."

Patty offers me a look of sympathy and a pat on the arm as she stirs the green beans that are in a skillet to sauté. "Your mother is a strong woman, Piper. She'll be fine. How about you? Are you seeing anyone these days?"

"Uh, no. I think I'll take a break from dating. My track record isn't the greatest. I think my picker is broken." We're both laughing as Ben walks in through the slider.

"What's so funny in here, ladies?"

"Nothing, honey. Just girl talk. These beans are about done, how about the rest outside?"

"Yep, just coming to tell you we're all set. Do you need help?"

"Actually, would the two of you mind bringing these out? I'm just going to grab a sweater."

Left alone with Ben, we work in silence transferring the green beans to a bowl. The sound of him clearing his throat stops me as I turn to walk toward the slider. Raising my brow in question, I wait for Ben to say something.

"I'm sorry if I offended you earlier. I just think you deserve better than someone like Tony Dominguez and it … well, it just looked different than you said."

"There's nothing to be sorry about. Thank you for being concerned but I promise I am not getting back together with Tony."

Dinner is the usual banter amongst the family with more laughs than we've had in a long time. Having Ben home seems to have brought a new element to our dinners and his parents are obviously thrilled to have him back.

Once dinner is finished, Ashton and I find ourselves elbow deep in dishes. Well, I find myself elbow deep, she's complaining about doing dishes. These are the battles with Ashton I don't fight.

"We need to talk Halloween, Pipe. What's our theme this year? I'm thinking Vegas Showgirl."

Shaking my head, I simply reply, "No."

"Come on, Piper! It's my year to choose. Last year we did the good witch bad witch thing like you wanted. By the way, I totally should have been the good witch but whatever. I want to sex it up already!"

Just as I'm about to reply Jameson and Ben walk in the kitchen. "Who is sexing what up?" Jameson asks.

"Us. Well, I want Piper to sex it up a little for Halloween but you know her, she's anti-sexy."

I splash water at her following that response and Ashton lets out a screech that probably has the neighbor's dog howling.

"Nah, Piper's hot already. She doesn't need to sex it up. You could probably sex it down anyway, Ashton." I'd expect something like from her big brother, but it's Jameson who makes the comment.

"Kiss my ass, Jameson. I don't need to down anything but a shot on Halloween. Now, as I was saying to *Piper,* we need a plan."

"Why don't we do a group thing this year?" This time it's Ben speaking and I turn to look at him.

"What if we do an adult version of those costumes from the best Halloween ever? The one where we all went to the youth center party. You remember, Ash?"

More screeches and now claps. I close my eyes as my ears ring in response.

"Yes! Oh my goodness, Ben! Brilliant idea!! Dolly now

will be so much more fun than Dolly before I had real boobs!"

"Wait, what was I?" Jameson asks.

Ashton and I look at each other and start laughing.

"Whoa, déjà vu," Ashton, Ben, and I say in unison.

"Oh yeah, Neo! That costume was the shit. I'm down."

"How about you, Princess? Are you in?"

I look at Ben, who has a huge smile on his face that I can't help but return. "I'm in."

"Yay! I'm totally sexing up your princess costume, Piper."

Everyone laughs at Ashton and I have no doubt I'll be stuffing my boobs back in their place all night long. Thank goodness I have weeks to attempt at toning down whatever Ashton has in mind.

Chapter 14

Ben

Since the last weekend at the lake, I've gradually started putting distance between myself and Piper. Seeing her is a little like putting a cupcake in front of a kid and saying look but don't touch. Simply put, Piper Lawrence is my temptation. Everything about her entices me. Once she put the brakes on anything else happening between us outside of friendship, I needed space.

That space will be put to the test this weekend since its Halloween. While we've seen each other at school, as co-workers, we haven't been social in over a month. I have been opting to work on the house instead of attending family dinners, much to my mom's chagrin.

Today is the school's fall festival. I know Piper is in charge of the cake walk while I volunteered to work on set-up. The cake walk was my favorite part of the school carnival when I was a kid. We thought we were cool because unlike the little kids playing musical chairs, we had the cake walk.

The joke was on us though, a cake walk is essentially musical chairs just without the chairs and the winner walks away with a cake.

Tonight, I've opted to stay with the cowboy theme I'll be wearing tonight but a scaled-down version. Dressed in jeans and a plaid shirt, I put on my Stetson before heading into the gymnasium where the festival is being held.

I see a few of my students and their parents on my way to the cake walk. The fact that I have compared Piper to cake and temptation is not lost on me at this moment. From a distance she stops me in my tracks. Dressed in all black, she has on a large witch's hat with feathers hanging off the ends. Only, it isn't what she is wearing that stops me. It's the way she is crouched down talking to a little boy. Smaller than most of the kids, this little guy is dressed to the nines as Darth Vader. Piper is smiling at him like every word he says is the most important thing to her.

She's beautiful. Time away has done nothing for me. Her laughter wafts across the room and hits me in the gut like a bullet. After a few minutes she stands and catches my eye. Her smile grows a little bigger and she waves. I wave back. God, I'm such a pussy. I'm standing here in the middle of the elementary school gymnasium dressed as a damn cowboy waving at the pretty girl.

"Hey, Mr. Sullivan. Wow, Miss Lawrence sure is pretty. Is she your girlfriend?"

I look down at one of my students.

"She sure is pretty. No, Will, Miss Lawrence isn't my girl-friend; she is my friend though. Would you like me to tell her you think she's pretty?"

"What?! No way! I'm going to the fishing booth. See ya!"

I laugh and walk over to Piper.

"Miss Lawrence, you're a very pretty witch."

"Well thank you, Mr. Sullivan. You're a pretty snazzy-looking cowboy. Jacob, this is Mr. Sullivan. He is your sister Clementine's teacher. Mr. Sullivan, this is Jacob Thorne and Mrs. Honeycutt."

I shake Mrs. Honeycutt's hand and turn my attention to Jacob. "Don't mind Miss Lawrence, Mr. Vader. She is obviously very confused as to who you really are."

Giggles come from beneath the mask as he pushes it up over his head. "It's me! I'm Jacob Thorne, silly!"

"Oh, my mistake. You sure do make a great Darth Vader. Are you having fun, Jacob?"

"Yep. Mrs. Honeycutt said she is taking me to the fishing game. If I win I get to take a fish home! Did you know that? Clem will probably make me keep my fish in my room but I don't care. It's going to be awesome!"

Jacob's enthusiasm is contagious and I'm considering joining him to catch my own goldfish. Before I can contemplate this odd thought, Mrs. Honeycutt excuses herself and Jacob. Alone with Piper, I suddenly feel awkward.

"How have you been, Ben?"

"Good. You?"

"I'm good. You're lucky you don't have to leave here to get ready for tonight. I'm a little frazzled. I haven't even seen my costume. I can't believe I let your sister make it for me, sight unseen."

"Wait. You haven't seen it? Are you nuts?"

"Why, have you seen it? Oh my God! What did she do?" Piper looks around, almost checking to see if anyone can hear us before she lowers her voice to a whisper. "Am I going to look like an extra in a porno?"

Her words combined with the look of horror on her face have me laughing so hard I'm crying. "No, I haven't seen it, but it's Ash. The likelihood you'll look like a stripper or porn star is pretty good."

A groan from her has me putting my arm around her shoulders. "Don't worry, you'll have your very own Village People and Neo to protect you."

"Not helpful," she says, burying her head in her hands.

"I don't mean to interrupt, but is the cake walk happening?"

I feel Piper tense immediately. Before I turn to the voice full of contempt and attitude, I give her a little squeeze. Once I turn to face the condescending woman who has obviously affected Piper, I'm not surprised to see Felicity Remington-Thorne.

"Oh, Ben. I didn't realize that was you. Is something wrong?" Suddenly the tone has gone from one of contention and annoyance to saccharine sweet.

"Nothing is wrong, thank you for your concern. Clem, you look lovely."

"Of course I do, Mr. Sullivan. I'm a princess. Mother, I would like a cake now."

"Just a minute, Clementine. The adults are speaking. I'm sorry, I don't think we've met. I'm Felicity Remington-Thorne," Felicity says to Piper, extending her hand.

"Yes, Felicity, I know who you are. I'm your son's teacher and you and I grew up together."

"Really? I don't remember you."

I look at Piper to make double check that smoke is not filtering from her ears as she puts her sweet-as-pie smile on and looks from Clem to Felicity before she responds. "I can assure you we did. Now, Clementine, how about you and I find a few more participants and we'll get this cake walk happening."

"Oh I don't want to walk; I just want a cake."

Before Piper can retort I step in. "Clem, that's not how it works, but it'll be a fun reward if you win. How about you run and find a few classmates or kids from other classes and we'll get a round going. Piper, why don't you make sure you have the music cued." Once I've sent Clementine and Piper off, hopefully avoiding a meltdown by one and a cat fight by the other, I turn to Felicity.

"Ben, you look quite handsome. The cowboy look suits you." This woman has got to be kidding me. She's practically petting me as she purrs her words at me. Removing her hand from my bicep, where she's managed to caress me into the uncomfortable zone, I side step her as I see Clementine making her way across the room with a few kids.

"Thanks. Look, Felicity, you did grow up with Piper and maybe you could be a little kinder to her now than when we were kids."

"Piper? Who is Piper?"

"Piper Lawrence? The woman you were just rude to and the one who is your son's teacher."

"That's Pathetic Piper? No way! Wow, she must have paid big bucks for a makeover."

I'm momentarily stunned silent as I process what has just been said. Managing to corral my anger at the insulting words this woman has said, I return to the spot I just vacated so there is no question she can hear me. "Do not call her that. Ever. Do you understand? That is cruel and not appropriate behavior for a woman and definitely not a mother to a young girl. I'm going to walk away now, please do not be rude to Piper."

Instead of staying at the festival, I've decided to leave and put some distance between myself and what just happened at the cake walk. Piper told me that Felicity had been awful to her growing up but I didn't know the extent of it until that moment. I'll never understand the cattiness of some women and frankly don't want to understand it. I lost my temper a little but I'll be damned if I'll let anyone speak to Piper that way.

I have a few hours before we're all meeting at Country Road. Plenty of time for me to get out to the house, work off whatever has me behaving like a caveman. A few hours swinging a hammer should help release some of the frustration and tension.

I managed to work myself into exhaustion and contemplated blowing off Halloween all together. I'm not sure if it's the idea of spending the night with my *friend* Piper or the ridiculous amount of text messages I've received from the guys that has me parked in front of Country Road. To top it all off, I'm dressed as some throwback version of the Cowboy from Village People. When we first joked about reliving a Halloween of our youth, I wasn't expecting everyone to be this pumped, but damn if they aren't.

Ashton has been cutting and sewing until her fingers bled for weeks. She not only made her costume and Piper's but she helped spruce up both mine and Owen's.

Unsurprisingly, Jameson didn't need help with his Neo look; then again, a pair of sunglasses and black coat aren't the hardest costume to put together.

Owen is living out his childhood dream as a policeman. He explained that every year his mother forced him to dress as a clown when all he ever wanted was to dress as one of the men in blue. This was his chance to live that childhood dream so he turned to Ash for "flare," whatever that is. Landon completed our band of misfits in a no-nonsense construction worker look. Which, is also his everyday wardrobe. Basically he's dressed up as himself. Why couldn't I have wanted to grow up to be a teacher and not a cowboy? Maybe I'll tell my students to keep this in mind for their future Halloweens.

Yep, together we'll look like half of the Village People even though that wasn't the plan. Ashton did an excellent job on our costumes and insists we are all going to rule the costume contest. Considering I'm getting here closer to the end of the night than the beginning the chances I've missed out on standing on the stage being judged for my costume is pretty high. Thank goodness.

Before I can even open the door I feel the music pumping through my body and know the place is likely packed. Not looking forward to mindlessly searching for my friends, I sent a text to Owen when I parked. A quick check of my phone confirms he hasn't responded.

Instead of wandering around like a lost puppy, I decide to head straight for the bar to see Ashton. The closer to the bar I get, the less I want to be here. That is, until I see Ashton. Nothing my sister does surprises me but seeing her as Dolly Parton stops me in my tracks. Choosing to portray her favorite character from her favorite Dolly Parton movie, *Best Little Whorehouse in Texas*.

With her dark hair hidden beneath a platinum wig, Ashton is covered in head to toe pink. The feathers from her poor excuse for a robe fly around her like a cloud as she mixes a drink. She's painted her lips fire engine red and her long acrylic nails look more like weapons. I shake my head as I notice she's added to the bust of the nightgown she's wearing. If it wasn't Halloween, I'd go into big brother mode and toss a sheet on her to cover the parts of her she clearly hasn't.

"Brother of mine! About time you got here. The douche crew is in full effect; you may need to save them."

"Yeah, I'm not saving anyone except whoever may get stuck with those things in their face." Gesturing to her ample, yet fake, bosom, I wink and take the beer she offers me.

"Oh please, this is every man's dream."

"Not mine. I'm done after this," I say, signaling my beer. "I have to be up early to get out to the house."

"Of course you do. You spend more time with that house than your own family. We'd like to see it one day, you know."

I guess I should at least take my family out to the property. I kind of wanted to wait until it was closer to done than not.

"Noted. We'll make plans soon, okay?"

"Deal. Anyway, the guys and Piper are over there on the upper level. It doesn't look like I'll get a break anytime soon so say hi for me."

"Will do."

Just as I turn to walk away I hear Ash call my name.

"Hey, will you check on Piper? I think she's upset or something. Maybe one too many shots, I'm not sure."

"Was Dominguez here? Did he say something to her?" I feel the heat rising in me at the thought of that asshole upsetting Piper. Again.

"Whoa there, cowboy. Literally. He was here but it was fine. She's just been really quiet and seems pretty down about something. Maybe you can just talk to her or something. I've got to go. Taylor can't handle this by himself."

"Sure. Oh, what does her costume look like? So I can find her?"

A very evil smile takes over my far-from-angelic sister's face. "Oh you'll know when you see her."

That's all she offers as she walks away laughing. It's actually more of a cackle than a laugh. She should have dressed as Cruella de Vil. Shaking my head, I start out on my quest to find Piper and the guys. The moment I spot her I stop dead in my tracks.

Holy fuck.

My sister is equally my favorite and least favorite person right now. When we agreed to these costumes Piper was supposed to be dressed as a princess. In my mind she was going to be dressed in some sort of big poufy pink monstrosity of a costume. Hair piled high with a crown or something on her head. Of course, she'd look jaw dropping and exactly as a princess should. Maybe a little sexy in the cleavage department but that was about it.

What stands before me is far from that. She's a princess, only instead of inspired by Cinderella she's a modern version of Princess Leia. Golden bikini Leia. A princess that my dick obviously approves of.

Giving myself this undetected moment, only this moment, to take her in. I swear on whatever anyone wants me to swear on that as soon as I take in this beauty in front of me from head to toe I'll go back to seeing my friend. *My platonic friend.* Screw it, I'm starting from the bottom and working my way up to those eyes.

Her long skirt just skims the floor as she stands there. It sits low on her hips, so that her perfect belly button draws my attention to a part of her body that suddenly causes my mouth to go dry. I visibly gulp as it becomes evident that Piper is not only an avid runner but must also spend a lot of time doing crunches. Mindlessly taking a drink of my beer, my gaze finds the swell of her breasts. Nestled in what some would call a bathing suit top, a top that should only be worn in private, I am stunned stupid. It's a top that should only be seen behind closed doors and finding its way to the floor. My floor.

I may be a good guy, but I am a man in the end. And a liar since I basically told my sister not less than five minutes ago that I wasn't a boob man. Which is technically true. I'm a woman man. I like women and don't find myself attracted to one body part. Even with Piper this holds true, I'm a fan of the entire Piper Lawrence package. My dreaming self is to blame for the boob part.

Now that I've said boob in my head enough to make these jeans extra tight below my holster, I need to refocus. Forcing my gaze from the distractions at chest level, I linger for a brief moment at the clavicle. How does this woman make a collar bone sexy? I'm not sure, but she does.

When my eyes finally reach her beautiful face, my breath catches. Her lips are plump, like she's been biting them, or even kissing someone, as she wraps them around the tiny straw in her glass. The thought of the latter option for their plumpness makes my blood boil. Her cheeks are flushed and I think Ashton is right. She seems to be a little more than tipsy and a lot more than distracted or unhappy. Looking down into the glass of amber liquid, she doesn't seem to be aware of my recent assessment of her. Just as I'm about to turn back for the bar to grab her a glass of water in case it's the former, she looks up and catches my eyes.

I swear time stops for a fraction of a second. Suddenly the music is gone and the voices are a dull hum. The only noise I hear clearly is the blood pulsing in my ears.

Then a smile takes over Piper's face and all I can think of doing is taking her out of here and kissing her until those lips are swollen from mine. I return the smile instead and walk toward her.

"Princess."

"Ben." Her voice is raspy as she sighs my name. That voice that is always honey sweet wraps itself around my insides and tugs.

"Well that is certainly some outfit you have there. I wasn't expecting *this* princess."

Rolling her eyes at me as she sets her glass on a nearby table, she laughs. "Neither was I. Your sister is a bitch. But I love her and didn't have a backup plan. So, here I am. Princess fucking Leia. It's awful, isn't it?"

She begins to pat away lint from her skirt that doesn't exist, fidgeting enough that I begin to worry that top will not contain her assets.

"It's something, but it most definitely is not awful. You look a little tipsy there, Princess. You want a water?"

Furrowing her brow, she isn't given an opportunity to respond before Jameson slaps me on the back and loudly exclaims how hot Piper looks. It's my turn to shoot him a look through a furrowed brow. I can tell the moment my dislike of his comment registers because he slowly removes his hand from the spot on my shoulder where his hand landed.

"Sorry, Pipe. But you really do look hot. Where ya been, man? You missed some hot chicks tonight."

"Excuse me, guys, I'm going to the restroom," Piper grits out between her teeth before scurrying away.

Interesting response to a simple comment. Very interesting. Her reaction isn't lost on me, or Jameson for that matter.

"What's her problem? She's been like that all night. The only time I've seen her look like she's having any fun was just now with you two talking. I thought you agreed to only be friends?"

"We did. We are. I think she's just uncomfortable in that outfit. Where are Landon and Owen?"

"They took off already. Twins."

"Got it. No twins for you?"

"Twins? No. A girl? Yep. She's saying goodbye to her friends before we take off. I just wanted to see if Piper needed a lift. Sasha isn't drinking tonight and said she'd give Piper a ride. Ya know, before she gives me one." Obviously his own favorite audience, Jameson is quite pleased with that innuendo.

"Really? You kiss your mom with that mouth? Shit, you kiss *my* mom with that mouth? You're a dick, you know that?"

"Lighten up. I'm just kidding. But really, we're going to take off. Maybe you should offer to take Piper home. She rode with us so she doesn't have her car anyway. You know, maybe spend some time with your *friend*. And that costume."

Without waiting for a response Jameson shouts to Piper that I'll take her home and walks up to the girl who must be Sasha, scooping her up and causing her to let out a squeal as he starts carrying her toward the door. Another blonde in his long string of blondes. I guess when you have a type, you have a type.

"You don't have to take me home, Ben. I can take a cab. That was the plan anyway."

"That's silly, Pipe. I'm already here. Besides, I am so over this costume and it's only been on an hour. Should we tell Ashton you're leaving?" We both look to the bar and see a line three people wide and at least thirty people deep and agree not to bother Ash.

As we walk out the door and start toward my truck I notice Piper isn't as graceful as she usually is. "You okay there, Princess?"

"Yeah. I didn't drink that much, I swear. I'm just not that graceful."

"Well, come on then, let's get you home." I offer my hand to help her and am surprised when she takes it. Like each time before that she's allowed me to hold it, I savor the feeling of her tiny hand in mine. I know this moment may end at any time. One day she won't grant me this small gift and that will devastate me just a little.

"Ben?" she asks me as she slows her pace so I am forced to stop and turn to her, never letting go of her hand.

"Will you take me to your house? I don't want to go home."

"Piper, you're drunk. You don't want to drive all the way out to my house. Another time."

I can't believe I just told her no.

"I'm sorry. I get it. You don't want to hang out with me." Dropping my hand, she continues, "I'll just get a cab instead. Have a good night."

Before she can turn and take a step, I grab her hand back. This time I interlock our fingers and tug her toward me. "I want nothing more than to hang out with you, Piper." A small smile takes over her face, making it hard to resist her. But I do.

"I'm not drunk, Ben. I may be a little tipsy, but by the time we get to your house I'll be fine. I just don't want to be alone. I'm tired of being alone. Please?"

"Woman, you are killing me." A half smile appears on her face. Perfection. "Let's go."

"Yay! Okay, come on!" she shouts and drags me to my truck. Never letting my hand go.

Chapter 15

Ben

The moment we got in the truck I offered Piper my coat. It's fall and the temperature is far from bathing suit top friendly. Gladly accepting the coat, Piper began letting her Princess Leia buns down, cursing Ashton the entire time. While the overall look is something I'll never forget, I'm pleased to see her long hair once again flowing around her shoulders. Once she was more Piper and less Leia, she fastened her seat belt and slightly curled into a ball next to me. With her cheek resting on the back of the seat, we both seem content to just be.

During the slight break between songs filling the cab I notice her breathing has slowed. A quick glance her way confirms that she's asleep. I briefly consider turning around and taking her home but if I know anything about Piper, it's that she'll be more than upset if I don't follow through with the plan to go to my house.

I take this opportunity to simply appreciate the quiet

and how this is the most relaxed I've felt in weeks. Avoiding time with Piper has been intentional and it has sucked. Royally sucked. A soft murmur from her has me looking at her again. She's moved her hands so they make a pillow of sorts. She looks angelic and, as usual with these simple moments in Piper's presence, I find myself hating my good guy self. Sometimes I wish I was less concerned about other people and willing to say screw it and push Piper to see where our feelings will take us.

I recognize all the ways this detour can go wrong. The most obvious issue is the fact that I may actually die from not be able to touch her. Then there's the possibility that we'll have another talk and Piper will remind me of the "friends only" agreement. Of course there is the slightest chance that nothing will happen. There is the chance that we'll avoid an awkward moment, avoid deep conversation, and, God willing, no friend zone talk.

While I'm contemplating each scenario in complete detail, I hear the seat belt unbuckle and Piper scoot next to me.

"Piper, what are you doing?"

"I'm cold."

"Let me turn up the heat."

Before I can reach for the dial to the heat, Piper curls into my side.

"This is fine. You don't mind, do you?"

"Uh, no it's fine."

I inhale through my nose and exhale through my mouth as I attempt to slow my heartrate.

"Don't wreck us, okay?"

"I won't. I will keep you safe, Princess."

"I know," she says through a yawn. "I'm just going to

close my eyes until we get there." Her last words are barely a mumble before she dozes off again.

These small moments she grants me give me the slightest glimpse of what we could be. How perfectly she fits into the crook of my arm and how her body molds into mine as if it was and is meant to be there.

Then the unthinkable happens and her hand drifts to my thigh, only inches from Mr. Happy. This woman is going to be the death of me. I shift my leg just enough, hoping she'll move her hand. She doesn't. If I didn't know better, I'd say her hand was intentionally gripping my leg and not just resting there.

The turn off to my property can't come soon enough and I let out a sigh of relief the moment I stop in front of the house. Unable to use my right arm to put the truck in park for fear of startling Piper, I reach across the wheel and use my left hand. Once the truck is safely parked and the ignition off, I use my same hand to move the hair that has fallen in Piper's face away. This tiny gesture has her slowly waking.

"Piper, baby. We're here."

"Hmmm."

I watch as her eyes flutter open and she takes in her surroundings. Slowly rising from where she is leaning against me, she looks into my eyes. My hand still on her hair where I just moved it.

"You always do that."

Never breaking eye contact, I offer her a small smile. "That's because you are too beautiful for your hair to hide your face."

I slowly move my hand so that my thumb is making a slow descent down her cheek until it reaches her chin. Her eyes take a quick break from mine and I see her look at my lips before returning my gaze. Our faces are close. Hers only inches from mine, I can feel her breathing, smell the whiskey on her breath.

I only notice my hand is still holding her face when her own hand grasps mine and she smiles. It's the smile that brings out the golden flecks in her eyes and causes her to scrunch her nose. The smile I can't help but return.

"Thank you," she whispers.

I clear my throat and put a little space between us. This movement successfully cuts through the thick tension – sexual tension – that made its way into this suddenly too small of a truck.

"Do you want to see what I've done so far?"

"Of course. Do you have electricity?"

I let myself out of the truck and walk around to help Piper out. Again, she lets me take her hand. I reach inside the rear cab and grab a blanket.

"I do have electricity. It was the first thing I had inspected and updated. Unfortunately, there isn't any heat so we shouldn't plan on being here too long. I'll bring this in case we want to sit for a bit," I say, raising the blanket.

We begin walking toward the house. Again, Piper lets me lead her while still holding her hand. She's holding her long skirt with her free hand when a slight breeze picks up and she releases my hand to pull her hair back. I'm taken a little aback when she finishes and resumes holding my hand. I offer her a little squeeze in recognition.

"Your mom was telling me that you haven't had your parents or Ashton out here yet. Why?"

"I don't really know. I guess I don't want them to see

what a mess it is and question why I made this decision. Honestly, Jameson has only been out here once and that was to help me with some demo. Otherwise, you're the only person to be here besides the various contractors."

"Really? I'm honored. You should bring your parents. Everyone should see this place."

"Thanks. I'll bring them out soon. I just want to keep it to myself for now."

"I'm sorry. I shouldn't have asked to come here. This is your home and I just barged into it."

Stopping at the foot of the porch, I turn to Piper. "Do not apologize. I love that you wanted to come here. Come see what it looks like with missing walls."

"Oh Lord. You are such a man! Tearing down walls and using power tools. Please tell me the stained glass in the kitchen has made it unscathed."

Laughing, I lead her into the house and flip the lights on.

"What can I say? Men see a power tool and a wall must come down."

Shaking her head in disbelief, Piper is laughing as she walks away from me. As I expected, her first stop is the kitchen. I hear her sigh in relief as she confirms that the stained glass is safe.

"Told you."

"You did, but I needed to check."

"Come on, you need to see the rest," I say with a toss of my head toward the main part of the house.

After a tour of the downstairs and showing Piper the plans for the upstairs master suite and additional two bedrooms, I grab the blanket and lay it out in front of the non-functioning fire place.

Piper takes a seat on the blanket while I lay down on it. She's still wearing my coat, but has twisted her skirt so that she's sitting with her legs crossed in front of me. I watch as she fusses with her hair, closing her eyes and massaging her scalp. Thankfully I have enough sense to look away before she catches me.

"I wish that fireplace worked, you have to be freezing since I have your coat."

"I'm fine. Sorry I'm not exactly prepared for entertaining. I actually called a chimney inspector last week. I figure if I'm going to be here working this winter I should get it functional. Obviously the one in the master will have to wait until the work begins up there."

"I can't believe your master is going to have a fireplace. That's a dream bedroom."

Piper tries to hide a yawn but fails.

"We should go, you're tired and it's late."

"Just a few more minutes. This floor is hard on my butt though. I'm going to lay here."

Laying down on her side, she's positioned so that we're facing each other. I lift myself up on my elbow so I'm looking at her. This is a really bad idea.

"Ben?"

"Yeah, Piper?"

"This friends thing is really hard."

"You're telling me. It's even more difficult with you running around as Princess Leia."

Smiling at my statement, Piper begins fiddling with the button on my shirt.

"You don't like my costume?" The innocence in her

voice is deliberate. I roll my eyes at her.

"Piper, I think we covered how much I like your costume at the bar. I don't think I like that all those guys at Country Road were looking at you in it before I got there."

"I doubt anyone was paying attention to me. I look ridiculous," she mumbles while still fiddling with my button. I still her hand, which causes her to look into my eyes.

"A man would have to be dead to not pay attention to you regardless of what you're wearing."

The smile I swear was made just for me takes over her face as I look into her eyes.

"Ben?" My name is a question, barely audible above the thundering of my pulse in my ears.

"Yeah, Princess?"

"Will you kiss me?"

"We agreed," I say as we both start gradually moving closer to one another. My heart is beating out of my chest and my palms are sweating. I know we are about to make a choice we can't take back. A choice I won't want to take back.

"I know, but right now I don't care. I'm not thinking about consequences, choices, or promises."

That's all the permission I need before I have her flat on her back and I'm positioned over her.

"Tell me to stop," I beg. Instead of doing as I ask, she tightens her grip on my shirt just above my waistband and gives a little tug.

I don't hesitate and give her what she asked for. The moment my lips touch hers, everything else slips away. The cold air, the hard floor, the broken agreements, and all the reasons we shouldn't be doing this are gone. The only thing that matters is this woman in my arms and her incredible lips on mine.

My kiss is gentle at first. I barely graze her lips with mine. I'm giving her another out. We can stop this. We can go back to the way things were. Instead, she relaxes more, slightly parting her thighs to make room for me. My arousal is evident and she seems to melt farther into the floor, taking me with her. This is the permission I need. I increase the pressure of my kiss, lightly licking her lower lip with the tip of my tongue as she gladly opens her mouth to me.

Piper releases a slight purr from the back of her throat that has me wishing there was a mattress in this shell of a house. As I'm thinking this very thought, Piper's hands find their way to my waistband, pulling my shirt from where it's tucked in my jeans. Her hands touch my skin; like ice cubes to hot coals. It sends a shiver down my spine. Another purr from her has me claiming her with this kiss.

Overwhelmed with a need to taste her skin, I begin my descent to her neck, which she turns slightly, granting me more access. This time it's a noise from me that fills the room. A sound that is more growl than anything else.

My hand has found its way to the opening of the jacket. I part the lapels and slowly move my hand up her side until it is just below her breast. I make my way back to her mouth as she arches her back enough that I know she is begging for some sort of relief.

Giving her what she wants, I slowly move my hand so that my thumb finds her pebbled nipple. Her breaths increase as I make feather-like movements over her nipple. She's lightly running her nails along my back in a pattern I don't even bother to try and figure out and, instead, I sink a little more into her. Piper responds in kind by lifting her hips to me. My senses are overloaded and I feel like a teenage boy about to explode in my pants.

This top that seemed far too tiny earlier suddenly seems as big of a barrier between us as a ten-foot wall. I've moved my lips from hers to the spot below her ear that, by her reaction, is *the* spot I should make note of.

"Please, Ben," she pants as she continues to run her hands up my back.

"What, baby? Tell me. Tell me what you want," I demand while never stopping my assault on her sweet spot.

"Please touch me."

That statement gets my attention and I turn my gaze to her. Stilling my hand that remains on her breast, I see so many emotions in her eyes. Lust, passion, kindness, a little bit of fear, and trust.

"Are you sure? Piper, if we stop now we can go back to how it's been. If I touch you, I don't think I can go back to friends. We have to break promises."

"I know. I'm sure. Please touch me."

She doesn't have to ask me twice. While it's only been months with Piper, it feels like I've waited a lifetime for this. The feelings I have for her are beyond attraction and physical. I know if we cross this line my heart will be hers. I can only pray hers will be mine.

I gently tug her top down, exposing her breasts. "Perfect," I whisper more to myself than her. Without a second thought, I lean in, taking her hard nipple into my mouth. Rolling my tongue over it, I am aware of the sounds coming from Piper and they only encourage me. With a slight nibble she lets out a whimper and I take that as a cue to turn my attention to her other breast.

Still nestled between her legs, I begin rotating my hips slightly. A movement she returns by lifting her hips and rolling them just enough to cause friction. I am so consumed with all things Piper I can barely stand it. While still holding myself up with one arm, I pull my hand from her breast and lower it to where her skirt has ridden up. I gather the skirt up so that her thigh is exposed. My hand, calloused by the work I've been doing, grips her thigh and I feel her quiver as I let my hand make its way around to her perfect ass. I release an animalistic growl when I realize she's wearing a thong.

Still offering as much attention to her mouth as her neck and breast, my hand finds the band to her panties and it's her turn to voice appreciation.

"Oh God," she whimpers.

I take that as an invitation to move my hand around to the front of her panties, easing myself to the side for access.

"Fuck, Piper. You are so wet."

"Please," she begs.

My thumb finds its way beneath the silk of her panties and automatically begins a circular motion over her clit.

"Let go, Piper." My voice is hoarse and full of lust. I remove my lips from her skin as I take in the sight before me. With her head tilted back, her neck is exposed, begging for me to kiss it. I don't. Instead, I watch as her still-closed eyes alternate between relaxation and squeezed so tight she looks to be in pain.

Her breaths become more ragged and labored as I dip a finger between her folds. Pumping my finger in and out of her while simultaneously rubbing her clit with my thumb, I see the moment she approaches her climax. I want nothing more than to release myself from these jeans and sink into her. Then the realization of where we are hits me and I know I don't want our first time to be on a dirty floor in a house filled with debris and power tools.

"That's it, Princess, let go. Let me see you come."

She does. I feel her spasm around my finger and let out a moan as she says my name. Dropping my forehead to her chest, I'm panting as her fingers come up to my head and tug at my hair, causing me to lift my eyes to hers.

Time freezes as I look at her. Her eyes are alive and she's looking at me like nothing else matters in this world. I pull my hand from between us so that I'm able to hold myself up over her. Never removing her hands from my hair she nudges me toward her. Instinctively I smile at her and drop a tender kiss to her lips.

"You are always beautiful, Piper. But, watching you come is majestic."

With my lips still on hers she smiles and laughs.

"Majestic? What am I, a unicorn?"

To that I can't help but laugh too.

"Baby, you are most definitely my unicorn."

I drop a kiss to her nose and tug the coat shut as I lift myself off of her. Sitting up, she follows suit and suddenly her expression changes from euphoric to one of concern and perhaps slight embarrassment.

"We should probably talk."

Her only response is a nod and a sigh.

Chapter 16

Piper

Talk. He wants to talk. Of course he does. As usual, he seems to have all the answers. Unicorn. I can't be his unicorn. That is far too much pressure for this girl.

Let us not forget the fact that I just acted like a complete whore. A cheaply dressed, panting, spread your legs at the first compliment kind of whore.

This has been a ridiculous night from moment one. I should never have trusted Ashton to make my costume. When I said princess I meant Cinderella-level princess, not stripper.

Fine, I'm Princess Leia. Whatever. Ashton took advantage of my distracted state the last few weeks and my options for tonight were to accept her costume or stay home. Staying home is all I've done lately and, quite frankly, I was getting sick of myself. I've read every ugly cry book I could get my hands on, watched *The Notebook* no less than twenty times, and had enough quality time with Ben & Jerry to declare my own intervention.

I've relived that moonlit conversation with Ben at the lake over in my head so many times. He laid it all out for me and I still ran scared. The reality is, we could pursue this thing we have between us. We could tell Ashton and yeah, she'd probably freak at first but in the end she loves us both. I'm sure there would be some sort of ceremonial vow or declaration from both of us that we wouldn't blame her if (when) we broke up, but she'd be okay with it.

I wouldn't. I know myself enough to admit I would likely screw something up and our, whatever this is, would end and I'd be outcast. Regardless of how close Ash and I are, Ben is her brother. Family trumps friend every single time.

Other than a few encounters at school and the occasional dinner at his parents, Ben has been pretty scarce since the last weekend at the lake. Sure, his disappearance has ensured the awkwardness we seem to ooze every time we are together be non-existent. Only, it's made me a little too emo for my liking.

Tonight when we talked at the school festival I felt more relaxed than I have in weeks. I knew then that it was stupid to deny that I missed him. After he stepped up and handled Felicity I knew I needed to pull him back into our group. He's my friend regardless of any attraction we have and I've missed him. Plus, he seems to bring a calm to the group, and if I have to listen to Ashton and Jameson insult each other one more time I may start looking for a new place to call home.

That was how I found myself in this barely legal costume at Country Road. I knew Ben wouldn't disappoint Ashton and blow off the night. It was my one chance to talk to him and clear the air. Only, the moment I saw him I wasn't thinking about my friend and how he could run interference between Ashton and Jameson. No, I was thinking how I really have a thing for cowboys and how I was almost willing to beg Ashton for her blessing to jump her brother's bones.

I wasn't even really drinking. I had one shot and had been nursing an actual soda I played off as a cocktail. Taylor was sympathetic to my plea for help passing off my drinks as alcoholic so that Ashton wouldn't worry I wasn't having fun. As the night went on and on I began to think Ben wasn't going to show. Then he was there.

Perhaps it was all of the romance I had been reading and watching, but I swear the room faded away and he was the only other person in the room. I was overcome with relief and happiness. Genuine unbridled happiness. Of course, the fact that he looked like a fantasy come to life didn't hurt either.

Then Jameson had to remind Ben that he missed out on hooking up with hot girls and that happiness morphed into hurt. The reality of only being friends with Ben became very clear. Friends are happy for their friends when they date and meet new people. If we're friends, I will have to watch him with other women. Looking for a new home may still be in the cards.

Of course Ben would be the good guy and offer me a ride home. And, because I'm a masochist, I had to let him hold my hand. Multiple times. I had to curl up next to him. I had to almost kiss him. I'm my own worst enemy and obviously I hate myself.

Then I lost my damn mind and begged him to kiss me.

Not just kiss me, but I practically asked him to ravish me right here on the dirty-ass floor of his home. Whore. It's a wonder I haven't gone up in flames. That may only be because this isn't a church. I have no idea. Maybe I should go to church and ask for some sort of forgiveness.

"Hey, you need to stop that." I'm pulled from my self-loathing by Ben's voice and his hand on my leg. Looking down at his hand, I can only think of where those fingers have just been and, I won't lie, I'm about to ask him for a second go-round.

Whore. Oh my God, I'm awful.

Burying my face in my hands, I can only shake my head.

"Come here," he says, grabbing me and pulling me so that I'm nestled between his legs, my back leaning against his chest. His really hard and muscular chest. I let him wrap his arms around me and, without a second thought, I relax into him and release a sigh. And start crying.

"Whoa, whoa there. What's wrong?" He pulls me closer, if that's even possible, and delivers a soft and gentle kiss to the side of my head near my temple.

"Sorry, I just … it's." I have no words, just snot and tears.

"Tell me. Piper, you can trust me, what's wrong?"

Why not? I've just thrown myself at him, had the most mind-blowing orgasm of my life, and am dressed like a trollop. What do I have to lose? Nothing. My pride is somewhere over there by the nail gun.

"You must think I'm pathetic. I have been sending signals as mixed as a batch of cookie dough full of nuts and not only begged you to bring me here but then I threw myself at you. I'm so embarrassed." I begin to pull away from him, but instead of letting me go, he turns me to face him.

"Up here," he says, patting his leg for me to climb on his lap. Hell to the no. I shake my head vigorously so he knows I really mean no.

"Yes, Piper. Up."

I don't even attempt to argue more and climb up on his lap so I'm facing him. Straddling him. This is so many different kinds of bad. But I'll be damned if this doesn't feel perfect.

"First, I swear you are going to be the death of me with your constant need to put yourself down. I would like to know who is responsible for making you think that you are less than worth every single amazing thing this world has to offer you. I think that person and I need to have a serious conversation."

I don't respond to his comments, I just listen and enjoy his arms around me. This is all going to end and I want to always remember this night and what we've shared.

"Now that we have that out of the way, can we talk about how we tell Ashton about us? I think we need to have a plan since she can be a little unpredictable."

That has my attention. My eyes are wide and his smile is sweet and gentle.

"What? Us? What *us*?"

Chuckling, he reaches for my hair and I know he's going to push it away from my face. I do it before he can and his hand stops mid-air. He seems a little bummed that I took the task from him.

"Us. You and me. We should probably have the conversation sooner than later."

"There is no us, Ben." I drop my chin to my chest and begin to pull my leg away so I'm no longer on his lap, but he stops me. Placing his hands, his very lovely hands, on my thighs, he begins lightly forming circles with his thumbs.

"Yes there is, Piper. The only thing that kept me from making you mine completely was the fact that you are too good for that to happen here in my freezing-cold house on the damn floor."

No words. I have no words. I lift my chin to look at him. Staring at him speechlessly, he scoots a bit so I am able to remove myself from his lap. This gives Ben time to stand and offer his hand. I put my smaller hand in his and he tugs me up. Still at a loss for words, I look up at him and don't argue when he kisses me. Gentle at first, he begins to deepen it as I lean in to him. Just as I'm about moan in delight he pulls back and rests is forehead to mine.

"Us, Piper. I can't go back. I told you that. I like you and want to see where this goes."

"I … I." Stuttering, I am unable to complete a thought before he's kissing me again. His kisses are gentle and full of promise. Not only does he render me unable to argue, but I want nothing more than to live off these kisses. A few more sweeps of his lips across mine, he pulls back to straighten the coat I'm still wearing.

"Let's get out of here. It's fucking freezing."

I laugh and realize that with every word he speaks little puffs of air are visible. I nod and he leads me out of the house, turning off lights as he goes. Not releasing my hand until we reach his truck, I hop up into my seat and he pinches my rear, causing me to yelp and giggle.

"Sorry, I couldn't resist."

I only smile and shake my head in response before he closes the door and is taking his place behind the wheel.

"I preferred you over here against me."

"I think it's best if I stay over here."

"Piper." He says my name so that it draws out enough to sound like a plea.

"Fine, but eyes on the road," I relent as I slide over to lean against him. I'll just enjoy these moments until he drops me off at my place. It can't hurt.

The drive to my apartment is quiet but comfortable. I used to imagine moments just like this with Ben when we were younger. Of course, I was a stealthy crusher. I don't think anyone ever knew how in love with Bentley Sullivan I was. I went through more notebooks in high school because I doodled hearts, flowers, and "Mrs. Piper Sullivan" all over them instead of using them for their purpose. The one thing I never imagined was a sexual experience with Ben. As a teen my fantasies consisted of nothing more than kissing and maybe a boob grab. Tonight was even more than my adult dreams. We didn't even have sex and I can't imagine ever imagine having an orgasm to top the one I just had.

Bentley Sullivan has both fulfilled my greatest teenage fantasy and single handedly ruined me for future men. Fabulous.

Just as I realize that I am destined for mediocre orgasms from this point forward, Ben pulls up to my building and puts his truck into park. I'm about to ask why he's parked, when he opens his door and, before I can protest, he's opening my door and smiling at me. Processing, I slide across the seat to the door and accept his hand to step down.

"Do you have a key somewhere I didn't see on this costume?"

I laugh at that.

"If I did, I'm sure you would have found it. No, I have a spare under my mat."

Not waiting for the lecture I'm sure to get on safety, I start walking toward my apartment. While I want to say goodnight and thanks for the ride, I know it will be pointless and he'll follow me to the door. Bentley Sullivan is a gentleman, well unless he has me flat on my back doing wicked things to my body, and will walk me to my door. At the thought of the wicked things he's done I feel a tug in my lower belly. Damn orgasm ruiner.

I pull my key out from under the mat, but before I can open the door his hand is on mine. "Let me look around first. You never know if someone is lurking inside."

"So you think a lurker came here knowing I wasn't home, found my key, let himself in, came back out and placed the key back under the mat and locked the door before hiding in my apartment?"

"Don't make light, Piper. It could happen."

He's completely serious. And adorable. It's my turn to place my hand to his cheek.

"Don't worry, Cowboy. I had my neighbor put the key under the mat at midnight. I knew I wouldn't be home before then. So, it's only been there about an hour. I think I'm safe."

"You brat. You let me think it had been there all night."

Shrugging, I turn the key to open my door. As soon as I step inside I turn to face him as I strip off his jacket. Just as I hold it out to him he walks past me inside. Not less than ten steps in he removes his boots and sets them to the side and walks to the kitchen.

Closing my eyes, I ask for someone to give me strength.

Not only does this man cause every emotion to flow through my body, but he can draw more sighs from me than should be allowed. Resigning that he's not leaving anytime soon, I hang his coat on the hook next to the door and, instead of walking toward the kitchen to join him, I make my way down the short hallway to my bedroom. Quickly stripping off these gold pieces of fabric, I throw on my favorite sweats, T-shirt, and slippers.

As I walk down the hall I am greeted by smell of something cooking and suddenly my stomach is very happy Ben stayed.

"Sorry I made myself at home but I realized I was starving and a grilled cheese sounded good. Do you want one?"

I sit down at my small bistro table, pulling my knees to my chest. "Yes, please. You seem to have made yourself right at home."

With nothing more than a wink he simply turns back to making our sandwiches. Is this what life would be like with Ben? Easy. Life with Ben would be easy. Enjoying being together, laughing, making dinner, watching a movie, and yes, mind-blowing orgasms would be a bonus. Simple, uncomplicated, and perfect.

Just as I have this thought my phone pings that I have a text message. Since I didn't exactly have the means to carry it tonight the phone has been on the counter all night. I pick it up and the reality of everything comes to a screeching halt.

Ashton: Just closing up for the night and wanted to make sure you got home ok.

Me: Yep. Just hanging out in my sweats getting ready for bed.

Ashton: Good deal. Sorry I was so busy tonight.

Me: You were working, silly.

Ashton: Don't remind me. Did you meet any guys? You looked smokin'.

Me: *eye roll* No I didn't meet anyone. I felt like an idiot. Payback is a bitch you know.

Ashton: Lol. Yeah I know but thankfully you aren't a bitch. I've gotta go. TTYL

Me: Okay. Night.

Just as I'm about to put my phone down it pings again.

Ashton: Did Ben leave with anyone?

Me: What?

Crap.

Ashton: I was hoping he'd hook up with someone. He's been a grumpy slug for weeks and figured he needs to get laid.

Choking on her last statement, I accept the glass of water that appears in front of me.

"Are you okay?" Ben asks, concerned.

"Yeah, sorry. Wrong pipe."

Me: I wouldn't know.

Ashton: Whatever, he's probably off being boring. I really have to go now. TTYL

I don't bother replying and set my phone down as Ben turns toward me with a plate of sandwiches and a few napkins.

"Do you mind if we sit in the living room?"

"Of course not. Do you want anything to drink?"

"Sure, surprise me," he replies as he makes his way to the living room.

Ashton's text is still on my mind when I join him on the couch. Ben should be hooking up with someone. He should be going out and meeting women like his friends. This is so messed up. The thought of him even talking to a strange woman at a bar has me losing my appetite. I just nibble at one-half of my sandwich but note that Ben has already consumed two full sandwiches.

"Hungry?"

He smiles and nods but, ever the gentleman, doesn't respond until he has swallowed the last bite.

"Yeah, I tend to forget dinner when I'm working at the house."

Nodding, I set my sandwich back on the plate and nestle into the corner of the couch as far from Ben as I can get. This movement doesn't go unnoticed.

"Why are you all the way over there? Scooch here," he says, patting the spot next to him.

"Nope. We need to talk and I don't trust you to use words if I'm over there."

"Good point. Okay, so let's talk."

After finish finishing the glass of water I brought him in a single drink, he mimics my position on the other end of the couch.

"First, thank you for taking me to your house tonight. It's really going to be magnificent and I am so excited for you." He doesn't reply, only smiles. Okay, I guess I'll keep going. "And, I uh, thanks for everything else, too?" The last part of my statement more of a question laced with nerves.

"Did you just thank me for an orgasm?"

"Oh my God, please don't talk about it!" Mortified, I bury my face in my hands. I feel his hands tugging mine from where they are hiding the horror of this moment from him.

"Princess, look at me."

I do. Through my fingers. Expecting to see him laughing at me, I am instead faced with a solemn expression and kind eyes.

"Why wouldn't I talk about it? It was probably one of the single most spectacular things I've ever seen and I, for one, cannot wait to see it again."

"Oh, God!" I declare, not only using my hands to cover my face but the tops of my knees to really send home how mortified I am. This time, he responds like I expected a few minutes ago.

"Yep, just like that but with more passion."

Grabbing the pillow from behind me, I throw it at him, making him laugh even more. I join him this time.

"Seriously though, Piper, please don't be embarrassed. I think we should table the orgasm talk for now and focus on the bigger issue."

"Ben, I told you it can't happen again. It was a lapse in judgment. I've just…"

"You what?" he asks me as he inches closer to me and I remain still.

"I just … This is so stupid. I missed you, okay? I did. I missed hanging out and talking. I thought we decided to be friends when we talked before and then you just went away. You stopped coming to family dinner and you have barely even talked to me at school. I thought that tonight we would hang out and it would be fun. I mean, it was fun but I wasn't expecting *that* kind of fun."

Now invading my personal space, he's pulled my feet so I'm forced to climb onto his lap, straddling him. This position makes it almost impossible to not look at him. He never stops looking me in the eye and never once do I break the eye contact. Normally this much eye contact makes me uncomfortable. Ben doesn't make me uncomfortable in the usual sense; I feel connected and natural with him. *That* makes me uncomfortable.

"My turn?" I confirm it is in fact his turn to respond with a simple lift of my chin.

"I've stayed away because I needed space. Piper, I was honest with you at the lake. I know that we have something I want to pursue but I also know that Ashton is likely to lose her shit if we choose to take this step. But that's the thing, I believe it's worth it. Don't you?"

I open my mouth to reply but he cuts me off. "Don't answer that, let me finish." I nod ever so slightly.

"I love my sister and you love my sister. Do you know who she loves?"

I shake my head.

"Us. She loves us. I know she's kind of bitter and anti-love or whatever but I think once she gets over her initial shock and selfishness she'll see that you and I make sense. We make sense, Piper."

Oh great, now he's got me all swoony and girly.

"If you want, we can take it slow and keep this between us for a while. Just spend time together as friends. Friends that are getting to know each other and see where it goes from there. What do you say?"

He makes it sound so simple. And I think he has a point. I know there's something between us but I also know that I will never do anything to hurt Ashton. Maybe if we're just friends hanging out we'll discover there's nothing really there and I'll have worried for nothing. But those kisses.

Friends don't kiss. I slowly run my tongue over my bottom lip at the thought of Ben's kisses.

"Oh and I have a few rules before you decide."

That has my attention and I raise a brow at him while I tug my lower lip between my teeth.

"Rule number one is that we put an end date to this secret friendship. It's Halloween now so I say Christmas break. If, by the time we let out for Christmas break, we haven't gotten sick of each other and are ready to take this to the next level, we come clean with everyone."

I start to tell him that's two months of secrets but before I can utter a word, he places a finger to my lips to stop me.

"Rule number two, benefits are totally fine in the whole getting to know each other. What do you say?"

"Benefits?" I sputter out in response. Surely he can't mean for us to be friends with benefits.

With a sly smile and a hand on my hip, with the other making its way up my back slowly, he leans forward. "Oh yeah. Lots of benefits."

This time, it's me who stops with a finger to the lips. "Kissing. Only kissing."

"I promise to only use my mouth."

Before I can respond he's kissing me again, and while I'm quite certain I've just made a deal with the devil, I'm also quite certain I don't care.

Chapter 17

Ben

Somewhere around the time I managed to get Piper out of her shirt and on her back, we found our way to bed. I kept my promise and only used my mouth. Of course, not just on her lips. There's no way I could not have more of her, but I also recognized that I'm going to have to take this slow with Piper. I have to show her how good we can be.

The sun has risen and the light is setting off prisms in the room as I lay here watching her sleep. If she wakes up and sees me, she'll likely accuse me of being some sort of stalker creep. I've just never seen something as wonderful as Piper Lawrence lying next to me with her perfect lips pursed and her breathing shallow. She fell asleep with me spooning her and I swore in that moment that I would do everything in my power to find a way to make this how I fall asleep every night.

A few months ago I was starting over and secretly

wondering if I'd made the biggest mistake of my adult life moving home. Then this woman came into my life, back into my life, and nothing has ever felt more right. The realization that I should leave before anyone sees my truck parked outside hits me about the same time she releases a sound that instantly hits me below the belt and the jeans I'm wearing suddenly feel like a strait jacket to my groin. Regardless of how much I, or my dick, want to stay here with her, the last thing we need is for the Lexington Rumor Mill to get involved.

I'm deciding on whether to wake Piper up or just leave a note and let her sleep when her eyes begin to flutter open. Doing what has somehow become my response to anything she does, I push the hair that has fallen in her face behind her ear and she smiles at me. Her smile is sincere and pure. Like her.

I remember once when Laurel hosted her book club at our place. The topic of conversation turned to the deal breakers for each of the ladies with the types of books they would read. Personally, I didn't understand a word any of them were saying – tropes, forbidden romance, second chance romance. The one phrase that stuck out to me that I thought was ridiculous and wondered how anyone could take it seriously was "insta-love." When I asked Laurel about it she said that was her favorite and made it difficult for her in the group because the other ladies hated an "insta-love" book. I agreed with those women and said any book where the lead characters fell in love after a few days was completely farfetched and ridiculous.

Then I saw a beautiful woman across the room of my local watering hole and my perspective changed. As ridiculous as it sounds, I know that Piper Lawrence is it for me. That's the first time I've admitted it to myself and, truthfully, it feels good. Damn good.

"Hey," she says with a raspy and fucking sexy voice. Kill me now.

"Morning. I think I'm going to head home."

Her smile drops and my heart leaps. Placing a gentle kiss to her lips, I pull back before responding. I recognize it is morning and I haven't brushed my teeth yet.

"I don't want to go. I'd never leave this apartment if I had a choice. It's just that I figure someone will see my truck out front and that doesn't do much for our whole secret friendship plan."

Relief washes over her face and she smiles again. "Okay."

"I'll let myself out, you just go back to sleep. I'll call you later? Maybe we can do something tonight."

"Kay. I am really sleepy."

Before I can respond her eyes close again and I know I've lost her to sleep. Carefully lifting myself from her bed, I find my discarded boots. Before I let myself out, I spot the key Piper pulled from below the mat last night. I'll be damned if I'm going to let her keep sleeping with this door unlocked. As much grief as I gave her for it, I reluctantly place the key under the mat after locking the door.

After a few steps toward the stairs, I stop. I'm not even going to second guess my instinct. I retrieve the key. I might as well make a spare for myself so Piper isn't leaving keys out for any crazy to find. It's what a good friend would do.

Yeah, Ben, keep telling yourself that.

Once I'm in my truck I realize how little I slept last night. Honestly, how little I've slept the last few weeks.

Avoiding Piper became like a second job and now that we've come to some sort of solution for our situation I'm exhausted. Instead of driving through the coffee stand I head toward my parents' house and my bed.

My dad sitting at the kitchen table with the paper shouldn't surprise me, nor should the smirk on his face that tells me he thinks I've been up to no good.

"Have a good time last night, son?"

I know my dad, and as much as I want some quality time with my pillow, I'm going to need to give him at least a few minutes of my time. Instead of grabbing a cup of the coffee that smells like heaven, I pour myself a little juice and take a seat across from him at the table.

"It was fine. I was out at the house for most of it." That's not a lie.

"Well, unless you slept in your truck I'm guessing you didn't spend the entire night at the house."

"Dad," I say with a warning but respectful tone.

"You're a grown man, Ben. I just wanted to let you know that your sister is parked in your spot so I would gather she's aware you didn't come home last night."

His rustling of the paper signals that he's done with this conversation. I contemplate unloading on him but think better of it. Piper would likely die of embarrassment if she knew I talked to my dad about us, and honestly I'm a little worried about what he'd say anyway. With that thought I place my glass in the sink and walk toward the hallway, but before I make it too far I hear my dad clear his throat.

"Oh, and Ben?"

"Yeah, Dad?"

"Just tell your mother you slept in your truck. She's like

a dog with a bone."

I can't help but chuckle at that comment.

"Don't I know it. I'm going to catch a few hours of sleep before I head out to the house."

"Sounds good," he says without ever taking his eyes from the paper.

"By the way, I'd like to have you all out to the place before the weather turns. Maybe next weekend?"

That seems to get his attention because he turns to me. "We'd really like that. Next weekend sounds good. But, let's hold off telling the ladies. They may have you regretting the invitation by the end of the week."

I laugh and shake my head. Again, my dad is a wise man.

It takes less than a minute for me to strip out of my clothes and land on my bed. Pulling my comforter up to my waist, I throw my arm over my head and suddenly this bed seems very empty. How did one night with Piper make falling asleep a different experience?

I'm jarred from a string of Piper-themed dreams by the sound of incessant knocking at my door. Okay, Piper's boobs-themed dreams. I might be the nice guy, the perfect gentleman, but I'm a man, too.

Groaning, I hope if I ignore them they'll go away. They do not. I know it's Ashton by the whiney sound of my name being bellowed.

"What?!"

"Are you decent? Can I come in?"

I pull the covers up a little more and reluctantly admit her entrance.

"Hey, brother of mine. Eww why does it smell like boy feet in here?"

"Well, perhaps because I'm a guy and have feet? It doesn't smell bad."

"Whatever." The typical eye roll follows her response. "Anyway, I have the night off since I was stuck at The Road last night until what was closer to today than yesterday and want to do something so take me to your new man palace so I can see it."

"Whoa there, that was one heck of a sentence."

"Shut it. Get up!"

"How much coffee have you had?"

"What is with everyone's concern about my caffeine intake? I actually haven't had any! I just slept like eight hours is all. I'm recharged and ready to do something. Piper is claiming a migraine but I don't buy it, I think she's hungover. Besides I need to know who you met last night that kept you out later than me."

Her last statement catches my attention and, unfortunately for me, my reaction doesn't go unnoticed.

"Ah, so there was someone. You can tell me in the truck! Get up, lazy ass!"

Before I can offer a retort, she's gone and yelling to our mother that we won't be home for dinner. I reach to my nightstand and grab my phone. Hoping for a text from Piper, I am disappointed when there is only one from Jameson. I guess his friend from last night is turning into a two-day friend.

Jameson: So this Sasha is pretty cool. We're going to

hang out again tonight. **Want to grab a run and breakfast tomorrow?**

Me: Oh a 2 nighter. Serious business. A run is good but not before 9.

Jameson: Fuck you. I don't do serious. 9 at the trails.

I respond with a thumbs up and contemplate what to say to Piper. I want to see her and spend time with her but I am also a little worried about scaring her off. She's like a timid cat at this point and the wrong move could send me right back to the real friend zone. I actually want to hear her voice but again there's that skittish cat thing.

Me: Are you around?

If feels like an eternity, but is really only seconds, before my phone signals a response.

Piper: Yepper.

Yepper? Instead of responding I hit the phone icon. I'm almost worried she's sending me to voicemail before she picks up.

"Hello?"

"Hey, baby."

"Hey?"

"Are you not sure if you're saying hi?"

"What?"

"You said hey like it was a question so I'm curious if you are uncertain if you're saying hey."

"Oh. I didn't mean to. I think you just caught me off-guard calling."

"I wanted to hear you voice. It's one of my favorite sounds."

She laughs and I can hear the disbelief in her voice.

"Oh hush, it is not."

"It absolutely is. To prove it, I'm going to bring a phone book over and have you just read it to me. That'll show you how much I love it."

"You want me to read the phone book? That's just weird."

We both laugh and whatever tension she had in her voice when she answered seems to be gone.

"What can I say? I'm a weird guy. Regardless, your voice is one of my favorite sounds in this world. It's sweet, smooth, and gentle. The first time I heard you speak I thought it reminded me of honey."

I can hear her moving around and it sounds like she's settling in before speaking again.

"Honey, huh? That's a new one. And I'm pretty sure the first time you heard my voice I was five years old and sounded like a cartoon character."

"Ah you've got me there, Princess. I suppose that's true. I meant the first time I heard your current, adult, sexy-as-hell voice."

She makes a noise that's part sigh and moan and I can feel the blood rushing from my head to other parts.

"That's the sound I'm talking about. Honey. Don't even get me started on your eyes."

"My eyes? They're brown, nothing special."

"Oh but that's where you're wrong. They are special. Everything about you is special, Piper. I thought we covered this need you have to put yourself down. Your eyes are beautiful. They are bright, hopeful, and the perfect shade of brown that is the same as my favorite whiskey. When you get excited or have an idea they dance. And, Piper, when you come?"

"Yeah?"

"When you come, baby, they sparkle."

I can hear her breath catch at my final words. I smile to myself. My girl is good in all ways that matter, but she seems to like it when I talk about things some would consider a little dirty. Truthfully, I've never uttered anything remotely dirty in my prior relationships, but something about being with Piper makes me want to be different. Everything about her and me is different. I am still afraid she's going to run so instead of digging deep for the dirty version of myself, I clear my throat.

"So, about that phone book."

She responds with a laugh. The laugh that makes me smile and I'm pretty sure is the sound of angels singing.

"You think I'm joking but I'm not. That isn't why I called though."

"I thought you just wanted to hear my voice," she flirtatiously replies. Vixen.

"I did but I also promised I'd call you later and we'd do something. Of course Ashton was in here a bit ago waking me up demanding I take her out to my house. I guess I'll do that. She also said you had a migraine."

"Oh. Well, yeah I did tell her that. I maybe, sort of, kind of lied to her. I'm a horrible person, I know. If this secret friend thing we have isn't already bad enough, I also blatantly lied to her. I'm going to Hell."

I chuckle and throw back my covers as I get up and start finding clothes.

"I'm pretty sure lying is not a means for a visit with Lucifer. But out of curiosity, why did you lie?"

"Because it's Ashton. You know she'll want to know if I

met anyone, who I was with last night, what I did, and so on. I can lie over text but not to her face. I thought I'd cave and tell her everything so I just said I had a headache. I never said migraine. Regardless, I just can't see her right now. I need to practice my liar face."

"Well, we can always tell her. I vote for that option over the liar face. I don't want you to change your face. I'm a little partial to it."

"No, we agreed. Friends and get to know each other and see what happens. You gave me until Christmas Break and I'm taking it."

"Okay, well, if you change your mind let me know. Do you want to do something tonight? We'll have to figure out what to do with my truck if we hang out in town."

"I would like to do something. What if I meet you at your house and we leave your truck there? We could just come back here and maybe watch a movie or something."

"I like the plan of *or something*."

"Ben," she warns.

"What? I kept my promise last night. Mouth only."

"Good Lord. Okay, on that note I'm going to go and get some stuff done. You go spend time with your sister. I'll meet you at your house at like eight? How's that?"

"Sounds good. Have a good afternoon, Piper."

"Bye, Ben."

I set my phone down on the side table and grab my clothes before heading to shower. A very cold shower. Thoughts of Piper force me to stay under the freezing-cold water longer than normal and I'm immediately greeted with a less-than-kind Ashton when I emerge from the bathroom. I'm still ignoring her nagging when we both walk into the kitchen and I grab my truck keys.

"Where are you two off to?"

I don't have a chance to answer my mom before Ashton goes on another tangent about my finally agreeing to take her to my house. I don't bother interjecting that I didn't actually agree to take her anywhere, she invited herself. My dad is sitting at the table again, but instead of reading the paper he's working the crossword.

"Seven-letter word for bowl-shaped percussion instrument," Dad absently shouts at us, causing a slight pause in Ashton's rant.

"Timpani," Ashton responds without missing a beat in her one-sided conversation with Mom.

"Excellent, honey!" Dad declares before dramatically setting his completed crossword down on the table. I, on the other hand, am staring at Ash.

"What? I know things, Ben."

"I know you know things, Ash, but really, who even knows what timpani is?"

"Your sister, Ben. Be kind. Now since you kids won't be home for dinner would like for me to make a few sandwiches to go?"

As I'm about to agree Ashton tells my mom that she's ordered a pizza for us and we'll be taking it out to my house. Apparently I'm only along for the ride in this plan of hers. I don't even bother arguing with her at this point and grab my keys as we head out the door. This is going to be a long few hours before I meet Piper.

Chapter 18

Ben

I've managed to skirt Ashton's questions about last night. I didn't lie when I told her I spent the night at my house. I did spend most of the evening here; I just didn't sleep here. Omission is not lying in this case and I'm okay with that. For now.

I hadn't realized how important seeing this piece of my life was to my sister until we arrived. She not only called ahead and ordered us a pizza, she had chairs and blankets in the back of my truck along with a cooler filled with a few beers and some waters.

Once we got here she was like a kid at an amusement park. In awe at every little thing in the house and on the property, she's already planned multiple cookouts and bonfires for next summer. Unfortunately, I've ran out of distracting conversation and I know she's about to hit me with what she thinks is her given right as my sister – nosiness.

"I love this place, Ben. It's really wonderful and so you."

"Thanks. I agree, I'm glad I went for it. The work is hard but once it's all done it will have all been worth it. Sorry it took me so long to bring you here."

"It's okay. I know you've had a lot going on the last few months so I've given you the space you needed."

Laughing at her assessment of giving me space, I'm suddenly hit in the head with a plastic bottle cap. "Hey now, you don't want to have to walk home, do you?"

"Whatevs, you wouldn't make me walk home. Besides, you still haven't told me who you met last night. I know you had to have met someone so fess up."

"Nope, didn't meet anyone. Sorry to disappoint. Besides I'm not looking to meet anyone new."

All truths.

"Mmhmm, I'm not sure I believe you but I won't pry. I'll figure it out soon enough."

We sit in silence a few more minutes and I can tell by the way she's shifting that Ashton is about to ask to leave. It's getting colder as the minutes tick by and if I can get her to leave now I can drop her off at the house and get back here before Piper.

"Good grief, it's freezing. Can we get out of here before my nose hairs turn to icicles?"

"Dramatic much, Ash?"

"Don't give me grief. It's absolutely fucking freezing!" she exclaims as she leaps from her seat and hops up and down in some sort of weird-looking jumping jack.

"Yeah, come on. I'll take you home and then I'm coming back here for a bit."

Again, truth.

"Whatever, come on. I'm going to have to start singing

like a Disney princess if you don't get me out of here."

My sister is a mess and I love her. I take her by the shoulders and kiss the top of her head. She wraps her arms around my body, and this is why I have to convince Piper we make sense. So this person a fun, feisty, stubborn, loving, kind, and passionate human who we both love isn't hurt in the slightest.

The drive back to my parents' house is quiet and I welcome it. Ashton seems happy to have had a little brother and sister bonding time. It occurs to me that not only have I been avoiding Piper but, in doing so, I've avoided my sister. Once I've dropped Ashton at home, I turn around and make a return drive right back to where I came from.

I notice that although Piper's car is parked in front of the house, she isn't in it. I don't even wonder where she is, I immediately head toward the house and the kitchen.

Finding her standing at the kitchen looking out the window, I pause a moment to take her in. The way the moonlight streams through the window, she looks almost angelic. She's wearing a dress with her cowboy boots and a jacket. She's not dressed for this weather so I can only hope she's dressed for me.

The shadows cast around the room set a feeling of calmness that gives me a sense of home and peace. I clear my throat to get her attention but not startle her. Piper turns her head so she's peering over her shoulder toward me and smiles. My heart falls to my stomach. It's not fear that has me reacting so dramatically. It's simpler than that.

I love this girl. I'm not sure when or how it happened but all these flashes of what could be are in this moment. That smile is similar to the one she offered me this morning when she woke up. It's the smile I want every night before I fall asleep and the smile I want to greet me every morning when I wake.

I return the smile and swallow down every declaration of love running through my mind. It's too soon, even I know that. It's too much and almost embarrassing. Almost.

She turns completely and begins walking toward me and I step toward her. Meeting her halfway. The symbolism of this moment is not lost on me.

"Princess."

Another smile before she responds, "Bentley."

I grab her hands and tug her against me. She laughs and falls into me, placing her hands on my biceps. One of my hands goes around her waist while the other instinctively brushes hair from her face. This time, she leans her head toward my hand and my thumb gently caresses her cheek.

I could say so much to her right now. I could easily tell Piper how her smile makes me feel like the most important person in the world. Or how beautiful she is and with a single look she takes my breath away. I want to make her eyes sparkle as she comes undone beneath me. I want to tell her how having her in my arms is the only time I know everything I'm doing makes sense.

I say none of that. Instead, I lay my lips on hers. Gently and slowly, I deepen the kiss and she melts into me. With each second that passes, I increase the intensity. A slight nibble of her lower lip and she opens enough to grant me access. This isn't a kiss of passion or urgency. This is a kiss of emotion and promises.

I realize I have to slow this down. Not so much for her but for us. For the us I know we are and will be. I need her to know that this is more than physical attraction, that we are more than just something superficial.

"What's with the full name?"

"I didn't use your full name. If I had, I would have greeted you with 'Hello, Mister Bentley James Sullivan.' I did not so thus it was not your full name."

Once she's put me in my place she turns from me and all that sass that first drew me to her is back in full force. I can't help myself and I smack her ass. Lovingly, but hard enough she yelps and turns to glare at me. Before she can completely turn to reprimand me, I wrap my arms around her from behind so her head is resting on my chest. Rigid at first, she relaxes when I place a feather-light kiss to her temple.

"You know, Miss Lawrence, I've never been one for this whole alpha male thing. But, hearing you say my full name with that tone I may change my mind."

"Oh please. I'd laugh you right out of this house. Now, fine sir, what are we still doing here? I believe you owe me a movie night," she says, wiggling from my grasp.

"Fine. Let's go, where are your keys?"

"Umm, *my* keys are in my pocket. You don't need them, I can drive."

"I know you can, but you won't. I'm the man, I drive."

"Macho much? I don't think so. Look, Ben, I don't think this will work with us being just plain ole friends if you think you're going to be some alpha male that takes charge and expects me to be some timid wallflower. I will not…"

Not letting her complete her sentence, I grab by the arms and kiss her. If I've learned there's one way to stop Piper from talking, it's kissing her. This kiss is not tender or sweet. No, this is passion and fire. As quickly as I started the kiss, I break it while simultaneously plucking her keys from her jacket pocket.

"Hey! That wasn't nice!"

"I actually think it was very nice. Let's get something straight. I will never expect you to be anything or anyone other than you. I am very fond of the you that you are. *But I will drive because as the man in this friendship I will always keep you safe and make sure you are taken care of.* That is why I am taking these keys and driving us back to your apartment for movie night."

This time it's me who walks away and she doesn't stop me. Instead I can feel her mind working overtime. I decide to have a little fun with her as I keep walking and she follows. "Don't think too much, Princess. We're wasting precious time while you do. I hope you chose something scary so you have to seek safety in my arms."

Once we're at her car I wait for her to catch up and open the passenger door, leaning on it as she starts to climb in, then pauses and looks at me. "I'm sorry I was defensive. I'm just … I'm trying."

"I know, baby. We'll figure this all out. Now let's go get our movie on."

It was not a scary movie. No, in fact it was a movie from before either of us were born. A musical that Piper knew every single word spoken and every song sang. I wanted to muzzle her at one point. I tried shutting her up with kisses but even that didn't work. Instead she swatted me away and told me if I got between her and her "Cool Rider" I was sitting on the floor. I have never been so grateful for a movie to end than I was of that one.

"Did you love it? It's my favorite movie of all time. Michelle Pfeiffer was so pretty. I used to pretend I was her singing in the mirror."

"Love is a pretty strong word for what I'm feeling after that. You are much prettier than Michelle Pfeiffer was."

"Well, you're sweet. I am not prettier than her and of course I know I can't carry a tune but that doesn't mean I can't sing along if it makes me happy."

I feel like this is one of those moments that she's telling me a little about what lies beneath the surface. Something that drives her to be negative about herself. As much as I'd love to understand that more, it's been ninety minutes since I've had her in my arms and that's about all I can handle right now.

"You know what?"

"Nope, what?"

"I think you should pretend you are Michelle Pfeiffer like when she's on that ladder. My lap could absolutely pass for a ladder, ya know."

"Oh really?" she asks coyly, tugging on a strand of her hair and looking at me through her long lashes before looking away. I watch as her facial expression tells me she's thinking too much again. She's conflicted, and if I know Piper, and I think I do at this point, she is trying to avoid taking me up on my offer.

I remove her hand from hair and lace our fingers. "Hey," I say, tugging her hand to catch her attention. She looks at me again and I see her wariness. "Don't think, just feel. Piper, stop trying to talk yourself out of being with me."

"I'm not talking myself out being with you. This is just so far outside of my comfort zone; you're so brazen and outspoken. It should make me uncomfortable and shy."

"Should?"

Instead of a response she unlaces our fingers and slowly moves to straddle me. Her hands first land on my shoulders, then slowly make their way down the front of my chest, ultimately spreading across my pecs to rest on my biceps.

"Feel free to sing away. I'll be the perfect ladder and just sit here."

"I don't think I want that," she whispers, slightly leaning in to me.

"No?" I ask while my hands begin making their way from her knees to her upper thighs. Thankfully the skirt of her dress has ridden up on its own as she's settled in on my lap. She's moving her body ever so slightly, causing her breasts to rise and fall. Her neck is within range of my lips and the moment I connect with her skin she tilts her head back and releases a sound that I can only believe she's been holding in.

My hands have made their way around to her backside. With a squeeze of her ass her face comes down and it's she who kisses me this time. Her hands move from resting on my biceps to either side of my face. I let her take control. This is the first time Piper has given herself over to me. She's choosing this. I pull my hands from her backside and begin tugging at the straps of her dress. I know she was freezing at my house in this outfit and knowing she wore it for me gives me hope.

The top of the dress is tight and the straps only come down a little on her arms. I reach around to find the zipper, but I feel her tense as I do.

"I'm sorry. I didn't mean to," I say apologetically. I must

have really pushed too far because she's standing up from where she'd been perched.

I open my mouth to apologize more when she extends her hand to me. I place my hand in hers and before I stand she says the words that will forever change us.

"Let's go to bed."

Chapter 19

Piper

This entire night is completely out of my comfort zone. I am not this girl, never have been. Not even in relationships. Nope, I am not bold and I sure as hell have never climbed up on a man and straddled him. I was being honest when I said I should feel uncomfortable and shy. That's normally how I feel with men. Uncomfortable, insecure, shy, and out of my league. With Ben I feel confident and bold. He makes me want to step outside of my comfort zone.

Taking his hand, I lead him into my bedroom. I don't bother with light and am grateful my blinds are slightly open, letting in some moonlight. Regardless of how bold I felt walking in here, I suddenly feel very self-conscious and aware of the fact that I am asking Bentley James Sullivan to have sex with me.

I know he can sense the shift in my confidence because just as I'm about to tell him I can't do this, he steps toward me and pulls me into a hug. Not a sensual kiss, a hug.

"Hey, relax. There is no pressure here."

So few words with so much meaning. I melt into his embrace and welcome his warmth. He smells really good. I should know his smell better than my own since I spent the morning snuggling, in a non-creepy fashion, the pillow he used last night. I pull back from him and look up at him as he does his thing with my hair. I've grown accustomed to his need to keep hair out of my face and offer him a smile as a thank you.

"Before you start thinking again, I want you to know we are not going to have sex."

Say what? We aren't? Why not? Because he doesn't want that with me. Obviously.

"Nope, you don't get to go there," he says, cupping my face in his hands, one on either side of my cheek, and tilting my head up to look at him.

"I see your mind working a million miles a minute. We are not having sex because you aren't ready. Truthfully, I don't think I'm ready for that. I know for a fact the minute I have you it's game over and I'll be all in. Tonight, I just want to be with you," he continues, moving his hand so he's threading my hair with his fingers and slightly tugging me so that my neck is exposed.

I swallow the lump forming in my throat as a sense of relief comes to the surface. I am so not ready for sex with Ben. I'm already half in love with this man and if I sleep with him I'll fall so hard I don't know that I'll ever recover. Instead of kissing me like I expect, he brings his mouth close to my ear.

"I want to hold you." Each word he says sends shivers down my spine in anticipation as he continues, "And kiss you." His soft kisses along my jaw line have me gripping his forearms in an effort to keep myself upright.

"I'm going to kiss you now, Piper, and then I'm going to take this dress off of you." Oh dear Lord. My breaths are quick in succession and my eyes close instinctively as his lips touch mine. Loosening my grip on his forearms, my hands find their way up and around his neck. I give myself over to the kiss just as my zipper is lowered and my dress pools at our feet. He spins me and begins walking us toward my bed.

As my knees connect with the edge of the bed, I tug at the hem of his shirt. "Off." He complies and with one hand pulls his shirt off. My breath catches again at the sight of him. I feel myself falling. Literally and figuratively. I open my eyes to find Ben over me. The intensity in his eyes causes me to gasp. Not in fear but in awe. Something changes in this moment; I finally see the man who has haunted my dreams all these years.

The man I have known was coming for me and would be *the one*. I search for something, anything to tell me what is happening. His arms have him braced so that he's hovering just above me, our breaths mingling because we are so close, and his heart beating in time with mine. My legs instinctively fall open so he is hitting me in just the right spot.

Nothing separates us but a few layers of clothing and I want nothing more than to rip those pieces away. I want him inside me. I need him inside me.

"God, Piper," Ben sighs. His sigh is hard to distinguish. It feels like acceptance but sounds slightly like frustration. The latter thought has me tensing slightly. "Do you have any idea how beautiful you are?"

I shake my head in response. "So beautiful you not only

take my breath away but render me speechless. There are no words in the human vocabulary to fully express the way you make me feel."

"Show me," I say in a voice I hardly recognize.

His response is only a growl and then his lips are on mine. This kiss is different than those before. Something has shifted between us. Not just Ben shifting between my legs and sending my body into a frenzy. The friction between his jeans and the silk of my panties has me humming from the inside out.

As Ben increases the intensity of the kiss, my hands come up to his sides and I feel him shiver slightly. I love that he reacts to me this way and I begin taking control of the kiss. An animalistic growl comes from the back of his throat. My heart is beating in rhythm with his and we are in sync, our movements like a dance. His hand finds its way between us. The moment his hand reaches the band of my panties he pulls away from the kiss to look in my eyes. He's searching for permission. Permission I grant.

I push up on my elbows and reach behind to unfasten my bra before tossing it aside. Ben's eyes bulge like a cartoon character and that causes me to giggle. He smiles a smile that, if I couldn't feel the silk, would have me believing had just melted my panties.

I lay back down so my head is on the pillow and run my hands down my torso and watch as he visibly swallows. This reaction has me smiling like I have a secret. My hands rest on his waistband and begin to undo the button before his hand stops me.

"Don't. I meant what I said, we aren't ready."

I suppose he's right. I may agree but I don't have to like

it. Ben only allows me those quick thoughts before he has me lost in the moment. His lips feel like butterflies fluttering against my skin as he makes his way from my lips to my neck. His fingers grace my breasts with gentle caresses and slight tugs at my nipples. My breath is catching with each tug.

His lips replace his fingers on my breasts. Ben stiffens his tongue and teases my right nipple. With each stroke I feel the warmth soar through me. Arching my back, I beg for more without words. He gives me what I want when his fingers pull my panties to the side and he sinks a finger in me. Tugging my nipple with his lips, the dual sensations have me quickly approaching my release. Just as I am about to verbalize this, Ben removes his finger from me. The loss is immediate.

I'm gathering my wits when Ben pulls back so he's resting on his knees. I open my eyes and instinctively raise my hands over my head. His sly grin sends my heart a flutter. I return the grin as he releases a growl from deep in his throat. Laying a series of kisses across my abdomen and to my hip, I know where he's headed. This is unknown territory for me. I've been intimate and had sex. Sadly, I'm realizing until this moment none of the men in my life before Ben have ever made it about me. Equally, I've never been with a man who I've cared was selfish in bed.

The moment he pulls my panties to the side and his tongue makes contact with my most intimate skin, I feel my orgasm building. The heat is overwhelming and instinctively I attempt to close my legs. Ben nudges my knees apart with his shoulders and moans his approval of what is happening. The vibration of his moan increases the intensity of the buildup. With a mind of their own, my hands find their way to his head, slightly tugging at his hair as my own moans fill the room. His tongue is doing astounding things as he adds his fingers to the mix. The intensity of each lick stronger than the next and I feel like I am outside of my body looking down at us.

I've never been vocal during sex, but like everything else with Ben, I am now. Incoherent words flow out of my mouth as I struggle to maintain a steady stream of breaths. The moment I say his name the orgasm floods me. Like an erupting volcano I'm shaking and have replaced my grip from his hair to the comforter.

As I get my bearings, Ben removes himself from between my legs and kisses his way up to my face. This time I don't wait for him to move my hair. Once the blanket of auburn is no longer blocking my vision I look up to the most handsome face on the planet Earth.

"I could do that every single day for the rest of my life and never tire of it."

"Don't make promises you can't keep, my friend," I tease.

I note his reaction to the use of the word *friend* before he places a kiss to the tip of my nose. He nudges the covers from under me until I am under them, where he joins me. Spooning me once again from behind, he feathers my shoulder with gentle kisses.

"I don't break promises, Princess."

"Mmm," I offer in response.

"It's getting late. Let's sleep."

"But," I begin as I untangle myself from his arms and turn toward him, placing my hands on his chest.

"But what?"

Slowly moving my hands across his very sculpted pecs, I struggle to find the words. "It's just that, well, you can't possibly be ready to sleep. You didn't … I should…"

Ben takes both of my hands in one of his own, making me feel small and fragile.

"I don't need to and you shouldn't ever feel you have to."

I just stare at him, no response possible.

"Now, let's get some sleep," he says as I snuggle into his embrace.

One lash at a time, I slowly begin peeling my eyes open. I feel slightly out of sorts and stretch my arms over my head while pointing my toes when suddenly I inhale two of the best scents ever created by man - freshly brewed coffee and bacon.

The relaxation I felt from my quick stretch is immediately gone as the realization that someone has brewed said coffee and is cooking said bacon. *Ben.* With that thought, the events of last night flash through my mind. Ignoring the tug in my tummy and the smile on my face at the memories, I groan.

"Breakfast is almost done, sleepy head."

Apparently I groan loudly. Making a face toward the voice to reflect my unhappiness of having to get out of bed, I do just that. Thankfully, at some point during the night I managed to throw on Ben's T-shirt as my makeshift pajamas. Not daring to look at myself in the mirror, I quickly brush my teeth before heading toward breakfast and the voice.

A man who cooks is sexy. A man cooking with a little extra scruff, messy bed head, bare feet, while only wearing a pair of jeans is delicious. I allow myself a few minutes to take in the sight while his back is to me.

"Are you just going to stand there staring at me or are you going to come say a proper good morning?"

"Why are you so talkative in the morning?" I grumble while pouring a cup of coffee.

Leaning against the counter, I attempt to avoid a third-degree burn on my tongue with short puffs of air at the liquid goodness and slowly take a sip as Ben chooses to ignore my question. I watch him carefully as he places the spatula on the counter and turns the burner off. I continue holding the cup so I'm blowing on the coffee but instead of taking another sip, I'm mesmerized by the sight of Ben's back muscles as they twitch with each movement. Wow. Slowly he turns and begins walking toward me.

Check that, stalks toward me. Taking my cup from my hand, he sets it on the counter. Before I can even process what's happening he scoops me up by my butt. My hands instinctively reach around his neck as he sets me on the counter. With him standing between my legs, I look at him wide-eyed with my mouth in the form of an O.

"For future reference, a proper good morning includes a kiss."

I don't even have an opportunity to reply as his lips claim mine. My body responds instantly. The want, need, and desperation for this man consume me. My hands thread through his hair as my legs wrap around his waist. When I'm almost convinced we're about to consummate this friendship in my little kitchen he pulls back with a mischievous grin and plants a quick kiss on my cheek before pulling away.

"Hey!"

"Now, that was how you say good morning. Let's eat."

Rolling my eyes in an effort to calm my hormones, I hop from the counter and grab my coffee before taking a seat at the little table. Before me is quite the spread of bacon, pancakes, fruit, and juice.

"Where'd you get all this food? I'm pretty sure all I had in the fridge was some cream cheese and maybe an apple."

Shrugging, he begins making a large mountain of food on his plate. "I woke up early and went to the store. We're going to have to get some groceries if we're going to spend time here."

"I usually go shopping on Sundays so I can do all of my food prep for the week. I wasn't exactly expecting weekend company."

"Good, I'll add a few things to your shopping list if that's okay?"

I'm not sure when we went from not talking for weeks to making a grocery list together, but I'd be lying if I said it didn't make me happy. Full-heart happy. And scared out of my mind.

"Sure, the list is on the fridge," I say while I continue to note the domestic scene playing out. "What are your plans today? Are you hanging out with the guys?"

"I figured I'd run home and change my clothes and then we could hang out."

"I don't think that's a good idea," I say as I stand to refill my coffee.

"What do you mean it's not a good idea? I think it's an excellent idea," he says, grabbing my wrist and tugging me onto his lap. I'm acknowledging the comfort of this lap when he turns me so I'm straddling him in the chair. "Explain yourself, please."

I roll my eyes at his demand. To which he pinches my backside and I offer a screech.

"Hey there, no pinching."

He smiles and places a sweet kiss on my lips.

"I just don't think it makes sense for us to spend all of our time together. We both have real lives, Ben. We can't hole up here in my apartment and pretend otherwise."

"I consider *this* my real life, Piper. I thought we were on the same page here."

I am so not handling this well. I can feel the tension radiating off Ben. I remove myself from his lap and refill my mug before turning back to him.

"We are. I just need some space of my own. This is a lot for me to digest."

"Okay, if you're sure. Don't start over-thinking this."

Ben stands and walks over to me. I hold the cup in both hands like a security blanket.

"I'm going to finish my breakfast and then we're going to do the dishes. I'll go work on my house while you have your alone time. But, don't get used to me not being around. I plan on being here often."

Once his declaration is complete Ben resumes his spot at the table and continues eating his breakfast. I continue to stand at the counter watching him. Regardless of what he says, I need this time without him here. This isn't reality. At some point this man is going to realize I am not worth the risk. He'll accept that a passing attraction is not worth hurting his sister.

I am fully aware that in this scenario, it is me who will end up hurt. Any normal well-adjusted woman would put a stop to this insanity. I am not that woman. I am willing to take the hit if it means that for a short period of time I can feel the level of importance I have for the past two days.

Dishes with Ben include him trying to coerce me back into bed and my insistence that we actually get some adulting done. I know if he gets me back in that bed I'll spend half the day repaying him for last night. Instead I'm going to spend the day cleaning, grocery shopping, and trying to understand my feelings.

I'm a confused girl. My feelings are not the problem. Or, perhaps, they are. I'm not sure. I've loved this man my entire life. Except I've learned that the version of Ben that I've loved isn't the man he is now. Instead I had romanticized him over the years. I always knew Ben was a kind person. The kind of guy who always opened doors for women or helped the younger kids with their bikes. He always smiled and greeted everyone like they mattered. The only person he ever had a problem with was Tony. Knowing Tony, that was probably less Ben's doing than Tony's.

Over the last few months I've seen that in many ways Ben is exactly the same as he was. He's chivalrous and kind, yet he's so much *more*. He says all the right things at the right time and then there are the things he doesn't actually say but expresses. Each gesture giving me a glimmer of hope this could all work out okay.

I am trying to trust that everything he says is true and his feelings are real. Still, the doubt is there. Little voices in my head, voices that sound a lot like my mom, telling me I'm a fool. Men like Bentley Sullivan don't fall for girls like me. Eventually, he'll get bored and realize I'm just a small-town girl who wants a simple life. His future has always been filled with possibilities and opportunities; I shouldn't expect him to stick around.

Logic tells me I shouldn't doubt his sincerity and, above all, Ben has integrity. He would never lead me on to just leave. Yet, the normal everyday version of me can't seem to accept that as a reality. I acknowledge these last two nights with Ben have been more real and natural than any of the nights I spent with Tony or any boyfriend before him. That says volumes.

I hate that I can't go to the one person in my life I share everything with. Normally I'd go to Ashton and talk to her about how I'm feeling, accept her no-nonsense advice, and let her tell me how everything will be. Since I can't do that, I'll just pretend she's here listening to me ramble about Ben and imagine what she would say in response. I'll skip past the initial "Why are you screwing my brother" reaction and settle on what I know she'd tell me instead. She would remind me that Bentley Sullivan is one of the good guys. He's by far the most honest person in either of our lives and if he tells me it's going to be okay, it's going to be.

There is no reason to doubt him. There is no reason to believe he will be anything less than perfect. Which in itself is quite annoying. I mean, can't the guy pick his nose or something, anything. The only thing that stands to reason is that I can be my own worst enemy and my own insecurities stand in my way.

Chapter 20

Ben

When Piper told me she wanted to spend the day apart, I was pissed. We've just had two amazing nights together and she has to see how great we are together. Instead, she opts to spend her day grocery shopping and cooking. I did manage to sneak a few items onto her shopping list, which I consider a positive sign that she plans on having me over enough to keep my preferred coffee creamer in her refrigerator.

I woke early enough to run to the store and prepare a breakfast for Piper. This also meant I had to cancel breakfast with Jameson. I didn't bail on the run, but there was no doubt in my mind who I wanted to share breakfast with. By the time I had Piper drop me at my truck I was already running late.

I pull into the parking lot at the end of the running trails to see Jameson talking up a brunette with a large, and scary-looking, dog. As I lock up my truck I turn to see that he's in the early stages of his usual pickup lines.

Currently Jameson is leaning on the nearest structure, in this case a trash can, while combing his hand through his short blond hair like it's wet from the shower. From a male perspective, it's less natural and more like he's in distress. According to Jameson the ladies find it sexy and he'll usually have a number before he has to move on to the next step in the pickup – showing his abs.

I can guarantee that at this point in the conversation he's likely thrown out a plethora of compliments while downplaying his own attributes. If I'm reading her body language correctly, the brunette is buying everything he's selling.

As I approach I notice she is holding his phone, presumably giving him her phone number. I clear my throat as he takes her hand in his and places a kiss to her knuckles. I cannot believe this shit works.

"Oh hey, buddy. I didn't think you were going to make it. Thankfully Celeste here was keeping me company."

Offering a smile to Celeste, I ignore Jameson's dig.

"Sorry, I had a few stops to make. Are we doing this?"

"Don't mind my friend, Celeste. He's not always a jerk. Say hello, Ben."

He's right, I'm not a jerk and that did sound a little harsh.

"He's right, I apologize. Hello, Celeste, it's nice to meet you," I say, offering my hand, which she takes.

"It was nice to meet you as well. Ben, is it?" The purr in her voice evident. "I'll let you gentlemen get your run in. Call me soon, Jameson."

Neither of us answer as she turns and walks toward the other end of the park. I start stretching, but Jameson seems more interested in the excessive wiggle she offers him.

"Hey, put your tongue away. You may catch a fly."

"Screw you. Where have you been? I could have been here all day waiting for you."

"Yeah it looks like you were suffering. Do you find women everywhere you go?"

"Nah, not everywhere. Old man Connors doesn't have any ladies working at the gas station," he replies as he turns toward our preferred running trail.

We take off at an easy pace, but as the trail widens we each pick it up a little. This is what I needed. When I'm running I can always let go of things that bother me and the tension begins to lessen with each strike of my foot to the dirt. Tension is not an accurate word. Frustration. I'm frustrated with keeping Piper a secret. I know it was my suggestion to be friends with some benefits for a few weeks and ease her into us being something more. I regret that. I don't want to wait. This weekend has shown me what we can be and it's pretty fucking great. I don't think we are giving my sister enough credit. Honestly if I didn't think it would scare Piper away completely I'd just tell Ash myself.

I make it to the end of the trail before Jameson and take a long drink of my water as he comes around the bend. Stopping with his hands clasped over his head, he takes a few long breaths before speaking.

"Are you training for the Olympics and I missed it?"

"What?" I strangle out between breaths.

"Dude, you were running like you were on a mission. You pissed at something?"

"What? No."

"Uh-huh. Let's go grab a beer and you can tell me all

about it," he says, turning and beginning our return to the parking lot. This time he sets the pace and it's less intense than mine.

When we make it back to the parking lot I remind him that it is only ten in the morning and perhaps a little early for a beer. He in turn reminds me that it is in fact Sunday and it's perfectly acceptable to drink with brunch.

"Brunch? Since when do you brunch?"

"Ben, brunch is a perfectly respectable meal."

"Uh, yeah it is, but I wouldn't think of you as someone that brunches."

"Screw you. Fine, let's go eat but not brunch because that would obviously be unmanly. That better, Bentley?"

"You're a dick. Let's go," I reply as I shove him a little and he laughs in return.

We decide on a sports bar that serves breakfast on football Sundays. Once we're seated in a booth we immediately proceed with ordering two large beers and a couple of omelets.

"Are you going to tell me what has you wound up to the point that you are running like a Kenyan in the Olympics?"

"I'm not wound up. It's nothing. So are you going to call that girl from the park? What happened to the other one, Sasha was it?"

"No deflecting. Come on, man, I know when something is up with you. You've been MIA for weeks, blowing us off at every turn. Landon's poor little feelers were hurt when you didn't come to poker night. I've had to listen to him whine for two weeks about that shit. You need to man up and tell me what is going on."

"I haven't been MIA; I'm working on my house, you

know that."

"Yeah, the house nobody gets to see. I'm a fucking contractor, Ben. We could have all been working on your house and had it almost livable by now. There's more going on. Is it Laurel? Are you getting back together?"

"What? No. Why would you even ask that? I'm not getting back together with Laurel." The defensiveness in my voice is obvious.

Our food arrives and I'm given a reprieve in this conversation while we both devour half of our meals without a word exchanged. I guess that run took more out of me than I thought considering I already had breakfast with Piper.

"If it isn't your house and it isn't Laurel, it must be Piper."

I choke on the bite I just swallowed and take a drink of my beer to wash it down. As I set my mug down I notice the smug expression on his face.

"Thought so. You've been seeing Piper, haven't you?"

"No. I have not been seeing Piper. You just took me by surprise. Why would you even say that?" While I pause and try to limit the defensiveness in my voice, he only stares at me, waiting for me to continue. "We talked at the lake like you suggested and she blew me off. I've just been dealing with my house and work has been busy. That's all."

"Nope. Not buying it. You are totally seeing Piper Lawrence and Ashton is going to kill you. Not Piper. She loves Piper. We all love Piper. You, my friend, are a dead man."

They all love Piper. "What do you mean you all love Piper?"

Putting his hands up in defense he laughs. "Not like that, man. Piper is a cool chick and we like her. You know, like we do Ashton. Well, they all like Ashton, she's on my nerves half the time and makes me want to stab my ears when she talks. Regardless, Piper's good people and she's one of us."

I absorb his comments and don't offer a response. We finish our breakfast while watching one of the games playing on the TV. Although the topic of Piper and me is off the table it is still in the forefront of my mind. After we pay and are headed back outside, Jameson stops with me at my truck.

"Look. I think whatever you aren't telling me about you and Piper is a good thing. You guys actually make sense. That's why I sent you with her the other night. I knew she wasn't drinking much; she never really does but she was playing like it for Ash's sake. All night long she was cranky and mumbling under her breath about the costume and how she dressed up for nobody. Then you walked in. Dude, she was finally herself. I could see that from ten feet away, you have to see it."

I don't respond. Which is a response on its own and he continues.

"I told you at the lake that you needed to make your move. You tried and she blew you off. I know you and I've gotten to know Piper. If my instincts are right, and they usually are, you are both under some sort of impression that you are protecting Ashton. You both have this impression that if you were to get together somehow Ashton would be upset or hurt. I don't think you give your sister enough credit. She's a royal pain in the ass and can be a total bitch but…"

"Watch it," I warn.

"Sorry." I offer a nod in acceptance that my sister is both

a pain and often a little on the bitchy side. "Anyway, she *can* be those things, but at the end of the day Ashton cares about both of you. She plays tough and the whole 'hos before bros' thing is her mantra, but you'll never know how she really feels if you never ask. Plus, if she finds out you're doing the dirty and lying about it, she'll probably kill you both."

I'm left alone at my truck as he walks away. He's right. Not just about Ashton being a royal pain but also about the lying. Suddenly this plan of mine seems like a really bad idea.

I get the distinct impression that Piper is ignoring me. It's not so much the fact that she has limited our interactions during the workday to the break room or that she told me she had too much to do the last three nights and couldn't hang that tells me that. It was the text she sent that simply said, "Yes I'm ignoring you." I'm going crazy.

Tonight is the fourth night since we were together last and I've had enough. Armed with a bottle of wine, a pizza, and a bouquet of flowers, I arrive at her place with a lot of determination and a little trepidation. Once I'm standing in front of her door I realize my hands are too full to knock so I use my boot.

Like on Ashton's birthday, the moment she opens the door she takes my breath away. Dressed in a tank with a pair of leggings and her hair piled high on her head, she's holding a frozen dinner in one hand and a shocked expression on her face. I smile my best smile as her eyes widen.

"Not to sound all *Fatal Attraction* like, but I won't be

ignored, Piper."

"Ben," she sighs as I step around her and walk in her apartment.

I hear the door close behind me as I make my way to the small kitchen and open the bottle of wine. Just as I'm pouring the second glass I hear something land with a light thud in the trashcan and smile to myself knowing it's the frozen dinner. Turning toward her with the glass, I brace myself for her wrath. I'm instead greeted with a warm smile and an extended hand. Holding the glass close to my chest, I return her smile.

"Nuh-uh. What did I tell you about proper hellos?"

Instead of replying she walks up to me with a smile that has morphed into more of sly grin than anything. Just as I lean forward to accept her hello kiss, she grabs the wine glass from my hand.

"I believe you offered me an education on proper good mornings, not hellos. Thanks for the wine," she tosses my way as she walks into the living room. I guess she's got me there. Admitting defeat, I toss two slices of pizza on a plate and follow her to the living room. As I sit down I notice she has a bunch of papers strewn across the table.

"What are these papers?"

"My mother," is her simple response as she takes a drink of her wine and grabs a slice of pizza from the plate I'm holding. I hand her the plate as I lean over to get a better look at the papers.

"What's Tessa up to these days? These are mortgage papers."

"Well, she's in love. Again. She called me and said that she needed me to gather the papers for her house because when she gets back she's going to put it on the market. She says she's moving with whatever his name is to wherever it is he is from."

I can feel the frustration and sadness in her voice and take the plate from her before I pull her to me. I hold her for a few minutes before she finally relaxes into the embrace. Placing a kiss to the top of her head seems to be all she needs because soon we're sitting there wrapped in each other's arms and the tension leaves her body.

"Is this why you've been ignoring me? Dealing with this stuff for your mom?"

"Kind of. Not really. I don't know. I'm a mess, Ben. Do yourself a favor and run for the hills."

"Thanks for the warning but no. Tell me what's going on, Piper."

Pulling from me, against my will, she sits up a little, resting her head on the back of the couch. I mirror her as I wait for her to speak.

"I was busy trying to find all of this in my mom's version of a filing system so I was truthful when I said I couldn't see you. But, I was also kind of intentionally putting space between us."

I begin playing with her fingers as she talks, mindlessly rubbing circles on the top of her hand before linking our fingers.

"Why were you giving us space?"

"I just think it's for the best. We agreed to be friends and I don't even see Ashton every day. I just thought it would be better that way."

"I disagree. We agreed to some benefits too and it's really hard to benefit from you if I'm not around you."

Rolling her eyes at me, she looks down. "It's just too much and I'm overwhelmed. I need you to respect when I need space if this friendship thing is going to work."

"Hey," I reply, sitting up and tilting her chin to look at me. "I respect you always. All you had to say was you needed a little alone time. Don't shut me out though, Piper. But I think we need to talk about this."

"I knew it. See, this is why I needed space. If we'd spent these last few days hanging out this would upset me more. So just say it. Go on." Her voice is alternating between an emotional quiver to strained.

"Whoa there. I see that the only way we can have a conversation is for you to assume the position. Up on the lap, Princess." A shake of her head is the only response she gives. This forces my hand and I reach over, tugging her to me. I say tug but it didn't actually require much effort on my part before she has, in fact, assumed the position. Her eyes never meet mine so I just begin the little speech I hadn't planned to give.

"That's better. Now, I have no clue where all of that came from but I'll just assume it is a result of not spending time with me for four whole days. Lesson learned." I see a small smile appear at the corners of her mouth but her eyes are still focused on the collar of my shirt. "Eyes up here, Piper. Look at me." Slowly she does as I say.

"Now, eyes stay on me. Got it?" She nods in response.

"When I said we needed to talk I didn't mean have 'the talk.' I meant only that I have changed my mind." She closes her eyes tightly. "Nope, eyes open." She complies again. "I was wrong to suggest we only be friends and that we keep it from Ashton. Piper, as much as I think she'll react poorly at first, I think if we keep this from her then we'll only end up hurting Ashton more. It is best for us to be honest and tell her we are together."

"Together?"

"Yep, together. I told you before and I meant it. I want to be with you, Piper. I want us to go out to dinner, grab a coffee, go for runs, hold hands in public. I want to kiss you whenever I want and for the love of all that is holy, I want to bury myself inside of you as often as possible."

The last part of my statement is emphasized with a lift of my hips, which causes a quick intake of breath by Piper.

"But. But," is all she gets out before I kiss her. After a few minutes I pull away from her.

"It's going all work out, Piper. Now, let's eat this pizza, drink this wine, and figure out what kind of mess your mom has here."

"Why are you so certain everything will work out?"

"I'm certain we'll be okay because I believe in us. I know how I feel. While I know you aren't ready to hear about those feelings, I also believe you feel the same way. Everything will be as it should be."

"You know this means I have to take a leap of faith, right? I have to trust you. That's not the easiest thing for me to do. I could get hurt."

"You could. We both could. But, isn't the risk worth the reward? Instead of focusing on all the negative things that could happen, why not focus of all the positive. Not only do you get to kiss these lips whenever you want, you also get to wake up to this face in the morning. I'll even let you make me breakfast. That's how much I care about your happiness."

Piper rewards me with her beautiful smile. The smile

that lights up the room as bright as the morning sun and sets my soul on fire.

"Nah, I think I'll let you make breakfast. I enjoyed the way you handled yourself in the kitchen last weekend," she counters as she climbs off my lap and takes a bite of her pizza.

"Pipe, I want to tell Ashton, but I won't say anything until you agree."

"I'm not ready, Ben. Can we just figure this out on our own first? Give it a little time?"

Although it goes against my gut instinct, I reluctantly agree to give us a little time.

Chapter 21

Piper

Mornings have easily become my favorite part of the day. The moments before Ben opens his eyes are quiet and peaceful. The little twitches his eyes make the seconds before the alarm sounds are adorable and endearing. I've never asked him what he dreams of but whatever it is, he's happy.

"Are you staring at me again?"

"Nope." I totally am. "You're asleep anyway, how would you know if I was?"

Wrapping his hand around my waist, Ben pulls me to him and smiles while never opening his eyes. I smack at him because he knows I freak out about morning breath. He can tell me every single day that he doesn't care and I'll argue the fact. Sadly, I'm a sucker for his kisses so I let him kiss me before I squirm away.

I quickly get out of bed before he can get his hands on me again and begin pulling my clothes out of the closet. I turn with a skirt in my hands and am momentarily stunned. Propped up on one arm, shirtless, with the sheet low on his waist, he is breathtaking. His messy hair and beard send my hormones into a tailspin.

"I know you're staring at me when you think I'm asleep because I do the same thing to you. I watch your lips curve into a smile while you purr and wonder what I am doing to you in your dreams to make you sound like that."

There is no way I'm going to tell him the kind of dreams I have of him. It has been fifteen days, twelve hours, and fourteen minutes since Ben appeared at my door holding flowers, wine, and a pizza. He has slept in this bed with me every night since that night. And, he has refused to have sex with me. Sure, there have been sexy times, but the real deal? None. He insists on waiting until I'm ready. I've bartered and begged to no avail.

It has also been just as long since I fell completely one-hundred percent in love with Bentley Sullivan. That's not true, I was more than halfway in love with him by the time I was fourteen. But now, the man he is today and the woman he encourages me to be, all in. Of course I won't tell him that. Heck no.

I begin pulling on a pair of leggings to wear under my skirt and decide to tease Ben a little. "Oh, I'm not dreaming of you. Usually my morning dreams star Zac Efron. Sorry, pal." I'm laughing as I turn toward the bathroom to finish getting dressed when I hear him cursing under his breath and damning poor Zac Efron.

This is how our mornings are. Easy, natural, and filled with laughter. Anyone looking in from the outside would think I'm crazy for not committing to this man. I love spending time with Ben and he makes me feel good. Here, at home, without any outside interference. The unknown of what will happen if and when we tell people, especially Ashton, is what is holding me back. I also have a lingering doubt that he really wants to be with me. That at some point he's going to realize he can do so much better than his kid sister's best friend.

While I'm brushing my teeth I hear him in the kitchen starting the coffee and muttering to himself. I've surely ruined any chances of us watching a movie with Zac Efron in the near future. Whoops.

It doesn't take me long to get ready for a day with a room of five-year-olds, and once I'm ready I walk into the kitchen, where Ben is rapidly texting on his phone.

"Bathroom's yours. Do you want some eggs for breakfast?" I ask him. Curious who he's texting at this hour, I don't inquire, only wonder.

"Sure. I'll be quick. You look nice," he says as he kisses me and walks down the hall.

Just as I finish whipping the eggs to put in the pan there's a knock on my door. A quick glance at the clock worries me. It's that feeling like when the phone rings at three in the morning. Fear. I turn off the burner and wipe my hands as I cautiously walk to answer the door. I know it's irrational but I feel like if I take my time getting there, it won't be bad news on the other side.

I open the door and my first instinct is relief. Which is then immediately followed by dread. I almost wish for the fear feelings again.

"Baby girl! I hoped I'd catch you before you left for work."

"Mama, what are you doing here?" I ask as my mother walks past me like I'm not standing there stunned. I watch as she drops her bag next to the couch and assesses the apartment before turning to me, arms open for a hug.

"Sweetie, I've missed you. Come give me a hug."

I reluctantly comply. When Tessa is gone for more than a week she acts as if it's been years since we've seen each other. In this case it has been months, but it isn't as if we haven't talked and Skyped.

"So, Mama, what are you doing here? I thought you were doing well in Chicago."

"Oh I am. I love it and Michael is wonderful. I just wanted to come see you. Can't a mother want to see her daughter?"

I roll my eyes and walk back into the kitchen to finish making breakfast. Mama follows me and pours herself a cup of coffee. I hear the shower turn off and stiffen at the realization that she heard it too. Crap.

"Piper, is someone here? Oh no, did I interrupt you? Is it Tony? Did you two work things out?"

"First of all, rapid-fire questions are annoying. Second, no I did not get back together with Tony. Why do you keep asking me that? He cheated, Mother."

"Yes, well, you don't actually know that he cheated. You may have nipped that before anything happened. Tony isn't a bad guy, Piper. You loved him and he has a good job. You could do worse. Besides, you aren't getting any younger. You can't really be choosy at this point, now can you?"

"Look, I have to leave for work soon. I am not going to get into this with you again but, for the record, I was never in love with Tony."

"Of course you loved Tony. You two were together over a year. Besides…"

She doesn't get to finish her sentence because just as she's about to go into the lengthy list of all the reasons I should forgive Tony and beg for him to take me back, Ben walks in the room. Wearing nothing but a pair of jeans, he's towel drying his hair. I think my ovaries just exploded.

"Baby, do you know where my clippers are?"

I look from my mother to Ben and back. When I don't respond, Ben stops drying his hair to look at me and sees the horrified look on my face.

"Hello there, I'm Tessa Lawrence. Piper's mother." As she extends her hand to him as if she's the freaking Queen of England, Ben only stares open-mouthed as he looks from my mother to me and back.

"Hello, Tessa. I guess you don't recognize me," Ben says as he takes my mother's hand, and instead of kissing her knuckles or whatever she wanted, he pulls her into a hug. I find a smidge of humor in the look of horror on my mother's face as my half-dressed boy … err, friend, hugs her.

"Mama, you remember Bentley Sullivan, don't you?"

"Oh, I, uh. Well, hello, Bentley. This is a surprise. I didn't realize you two were together."

"We are."

"We're not."

We respond simultaneously. I shoot a death glare at Ben as he laughs.

"As you can see, Tessa, we aren't exactly on the same page with regard to our relationship." Ben walks toward me and kisses me on the cheek. "I'm going to get out of here and let you catch up a bit before work."

I nod in response as he excuses himself.

"I'll be right back."

I leave my mother in the kitchen as I follow Ben down the hall. He's tying his shoes when I walk in my room.

"You don't have to leave, Ben."

"I know, but you should talk to your mom. I have a feeling she's going to have a lot to say about the fact that I'm not Dominguez."

Ben's trying to sound nonchalant about this, but the way he says *Dominguez* indicates otherwise.

"You heard her." He nods in response. "I'm sorry. You heard me too, right?" Another nod. "Are you mad? You know my mom, she's very one track." Standing and walking toward me, he pulls me to him, wrapping his arms around me like we're dancing.

"No, I'm not mad. I am actually glad she's here. I feel like you need someone to talk to about this and help you work through your feelings. I don't think I would have necessarily chosen someone that wants you to be with Dominguez for the job, but at least it's someone. You have a little less than an hour before you have to leave, spend it with your mom. I'll see you at work, okay?"

"Okay," I reply, pulling him a little closer to me. "I'm sorry we didn't get to have breakfast; it's kind of my favorite part of the day."

"Me too, but I think I like the nights best," he says as he pulls me flush to him and I feel his heart beat. Placing a kiss on my lips, I long for him to deepen it, but instead he pulls back. "Go spend some time with your mom and tell her how amazing I am. Don't forget, we can still run away next week."

"We are not running away next week. It's Thanksgiving and your mom deserves to have you and Ashton at her table this year."

After a few kisses I return to the kitchen and start cooking the eggs I had whipped. Ben stops to say goodbye to my mom before he leaves. The moment the door closes my mom speaks.

"How long have you been seeing Bentley Sullivan, Piper?"

Wow, she's going to just jump right into things.

"He goes by Ben now and we aren't seeing each other; we're friends."

"Really? My friends sleep over and don't walk around my house half naked."

"Fine. A few weeks, I guess. I don't know. It just happened."

Silence fills my tiny kitchenette as I scoop the eggs onto two plates and put a few slices of fruit on each plate. I set a plate in front of my mom and refill both of our cups with coffee before taking my seat at the table. This is how it is with my mom. She's waiting for me to continue. She knows my mind is spinning.

Like a levy breaking in a flood, I dump it all on her. I tell her about Tony and how I felt after I found the online dating profile. The first kiss with Ben, the developing friendship, the talk at the lake, and I told her about the house. As I talked I never looked at her. I stared off at the clock on the stove, never seeing the numbers. My story ends with me telling her that Ben wants to take me away next week to show me what our relationship could be if we weren't spending all of our time in secret. When I finish I finally look at my mother.

I expect her to be bored or annoyed, her usual reaction to things. Instead, one hand is to her chest over her heart and the other is covering her mouth as tears pour out of her eyes.

"Mama, why are you crying?" I ask, handing her a napkin.

"Oh honey, you're in love. True blue love. He's the one. It's always been him, hasn't it? The man in your dreams. I thought you were just creative and an excellent storyteller but you were actually seeing your future."

"Yeah, I'm pretty sure I was not seeing the future. I had some dreams, I'm not clairvoyant or anything."

"Well, whatever it was, I think it's lovely. And it's so sad."

"How is it *lovely* and sad? That doesn't make sense, Mama." I grab her plate in frustration. This is just like her. I pour my heart out and she confirms what I know. I'm in love with Ben and then throws in something negative.

"Sweetie, it's sad because obviously you can't see him anymore."

"What? Why? You just said it was lovely!"

"It is. But, honey, this can't work. Not just because he's Ashton's brother. Men like Bentley Sullivan don't end up with women like us. No, it's best if you just break it off now and go back to Tony. He'll be a good provider and he has to have learned the error of his ways. He knows you're the best he'll ever get, Piper. Someone like Bentley? He'll leave, Piper. He's too big for this town; he left once before and he'll leave again."

"That's not fair, Mama. Not fair to me and especially not fair to Ben."

"Piper, this is real life. I've done you a disservice with those stories of princesses and white knights." Her frustration with me is infuriating.

"Mama, your stories weren't a disservice. All little girls want to believe in true love and happily ever after. I believe Ben cares about me and I also believe he's honest. If he says he's staying in Lexington, then that's what I believe."

My pulse is racing. I'm equal parts angry and hurt. I'm angry because she's my mother and should be telling me I'm lucky to have someone like Ben in my life and I'm hurt because her words hit too close home. Deep down I worry that everything she's saying is true.

"Look, baby. I get why you want to believe this could work but I'll tell you this, Bentley Sullivan reminds me a lot of your daddy. He left and Ben will leave too. Listen to your Mama and end it now."

I don't have time to continue this conversation, nor do I want to.

"I have to go to work. Will you be here when I get home later?"

"No, Mike should be picking me before you get home. I'll let myself out. Have a good day, sweetie. I love you."

I don't respond and instead gather my things and walk out the door. Driving to the school in a daze, I replay my mom's words in my head. Regardless of her opinions on the matter, I would never go back to Tony. That ship has sailed and I've made my peace with it. Likewise, I believe Ben when he tells me he's home for good and wants to be with me. He's shown me in more ways than one that he's all in. That he wants more than friendship with me and I just need to say the word.

Regardless of the rational thinking, pieces of her opinion stick in the back of my mind. I believe in my heart of hearts that my mom believes what she is telling me is for my own good. That, somehow, she is protecting me from hurt.

⚜

Thankfully my students were all cooperative and happy this morning. Five-year-olds are unpredictable and there are times I swear they add ten years to my life.

I left my apartment shortly after my mother's version of a pep talk and forgot my lunch. I have about thirty minutes to leave campus for lunch. While I hate being rushed, I hate being hungry more. The closest place to campus to grab something other than fast food is a bakery and deli. I call ahead and place my order so that when I arrive I can quickly pay and get back to the school before my thirty minutes are up.

As I park in front I glance to my right and think I see Ben's truck. I should have asked him if he wanted anything. It's silly that we're both here. This is a prime example of why I don't want to label us outside of friendship. My lapse in thinking of him for lunch would make me a bad girlfriend, but since there is no label, I'm just a crappy friend for the moment.

Once I'm in the door I am immediately greeted with the aroma of freshly baked bread and my stomach jumps to attention. Thankfully it's loud in here and nobody else is privy to the serenade of hunger happening from within me. It only takes three steps before the room spins, the voices turn to a dull hum, and my world flips.

Ben.

And Laurel.

I quickly take a mental tally of our conversation last night and our morning. Nope, no mention of Laurel. We definitely didn't talk about him meeting Laurel or the fact he'd be holding hands with her across the table.

As much as it pains me to admit it, my mother was right. This was never going to work. I've put him off too long. He wanted to take things beyond friendship months ago and I said no. I pushed him away and he's finally had enough.

My chest is tight, my breath is shallow, and I hear a ringing in my ears. I swear on my favorite book if I faint in this deli with Bentley Sullivan sitting nearby holding another woman's hand I'll never be able to handle the smell of freshly baked bread again. It will forever remind me of this moment and how every part of my being is screaming to run.

And I do. I don't pick up my lunch and I don't confront him. Instead, I turn on my heel and walk out the door I just entered. Somehow I make it to my car and pull out of my parking space before the first tear falls. The first of many. There can't possibly be enough tears in my body to convey the level of devastation I feel.

When will I ever just be enough? When will a man look at me and think, "That's the girl for me. She is everything I need."? I am beginning to wonder if that man exists. I knew over these last few weeks that I had fallen in love with Ben. I also felt deep down it was too soon and that telling him would make me vulnerable

I pull into the school parking lot and manage to pull myself together enough to finish the school day. The afternoon is a haze and the kids love me more than ever because they spent the afternoon doing an impromptu art project that didn't require me to have it together. I convinced myself I wasn't a bad teacher because we are going into a school break and its fun for the kids to have down time.

I'm gathering my things with the intent to get home before Ben stops by my classroom like he does every day. As I pull my purse on my shoulder I notice Jacob Thorne is still in his seat. I put my things down and walk over to him.

"Jacob, sweetie, what are you doing?"

I notice Jacob is fiddling with something in his lap, and as I lean over to look, he starts giggling.

"You can't see yet. I have to do the plan."

"The plan? Jacob, I need to get home soon. Is Mrs. Honeycutt picking you up today?"

Nodding, he finally blesses me with the sweetest smile that I return.

"Well, since I have to leave maybe I can take you up to the office to wait for her. How about that?"

"Nope. That's not the plan. Hold on," he says as he slides out of his seat. Taking a deep breath, he looks up at the ceiling.

"I'm membering so just a sec, mmkay?"

"Okay, but I really do need to go, sweetie."

"Miss Lawrence," Jacob begins.

It's obvious he's memorized something and suddenly running from this place and my own drama isn't my priority. This sweet boy who has something planned is.

"I think you are the nicest lady ever. My mommy says you are boring. My mommy is silly 'cause you are super fun and can color really good."

Felicity thinks I'm boring. That almost seems like a

compliment. Surely that wasn't her intent.

"I want to be a fireman when I grows up so I can protect you from fires. So I made you this," he tells me as he hands me a picture. Like with most of my students, it takes me a few seconds to process what I'm seeing. It's a woman who I assume is me being handed a flower by a little boy.

"Thank you, Jacob."

"Yep. Clem won't help me drawl a flower so it's not good but it's for you. I think you are the prettiest lady and I am sad I am going to the snow and you won't be there."

"Aww, Jacob. This is the sweetest gift I've received. I think you are going to have a great time with your family next week and just think, when you get back you'll have all kinds of stories to tell your friends."

That comment seems to pacify him because he offers me a full smile. I open my arms for a hug and he runs into them. I hear a throat clear and look up to see Mrs. Honeycutt at the door.

"He's been practicing that speech for a week. Thank you for letting him give it."

"Jacob, is that true? Did you practice all of that just for me?"

He nods as he pulls away. I smile and brush the hair away from his face. This sweet boy has no idea how much this means to me today. How, in the wake of having my heart broken by the only man who carries the power to do so, his words and kindness have lessened the blow.

A second clearing of a throat catches my attention and I see Ben has joined Mrs. Honeycutt at the door. With his messenger bag slung over his shoulder and his button-up shirt untucked with the sleeves rolled up, a flicker of desire sparks and I almost forget the pain I felt at the deli. Almost.

"Hello, Mrs. Honeycutt. What do we have here?"

"Hello, Mr. Sullivan. Jacob was just giving Miss Lawrence a gift. He's going to miss her over the upcoming break." With a whisper she continues, "I think our Jacob is a bit smitten with Miss Lawrence."

"I know the feeling," is mumbled in response. If Mrs. Honeycutt heard it, she didn't respond.

"Jacob, let's go. I'm sure Mr. Sullivan and Miss Lawrence have places to be."

"Thank you again for my gift, Jacob. Have a wonderful time on your trip and I'll see you when we get back.'"

"Okay," Jacob responds as he places one of his tiny hands on mine. "Don't miss me, okay, Miss Lawrence?"

Laughing for the first time all afternoon, I agree. Jacob leaves with Mrs. Honeycutt and the tension in the room is thick as I move to my desk and gather my things. My hands are shaking and I just want to get out of here. I turn to head for the door and walk right into Ben.

"Whoa, where's the fire?"

"I need to get home."

"I know, I wanted to see if you felt like ordering in tonight instead of cooking. I never understand how a group of seven-year-olds can be so exhausting."

"I can't. I have a headache and just want to go home."

"Okay, I'll grab something and meet you at your place. About an hour?"

"I just want to go home and sleep," I snap and start walking out the door.

I hear Ben walking quickly to catch me. When his hand grabs my elbow I stop with my back to him.

"Please just let me go home, Ben. I'm exhausted and my head hurts."

"Something is wrong. Tell me what it is, Piper."

Only shaking my head, I walk away, leaving Ben standing in the hallway.

Chapter 22

Ben

Swinging a hammer is therapeutic. It is for me, anyway. I've spent the last four hours working on the porch of my house. This will be the most secure set of stairs in the county by the time I'm done with them. I should be inside working but this is better for releasing the tension that's built inside me since I left Piper at the school. Or, more accurately, since she left me at the school.

The last few weeks have been great between us. We've grown closer, had quality time, and I thought we were on the same page with where we were heading in our relationship. I even planned to talk to Piper tonight about telling Ashton next week during Thanksgiving dinner.

I should've known this day would turn to shit when I had an early-morning text from Laurel. She'd started dating a guy she met through work so I hadn't heard from her in a few weeks. When I checked my phone this morning and saw a text from her asking me if we could meet for coffee today during my lunch, I knew in my gut something was wrong. Then Tessa showed up.

I will never say anything against Tessa because she's Piper's mother. That being said, I now know who is responsible for all of the self-doubt Piper harbors. I'm under no guise that I am the best catch in town, but to encourage Piper to go back to Tony instead of being with me is ridiculous. I don't know what else they talked about after I left, but considering her reaction to me this afternoon I can't believe it was anything positive or Team Ben.

Lunch with Laurel solidified my feelings for Piper. There was never any doubt on my part, but one of the first things Laurel asked me was if I was in love. I didn't tell Laurel that I was in love with Piper. That wouldn't be fair to Piper or our relationship. She should be the recipient of that information before anyone else. I did confirm that I was with someone and this was a forever kind of relationship. Laurel said she was happy for me. Then she started crying.

I knew something was wrong when she texted me this morning. Since our split, we have talked a few times, but mostly kept in touch via text. A little over a month ago she kind of fell off the grid and I hadn't heard from her. I knew she was dating again and figured she had met someone. There was nothing specific in the text this morning but it was just a feeling I had.

My instinct as she started crying was to offer her comfort, but she seemed to retreat from me. Instead, I held her hand and she started talking. Apparently the guy she was dating wasn't the good guy he had portrayed. He is possessive and controlling. Picking up on what she wasn't saying, I deduced he is also an abusive asshole.

Refusing to confirm or deny the abuse, she did confirm that she had secured a protection order from the bastard. I immediately saw red and wanted to hunt the guy down. Laurel said that since she began dating this guy, she hadn't seen or talked to most of her friends and that was why she reached out to me. Unfortunately, a piece of paper doesn't protect a person and he has still been bothering her indirectly.

I'm grateful Laurel knew she could come to me. Without a second thought, I invited her to stay at my parents' house for a while and to spend Thanksgiving with us. She balked at the idea at first, but relented when I reminded her the jerk couldn't find her here. I wanted to send her to the house immediately but she insisted on going home to pack a few of her things. I begrudgingly agreed after she promised to check in when she got home and come back tonight regardless of the time.

I wanted to get some time with Piper after school to check in from her talk with her mom this morning but also to let her know that Laurel was coming to town. I know that initially it may be awkward, but Piper will understand my need to help Laurel. Plus, if Laurel is going to be staying with my parents for the next week, we needed to come up with a game plan to explain why I'm staying with her for the next week. My personal preference is to just lay it all out and let the chips fall as they may. Like anytime I am able to just watch her, seeing Piper with her student reaffirmed how deep my feelings run and how amazing she truly is.

Then she served me her bullshit headache excuse instead of talking to me. I know it's a bullshit excuse because she used it before on Ashton to get out of lying to her face.

Obviously she doesn't have the same concern when it comes to me. I have no idea what happened from the time I left her apartment and I arrived in her classroom but, whatever it is, I know I'm not going to like it.

I put down the hammer and walk to the cooler, contemplating one of the beers I brought or a water. It takes all of thirty seconds before I choose the beer. This choice means I'm done working for the night. I opt instead to have a fire and try for the fifth time to call Piper.

Like I've done the other four times, I follow up the voicemail with a text.

Me: I hope you're feeling better. Call me so I know you're ok or I'm coming over.

This time, I receive a response.

Piper: I'm fine. Please don't come over.

Me: Tell me what I can do.

Piper: Just give me some space.

Me: Space? Is something wrong? Don't do this Piper. Don't run from me.

Piper: Please, Ben. Space. I just need to process.

Me: Can I at least text you?

Piper: In moderation. Don't be a creepy stalker.

Me: It's not stalking if you want me to do it.

Piper: Says every stalker.

Me: See if I was there we could debate my stalker status.

Piper: Nice try. Please respect my request, Ben.

Me: I always respect you. I don't like it but ok. Get some rest and sleep well.

Piper: I will.

Me: I won't. I'm used to you in my arms.

Piper: Ben...
Me: It's true. Sleep well, Princess.
Piper: Night, Cowboy.

It's not the same as talking to her, but at least it was a conversation. Since I won't be spending my night with Piper, I decide to text Jameson. I'm sure he's going out or has a date but it's worth a shot. When I scroll down to his name I note it's been over a week since I've called or talked to him. He's sure to give me shit for that.

Me: What are you up to tonight?
Jameson: Who is this?
Me: Screw you asshole.
Jameson: Oh is this that guy I know? Ben Sullivan?
Me: Hardy har har. Don't quit your day job.
Jameson: What's up dick?
Me: Nothing just seeing what you were up to. I was just finishing up work on the house for the night.
Jameson: I'm actually out your way, I'll swing by.
Me: Cool. I'll be here.

Twenty minutes later Jameson has joined me by the fire I started. Armed with his own beer, he takes the seat next to me. We're quiet for a few minutes and I welcome the silence because I know I'm about to get an earful about leaving my buddies hanging and about Piper. I still haven't confirmed there's anything going on between Piper and me, but Jameson has enough figured out to know where I've been the last few weeks.

"So, where's Piper tonight?"

That didn't take long.

"She has a headache."

"So we aren't skirting the issue, you're going to admit

you're together?"

"I'm not skirting. I've been respecting her wishes but I have a feeling something is wrong and I need to talk to someone."

"Mmhmm. I see. So I'm good enough when you need someone to unleash your secret relationship on but not enough to just hang out? That's cold, Ben."

I turn to him to defend myself and see he's smiling.

"Dude, I'm sorry. I've been a shit friend haven't I?"

"Nah, man. You're in love. This is what happens. I'm just giving you a hard time."

"Thanks."

"Wait, you didn't deny the love part."

I opt to not answer. I am committed to Piper being the first person to hear that I love her, but I won't deny it.

"I'm not talking about that with you. If I'm having that conversation, it's going to be with Piper."

"I see. Well, good for you. Both of you. When are you coming out?"

"I hope next week. I wanted to talk to her tonight and tell my parents first. Kind of use them as a buffer for Ash on Thanksgiving."

"Thanksgiving. Good call. Ashton is her happiest when there is pie."

Over the next few hours I relay my day to Jameson and he offers the spare room at his house for Laurel. As much as I appreciate the offer, I think Laurel needs to be somewhere she is familiar with. Plus, my mom will mother her to death and that'll also be good for her. Before we leave I promise to not be a recluse anymore and commit to a few runs this week and poker with the guys.

The drive back to my parents' house is depressing. Each mile that clicks away on the odometer is a reminder of how I'd rather be heading to Piper and her bed. I should've just stayed at the house tonight, but Laurel texted me that she's going to get in after midnight and I want to be there when she does. Plus, I need to run a little interference with Ashton before Laurel gets there. Ash has never really been a fan of Laurel's and I need to get her up to speed before she says something snarky.

I have a little time before Ashton should get home from work so I opt for a shower and a snack. After rummaging the fridge, I put together a mish-mash of a meal and am only about halfway through it when the kitchen door opens and Ashton walks in.

"Well, hello there, stranger. Finally come up for air?"

"Hey, sis." My response is not nearly as antagonistic as hers.

"Whoa, what's going on? Someone die? Are the parentals okay?"

Pushing my plate away, I take a drink of my milk before answering. "Yeah, they're fine. It's just been a shit of a day."

"Problems with your lady love?"

I'm taken aback by her comment. She couldn't possibly know about Piper and me. "Lady love?"

"Come on, you haven't slept here in weeks and if you've been at your house then you'd be in traction from sleeping on the floor. One can only assume there's a lady love in the scenario," she replies, sitting down as she takes my fork and starts eating the rest of my food.

"Anyway, I wanted to talk to you about something." I'm going to just skirt on by her comments about a lady love.

"Sure, what's going on? You're being weird, even for you."

I tell her about Laurel and how I invited her for the week. I expected a smart-ass comment from Ashton about Laurel, but I was wrong.

"Oh my goodness. Ben, that's awful. Is she okay? Of course she should stay here. Did she call the police and stuff?"

"Yeah, she did. I think she just needs a change of scenery and regroup. I figured this was a safe place for her. I felt really bad, Ash. Can I tell you something?"

She nods as she slides the plate away, the topic obviously effecting her appetite.

"I feel responsible."

"What? No way, Ben. You cannot assume the responsibility of this."

"Logically I know it's not my fault, but I can't help but wonder if I hadn't moved back home if this would have happened."

"Of course it wouldn't have happened." I'm stunned by her response, and before I can respond she continues, "You never would have broken up and therefore there would have been no asshole rebound guy. But, Ben, you weren't happy and since you've been home ... well, you've been different. I kind of like you now. You're not all stuffy and boring."

I laugh a little at that last comment. I was completely boring the last few years. I blame the ties I wore every day. Of course I know I'm not responsible for Laurel's current situation, but the reality of it all is that I ended things between us and she dated this guy. I wish I could call and talk to Piper.

Screw it. I pick up my phone while Ashton is lecturing me and send a text to Piper.

Me: Sorry it's late. I need to talk to you. Are you up?

After ten minutes, Ashton has wrapped up her lecture on how Laurel's life choices are not my responsibility and that she'll spend the next few days with her to help keep her busy. There's been no response from Piper. I realize how late it is and that she's probably asleep.

Suddenly the weight of the day hits me like a ton of bricks. While I wait for Laurel to arrive, I make up the couch as my temporary bed. A quick check of the time confirms that tomorrow is going to be a long day.

Laurel looks slightly overwhelmed with the attention my mom and Ashton are giving her this morning. The entire time we were together I would have sworn neither of them liked her or wanted her in this house. Now, I think they'd prefer I leave and she stay. Which I'll have to do at some point because they are planning a movie marathon. I heard something about avoiding all romances or movies with happy endings so I assume it's going to be Ashton's preferred collection of Dolly Parton movies. While they do have happy endings, they also are campy with a lot of singing.

I manage to steal Laurel away from them for a check-in. Grabbing our jackets, we make our way outside and each settle in one of my mom's deck chairs. Happily enjoying the quiet, I realize this is something that Laurel and I have always done. We've always been able to just be in each other's company and enjoy a comfortable silence. After a few minutes I can feel a shift in the mood.

"Thank you for inviting me here, Ben. Your mom and sister have been great. I could've sworn they hated me all these years."

I turn my head to look at her and she mimics the movement. "Honestly?" I ask and she nods. "So did I." We both laugh. "My family is kind, Laurel. Let my sister and mom hover and care for you." She offers no response so I continue, "How are you doing otherwise?"

"I'm okay." I notice that she absently tugs on the sleeves of her coat and rubs her forearms. I flinch as the thought of that asshole laying his hands on her. My own hands morph into fists in an instant. My desire to find this prick and pulverize him is high.

"I hate this for you. What do the police say?"

Turning her head to look off in the distance, her voice is flat and devoid of emotion. "Not much. I spoke to the prosecutor yesterday before I came to see you. It's his first offense." I scoff in response. "Okay, the first time someone has followed through with the allegations." She laughs in a way that kills me.

"That's what they call them. *Allegations.* Like he didn't…" I hear a hiccup as she pushes down tears and emotion.

"He'll likely plead it down and be ordered to some sort of anger management. No jail time."

"That's bullshit. Can't you fight that?"

"I'm not in charge. I really just want this to be over. I think I'm going to find a new place to live. One less way for him to bother me."

The pain in her voice is unlike anything I've ever heard from her. I reach over and grab her hand and offer a gentle squeeze. She never moves her gaze, but responds with a squeeze of her own. Another few minutes go by and she twists to her side and faces me, offering me a smile. I know what comes next.

"Tell me about the woman you're seeing."

My eyes go wide and she raises a brow at me. "It's complicated."

"Come on, complicated or not you need to tell me."

"Uh, actually I don't. How'd you know, anyway?"

"Ashton. She said something about not seeing you and how you were obviously hooking up with some girl you were ashamed of, otherwise why would you keep her away from the family."

I shake my head in disbelief. Leave it to Ashton to use Laurel for her dirty work.

"I see. Is this some sort of bonding experiment between you and Ashton? She's having you find out the details on my personal life since I won't tell her?"

"No, this is completely my doing. Come on, Ben. You look like you're ready to burst at the seams. Plus, you've checked your phone at least a dozen times since I arrived. What's going on?"

"I don't know that I feel comfortable talking to you about this."

"Hush up. We're friends, aren't we?" I agree. "I came to you when I needed help. That's what friends do. Let me reciprocate. Please, Ben. I need something good to happen for one of us." I can hear a quiver in her voice and know that she's trying so damn hard to be strong in all of this.

"Okay. If I talk to you about this, you have to promise to lock it up tight. Nobody knows." She smiles in response.

"I'm not kidding, Laurel. Do not use this as a bonding tool with Ashton. Especially Ashton."

"Okay, geez. Dramatic much? Hit me with your secrets."

"I've kind of been seeing my sister's best friend."

"Whoa." I nod in agreement.

"Have I met her before?"

"No, and actually I hadn't seen her in years until the night I moved back. I guess anytime we visited she wasn't around."

That gets me thinking a little. Piper never was around when Laurel and I visited. For years I came home for visits, sure they were far and few between but I visited, and never once saw Piper.

"Very interesting. So, nobody knows? Ashton?" I shake my head. "Is there some sort of reason nobody knows?"

I lay it all out for her. How I made a spontaneous move one night at the bar, Ashton's likely response, my trying to pursue something with Piper, her stance regarding Ashton, and her sudden headache yesterday. I stopped short of my feelings for her.

"You're in love with her." I don't respond. "You haven't told her, have you?" Again, no response. "I see. Well, I think therein lies your problem." The only response I offer is a motion of my hand for her to continue. To which she responds with an eye roll. "I'd bet that this woman, can I at least know her name?"

I smile. "Piper."

"Thank you. Piper, great name by the way, needs you to lay it all out for her. Tell her you love her, Ben. Make the grand gesture. You have to do this before it's too late. She's in limbo right now." My expression must show the confusion I feel. "You are an amazing man, but so very stupid."

"Hey!" I shout and she shushes me. I take it down to a whisper. "Hey, I'm not stupid."

"Oh, sweetie," she says, very patronizing, "but you are." She all but tsks me like a child.

"Here's the deal," she begins as she sits up straighter, and with a little fire in her. "You love this Piper and I'd bet my last dollar she loves you too. But, you're both so worried about doing things right you aren't being true to yourselves and surely you aren't giving Ashton enough credit. I don't know your sister well, but I can tell you from a female perspective, the secret will be worse than the truth."

Laurel stands up and begins to walk toward the slider when she stops and places a hand on my shoulder. "Follow your heart, Ben. Tell her how you feel and then tell your sister. If I've learned anything in these last few months, it's that life is too short and true love is something to respect."

I remain in my seat as Laurel returns to the house to begin her bonding time with my mom and sister. She's right. I have sat back these past few weeks trying to not scare Piper and all it has done is leave us in limbo. I love her and want to be with her. I see her living in my home, hosting our own Thanksgiving dinner, and as the mother to my children. I need to stop waiting for her to be ready and make the grand gesture.

Chapter 23

Piper

After work I came home and was relieved to see my mother had actually left as she said she would. There was the slight chance she's have some sort of maternal reaction and want to stay for a few days. I don't think I could stomach another one of her pep talks on my love life.

As soon as I was in my apartment I made a beeline for my room and changed into the only outfit I plan to wear in the foreseeable future – pajama pants and a T-shirt. Fine, it's Ben's T-shirt. The perfect ensemble for a recluse. I may have made a lot of changes in my life over the last few years but the ability to return to my reclusive ways is always easy. Wearing Ben's shirt is just an added level of my self-destructive ways.

I have all of my wallowing and post-breakup necessities ready in just a few minutes. Food delivery menus, my favorite pop and ice cream, salty chips, movies that make me cry, and a box of tissues are assembled and placed on the coffee table.

My wallowing list doesn't vary much from what I remember my mom having after a breakup. Instead of a few delivery options, pizza was our only option and my mom opted for wine instead of pop. The rest is pretty on point. I guess I'm no different than other women my age, I'm becoming my mother.

Over the last few hours I've experienced at least three of the five stages of grief. I managed to get through the biggies before my pizza was delivered and I poured my second glass of wine - denial, bargaining, and acceptance. I was in denial that Ben was actually at the deli with Laurel. Surely I had fallen asleep and it was a nightmare. That was followed by the acceptance that he had been there and I waited too long. The bargaining came around the time I put his T-shirt on and asked the heavens to let me go back to this morning and tell him how I feel.

I've consumed half a pizza and a bottle of wine since the bargaining went without a response. I can feel myself moving right on to stage four – anger. I'm pissed. How dare he? How dare he stand there this morning, looking sexy as all get-out, and be kind and understanding with where I am in my feelings? He knows me well enough to know I needed to unload on someone. Since my go-to person, Ashton, is out of the question, my mother was the next obvious choice.

Obvious choice if my mother were the nurturing, loving, and supportive type of mother, that is. Regardless, her words did hit a little close to home. Ben deserves someone who is his equal. Not the girl who is perfectly happy teaching kindergarten in her home town. I'm a creature of habit and not an outside the box kind of girl. He should be with someone who scales mountains. Or at the very least, has a passport.

A passport. Who really needs a passport? Not this girl, that's for sure. I don't need to leave this country to find adventure. The Grand Canyon is adventure. I'll go there. How about *that,* oh-so-perfect Bentley Sullivan? Suck on that.

I may need to reconsider this second bottle of wine I'm opening. Nope, I'm doing it. I'll regret it and that's fine because I'm doing something outside of my norm. Stupid Bentley Sullivan and his text message saying he's coming over. No, sir. I don't think so.

I knew telling him to respect me was going to be the only way to keep him away. Questioning Ben's integrity is a surefire way to get him to back down. God I love that about him. Nope. No love. Love is for suckers. I'm not going to be a sucker.

As I'm looking at the glass of wine I poured and arguing with the rational side of my brain that is telling me to dump it out and go to bed, my phone chimes a text message. I did tell him he could text in moderation. I'm sure he's just telling me goodnight. Or to lock the door. Or that he's back with Laurel and how happy they'll be. Probably that last one.

Jerk.

I set my wine down and grab my phone with the intent to tell him to go jump in a lake when I notice the text isn't from him.

Tony: Hey Piper. Are you up?

Great, just what I need. Little angel Piper on the left shoulder says not to be rude and answer him. Little devil Piper on the right shoulder says to answer him for a little revenge.

Me: Yep, what's up?

Tony: I was wondering if we could meet for coffee I wanted to talk to you about something.

Me: I don't think that's a good idea.

What could he possibly have to say? He's actually found two women who want to share him? I know he doesn't have a disease, I confirmed that at the doctor within a week after our breakup.

Tony: I thought we were friends.

Wine is in charge tonight.

Me: Fine. When and where?

Tony: Tomorrow morning, the diner at 8?

Me: Better make it 10. See you then.

I really am a glutton for punishment. Maybe this is a good thing. Maybe, just maybe, one of the town gossips will see us and tell Ben I've moved on. Well, not moved on since nobody knows about us because I'm a scared child, but gossip could be good for a change. Then stupid Ben can feel crappy for a minute.

Those are my final thoughts as I fall asleep on the couch with every intention of not dreaming of Bentley James Sullivan. I fail miserably even in sleep mode.

Being at Rosa's with Tony is not my idea of an ideal morning. However, a big plate of Rosa's huevos rancheros is the perfect way to spend a morning after drinking an entire bottle of wine. Tony was waiting for me outside in the parking lot when I arrived. I'm in no condition for small talk. The wine has turned to acid in my stomach, so we just walk in without more than a good morning between us.

As always, it's sensory overload in Rosa's. The smells are delicious as usual, but this morning they are like a sledgehammer and the noise seems abnormally louder than usual. The saving grace is an open booth. I make a beeline for the booth and slither in, laying my head down on my hands in a napping position.

"Rough night, Piper?" Tony asks as he takes the seat across from me.

"Yes. Obviously, or I wouldn't even be here. I had a momentarily lapse of control when the wine answered you."

Before he can reply to my snarky remark his mom is at our table, pulling me from my seat.

"Oh! Piper!" She's shouting so loud.

"Mom, maybe don't yell. I think Piper had a little too much wine last night."

Shooting him a look that tells him to shut up, I return Rosa's hug. "I'm fine. Just moving a little slow this morning. Nothing some of your wonderful food and coffee won't cure."

"Of course, m'ija. Let me get your food going. What are you feeling like?"

Tony and I place our order with Rosa and she scurries away, motioning for a server to bring us coffee. Once I've taken a few sips of the liquid gold I finally feel a little more normal.

"So, what did you want to talk about?"

"Gee, Piper. I thought we could at least catch up. How have you been?"

I don't reply, only shrug and take another sip of my coffee. What is there to say? Do I tell him that I was blissfully happy for the first time in forever until about noon yesterday? How about telling him I fell in love with my best friend's brother and now I'll have to spend the rest of my life pretending I didn't? I think I'll pass on all accounts.

"Are you still seeing Sullivan?"

That jars me from my bonding time with my coffee. My eyes go wide as I look at Tony, trying to process how to answer. Technically we were never "seeing" each other, just friends. I'm also the Queen of Denial in case there was any doubt.

"Umm, we're just friends."

"It didn't seem that way to me. What does Ashton have to say about it?"

I hesitate, and now it's his eyes that widen.

"Oh shit. She doesn't know." Letting out a whistle, he leans back as our food arrives.

"Just drop it, okay. There's nothing going on. At least, not anymore." The last part of my statement a mumble under my breath.

"I heard that. Is that why you spent your night at the bottom of a wine bottle? It's not like you to overindulge."

"That's a little dramatic. And sadly, the truth. Maybe that's the problem. I'm so straight-laced and predictable. Boring."

"Is that what he said? Did he tell you that? I'll beat his ass for being such a dick to you, Piper. Just say the word."

That statement triggers something in me and I break out in a string of laughter that sounds manic. It's absolutely ridiculous that both Tony and Ben are quick to blame the other for treating me poorly.

"I'll do it, too. I may not have been the best boyfriend

but I would never say those things to you."

"Oh no, instead you'd go behind my back and try to find someone else. Give me a break. You are in no position to try and be my friend. I am too tired and hungover for this. What did you want to talk about?"

"You're right. That's what I wanted to talk to you about."

I really can't deal with this, but I'm here and this coffee is spectacular. I motion for him to continue.

"I was a shitty boyfriend and I'm sorry. I can't apologize enough. I loved you, Piper, I swear that was true. I think you were right though; we weren't *in love.*"

For the next few minutes, I simply eat my breakfast and drink my coffee. Every few bites I look up at Tony and he's just staring at me. I enjoy this more than I should. I'm not a cruel person, but when it comes to Tony I am enjoying watching him uncomfortable.

I could use this opportunity to unleash all of the reasons Tony sucked as a boyfriend. The truth of the matter is, I knew who Tony was when I started dating him. Somewhere in my life I decided I wasn't worth more than what someone like Tony offered. That part I own. Overall, I enjoyed being the girl a good-looking and sought-after guy chose. We had fun together and for a majority of our relationship he wasn't a bad guy. In the end we were just going through the motions with no future.

The server refills our coffee, and after I add the perfect amount of creamer I take a drink before I finally respond to Tony's apology.

"True enough. We weren't in love." He begins to reply before I cut him off, "But, that doesn't mean I deserved to be treated that way."

"What about Sullivan?"

"What about him? I told you, we're friends."

"I'll admit, at first I was pissed you were together, but the more I thought about it the more it makes sense. Plus, anyone that's around you two for more than thirty seconds can feel the sexual tension."

I'm not able to reply to his comments because something catches his attention over my shoulder. With a sly grin on his face he sits up straight and places an arm on the back of the booth while he reaches for his coffee. Nodding to whomever is behind me, he takes a sip of his coffee.

Like a lead brick, my stomach drops.

I slowly look to my right and up at the person who is now standing next to me. Crap.

"Dominguez."

"Sullivan."

"Princess."

"Umm, hey, Ben. How's it going?"

"Fine. What's going on here?" The tension in Ben's jaw has me worried he's going to break a tooth.

"Piper and I were just enjoying an early breakfast. She needed the substance after last night," Tony replies and I shoot him a look to shut his mouth. His insinuation doesn't go unnoticed by Ben.

"Last night? I thought you weren't feeling well."

Just as I'm about to explain why I'm here with Tony, his name is called for a to-go order.

"Wow, that's a lot of food. Your mom isn't cooking?" I ask.

"This is for the guys. They're meeting me at my house to do some work. I haven't been spending as much time on the house as I should lately."

Excuse me if spending time with me was such an imposition. I'm sure Laurel would never demand so much attention. I don't say any of that. Instead I smile and grit out a polite response.

"That's nice of them. Well, don't let us keep you," I say while turning back in my seat so I'm facing Tony. Who, by the way, is smiling like the proverbial cat that ate the canary.

The dismissal evident in my voice, Ben says nothing and instead retrieves his order and walks out of the diner. I quickly look out the window and see him stop at his truck and look in my direction. Our eyes meet and the look in his breaks my already fragile heart into a million pieces. I'm not even aware I'm crying until Tony pushes a napkin in my hand.

"Damn, that was awkward. What did the guy do, Piper? I almost feel bad for him."

"He did what all the guys I'm with do. He chose someone else. I have to go. Tell your mom I said goodbye."

I rush from the diner, leaving Tony sitting in the booth alone. I haven't even started my car when my phone chimes a text message.

Ben: If you are trying to make me jealous it didn't work. Don't push me away.

The crocodile tears start and I don't respond. I need to be somewhere safe and full of love. That place has been with Ben. He fills the voids and hushes the loneliness. Ben challenges me and cares for me in equal amounts. I want nothing more than to talk to him and ask him to choose me. To tell him that I screwed up. I should never have treated what we had as something salacious when it was pure.

Instead I drive around for a bit before I find myself at the Sullivans'. Before Ben was my safe place, their home was where I feel my best. My haven when life is too hard and I seek something to stop the loneliness. When I pull up I gather myself and hope that Ashton will just be here for me without me having to explain what is happening. I can't explain it to her if I have no idea.

As I approach the kitchen door I notice the house is quiet and there are no cars outside. I check the door and confirm it's locked. I use my own key to unlock it and head inside. Even if there are no actual Sullivans here, the house itself offers me enough comfort. I'm filling a glass with ice tea when I hear footsteps and then a gasp. Startled, I drop the glass, which shatters across the floor.

"Oh shit! You scared me. Don't move, I'll get a broom."

Laurel. Of course she's here. Why wouldn't she be. I can't even move because there's glass everywhere. I'm stuck here in this position while I wait for her to return.

"Here, let me just sweep this up so you can move. You aren't cut, are you?"

I shake my head but don't speak. She is quick to clean up the mess I made and takes the dust pan of glass shards to the outside trash. While she's gone I attempt once again to pour myself a glass of iced tea. This time, using an unbreakable glass.

Laurel walks up to me with a tentative smile and extends her hand. "Hi there. I'm Laurel."

Because my mother imbedded manners in my psyche, I shake her hand. "Piper Lawrence."

"Oh. Oh!" she responds with some sort of recognition in her voice. Which is strange since we've never actually met. My confused look must register because she covers her mouth and begins laughing. "You must think I'm a crazy person. You're Piper. Ashton's best friend." I nod and relax a little. Ashton must have mentioned me. "Ben's Piper."

What in the what?

"Excuse me?"

"You're Ben's Piper. He told me all about you. Well, not all about you. He's rather mum about the whole being in love thing, but whatever. Semantics." Her hands waving like she's shooing something from around her. "I'm so excited to meet you. Thank goodness nobody is here so we can talk. You two really have made a mess of things, haven't you?"

"I'm sorry, what? I need to sit down."

"Oh sure, of course. Let's sit down. That tea looks good. I'm going to get some. Are you hungry? That's why I was walking in here, to get a snack. I'm starving. I haven't been eating much but for some reason, being here has retriggered my appetite."

I decline a snack and watch as she buzzes around the kitchen. She's obviously familiar with the setup. This should seem normal; she was with Ben for years and has been here before. Only, this triggers nothing but jealousy.

Ashton has always referred to Laurel as cold and closed off. This is not the person rambling on and on about crackers, gluten, and regret. I shake my head a little as if that will somehow make this less awkward.

"So, Piper. You're probably wondering what I'm doing here. I asked myself that same question this morning. It took me a few minutes to realize I was in Ben's childhood room. Patty should really redecorate the space."

I cough a little when she mentions sleeping in Ben's

room. They stayed here. In his childhood bed. Why wouldn't they? Could this day get any worse?

"Oh shit! That sounded really bad. I'm making things worse, aren't I?" I don't reply, I just stare at her wide-eyed. Some questions aren't in need of an answer. "Let me start with telling you that Ben and I are just friends. One hundred percent, we're just friends. I have some things happening in my life and really needed a friend so I called Ben. He insisted I come stay here for the week and celebrate the holiday with his family. With all of you."

I relax a little at her explanation. She must recognize it because she exhales what sounds like relief. "He slept on the couch." I nod. I have no idea why I can't speak, but my tongue feels like it has tripled in size. "Anyway, so this house is made for sleeping. I don't know if it's the house or the quiet but I slept like a baby. When Ben and I were together I was always on edge, not quite fitting in with his family, so I didn't appreciate how warm and inviting it is. I also didn't appreciate how kind his parents and Ashton are. Truly, they are wonderful people."

"I agree, they really are. I'm sure things will be different between you and them now. Different than it was before."

"Oh, I meant what I said. I am not here to be with Ben. I just needed somewhere to go that wasn't home. And, well, let's just say nobody would think to look for me here so it was perfect. Anyway," she says shooing the invisible flies again to indicate she's past that subject. "Enough about me. Can we please talk about what a mess you and Ben are making of things?"

"Look," I reply with a warning in my voice. "I'm not sure what you and Ben have been talking about, but there is nothing going on to make a mess of. We're friends. Co-workers."

"Oh, sweetie, that is so beyond crap it's not even funny."

"Why don't you enlighten me then, Laurel, because I'm pretty sure I know what my relationship status is and I'm not in one." Now I'm just pissed. Who does she think she is? She doesn't know me and couldn't possibly know anything about Ben and me unless he's been talking to her about us, which he promised he wouldn't do.

"Now, now, no need to get snippy. I'm on your side. I'm absolutely team Biper."

"Biper?"

"Yeah like Brangelina and Bennifer. You're Biper. Sorry, I love pop culture and maybe watch a little too much E! in my downtime."

Interesting, I didn't take Laurel as a pop culture and tabloid aficionado. "Maybe we could skip the nicknames and you could just tell me what you think you know about Ben and me."

"Deal. First, I haven't talked to Ben much in the last few months. We have texted here and there but nothing really. We were together a long time but in the end we were and are just good friends. The romance had died out long ago."

She pauses almost like a check-in to make sure I'm following along. When I don't respond she continues, "Then, like I said, I have some stuff happening in my personal life and I needed a friend. Ben was the only person I knew I could trust and wouldn't judge me. For some reason I feel like I should tell you everything just so you know I'm serious here. We are just friends."

"You don't have to tell me anything. I'm sorry you have

things going on but I'm glad Ben was there for you. Everyone should have someone to lean on."

"Thank you. Anyway, I text him yesterday morning and asked if we could meet for lunch."

Morning text and lunch. Oh no.

"It's funny; I called him because I needed a friend and it turns out he did, too. I was a mess and will forever be grateful he took the time to see me. But, I knew as soon as he sat down something was different."

This conversation is making me uncomfortable and I begin shifting in my seat.

"This morning over a cup of coffee, we had a few minutes to talk. We talked about my stuff but I pried and asked why he was being such a moody jerk. He told me about you."

"He had no right to do that."

"Didn't he? He needed to talk to someone. Ben cares about you, Piper. I think more than cares, and if your reaction to all of this is any indication, you care for him, too. I'd go as far as to say you love him."

I don't respond.

"Look, I'm no relationship expert," she says with a slight hitch in her voice. "But I know a little something about wasting time and taking love for granted. Ben has respected your wishes and not told Ashton about you. He's also been patient by letting you decide when and if you tell other people about your relationship. You can't expect him to sit around and wait forever. It's time to piss or get off the pot."

I cringe at her choice of words.

"Sorry, too much?" I shrug. "I'm serious though. I won't go into any details but will confirm that Ben didn't talk to me about his feelings for you specifically. That's a conversation you should have with one another."

I am relieved to hear Ben didn't talk to her about his feelings. Something about that would bother me more than I'd like to admit. Not that it's Laurel, but that he'd tell someone something so private before talking to me.

"Now, that we have all of that out of the way. The Ashton angle is a bit of a problem, isn't it? I don't know her well but I can see the trepidation. She's a little scary for such a little thing, isn't she?"

I laugh with Laurel and have to agree with her. What's the point in even disputing any of this? "I have to agree with you there, Laurel. I love Ashton like a sister but I am thankful I sit on her good side. That's part of the problem. As much as Ash loves hard, she can hold a grudge like nobody's business."

"Are you afraid she's going to be angry and not talk to you anymore?" I nod in agreement. "That's ridiculous!" I startle as Laurel smacks her hand on the table. "Whoops, sorry. It is ridiculous though. Why would Ashton be angry if you and Ben are together?"

"She has this motto of hos before bros. I've known her my entire life and don't know what happened, or when, but she has always made that her thing. She's backed out of important moments in her life to be with me when I needed her. Ashton and the Sullivans have always been my family and I will not do anything to mess that up. If that means I sacrifice whatever feelings I have for Ben, then that's what I'll do."

"Hmmm. I didn't take you for a martyr."

"I'm not a martyr."

"Well, then what do you call it? Selfish?" Laurel squints

her eyes at me like she's trying to figure me out.

"I'm neither a martyr nor am I selfish. Maybe you'd handle things differently but I'm doing what I think is best for all of us."

"I believe that, Piper. But when it comes to love, isn't the risk worth the reward?"

That's all she says before leaving me alone in the kitchen. This has been the strangest day. Breakfast with my ex-boyfriend to get some pseudo apology for sucking at the same title followed up by my … whatever Ben is … ex-girlfriend giving me relationship advice.

Although, some of what she says makes sense. Ben has been patient and he has respected my wishes. He's given me no reason to distrust him and yet I was quick to assume he was already moving on from me to Laurel in a split second. I let my own insecurities and past dictate how I responded to seeing him with another woman. I don't want to be that person. As much as I hate the phrase, Laurel may be right. It's time to piss or get off the pot.

I have a feeling this is going to be a long and strange Thanksgiving.

Chapter 24

Piper

*H*aving Laurel in town has proven to be a blessing. Ashton has been spending time with her and helping her deal with whatever is going on in her life. Ben's respected my request for space and has only sent me good morning and good night text messages. I miss him. More than that I thought it was humanly possible to miss another person. It's not just his touch that I miss. It's his chivalry, kindness, and his amazing laugh. Heck, I miss his loud eating and I'd even take his leaving the toilet seat up at this point.

I know it would only take a quick call and he'd be here. The ball is most definitely in my court at this point, I just have to decide what to do with it. Do I want to end things with Ben? No. If I were listening to a friend saying all of these thoughts aloud, I would be completely frustrated and want to shake some sense into her. And, I'd remind my friend that the guy isn't going to wait forever and if my heart is broken it's my own doing.

I've been completely selfish. Ben doesn't deserve this back and forth high school drama. I need to either lay it all out there or end things.

A knock at my door jars me from my thoughts. Ashton doesn't wait for me to answer and lets herself in.

"Hey, sister from another mister!"

Joining me in the kitchen, she tosses her purse on the table and leans against the counter, snatching a carrot from my cutting board.

"Watch it, you wouldn't want to lose a finger, would you?"

"Oh hush, you wouldn't cut me. I'm starving, what are you making?"

"I was just making a salad and cooked some chicken. I figured since we're eating big tomorrow we could eat light tonight."

"Excellent plan. I cannot wait for tomorrow. My mom was making a pecan pie when I left tonight. The house smells heavenly. God, I love pie."

"Yes, Ash, we know. Everyone knows how much you love pie. Want to eat in the living room?"

"Sure, take that in and I'll grab some drinks. No booze tonight, though. Laurel and I drank way too much wine last night. That girl is a lot of fun. It's too bad she was such a dud when she was with my brother. Maybe they wouldn't have broken up."

I don't respond to her statement and set our plates on the coffee table. Taking a spot on the couch, I remind myself that Laurel confirmed that the breakup was a good thing for both her and Ben. Regardless, the idea of them together stings just the same. Ashton joins me and places a glass of tea on the table.

"So, what's new? I know I haven't been around much, sorry. Heard from dickhead lately?" she asks, grabbing her plate and taking a bite of her salad.

"If you mean Tony, yeah, we had breakfast the other day."

Coughing while attempting to swallow her food, Ashton's eyes widen. I take mercy on her and explain.

"Oh, well, as long as you weren't like on a date or anything. You deserve better than him, Pipe."

"Thanks. What about you? Any new prospects?"

"Yeah, no. I'm on sabbatical from guys. Plus, I've been spending time with Laurel while she's staying with us. Ben's been working on his house non-stop. At this point he will be living there by Christmas."

"Wow, that seems fast."

"I know, but he's been working around the clock all week and I think he finally hired Jameson to have professionals finish it. Something is up with him. At first I thought it was having Laurel around, but they both told me it's not a big deal. He's been a grumpy asshole again so I assume his secret girlfriend dumped him. I wish I knew who she was so I could ask her to take him back."

"Secret girlfriend?" I ask, my stomach tightening at the idea of Ashton knowing about us.

"Yep. Didn't I tell you? Ben had some secret girlfriend. He basically disappeared for a few weeks and we hardly saw him. But when we did? He was happy and fun to be around. He reminded me of how he was when we were growing up. I liked him again. Now he's back to being boring and on edge."

I know the feeling. "Did he tell you he had a girlfriend?"

"Nah, I figured it out, but he didn't deny it either. I don't get the secrecy. I mean, unless she's married or something. Ben wouldn't do that though. He's the good guy."

"I agree. Maybe he just wanted to have something for himself. Keep it private for a while."

"That's ridiculous. We're family, why wouldn't he want us to meet her? Is he embarrassed by her? Oh my gosh! You don't think it's Felicity, do you? I heard her and the Mr. Thorne were having problems. Jenna Showalter was in Country Road the other night and said she was in Burlington last week shopping. She saw Felicity shopping at Target. I don't think she's stepped in a Target since 2003!"

We both laugh at that. I can't imagine seeing Felicity walking around Target decked out in her Gucci pushing a red shopping cart comparing toilet paper brands.

"We shouldn't laugh, but it is funny. Besides, I can guarantee it's not Felicity. At the school's Fall festival Ben was not impressed with her when she was rude to me."

"See, that's what I mean. Good guy. One day that good guy thing is going to bite him in the ass. His holier-than-thou noble attitude is going to screw him over and I'm going to laugh."

I was hoping there would be an opportunity for me to casually bring Ben up to Ashton tonight. I'm closer to deciding what to do with that ball in my court and this is the last part of that equation.

"That's funny. You're right though. He is a good guy. Did I ever tell you I had a crush on him?"

"Eww, on my *brother*?"

"Yep. Probably off and on from the time I starting liking boys."

"That's weird and a little gross." She visibly shivers and I laugh. "I guess I can see it though. You guys are totally alike. Plus, even I can admit he's not completely gross-looking. I mean, for my brother and all. Did you ever, you know, hook up or anything? This is a weird conversation."

"For the record no, your brother is far from gross-looking. You can relax, I never made a move on your brother." Truth. Well, semi-truth. I did beg him to have sex with me a few times. "Besides, it's not like I was ever on his radar anyway. You know it took me until I was in college to really have any confidence."

"I've never understood that but yeah, I remember. Well, this is an interesting development. Maybe you guys should get together. Then he'd stop being a complete jerk all the time."

Ashton's comment comes at the exact moment I take a drink. "What?" I spit out, along with half of my tea.

"I said maybe you guys should get together. But the more I think of it that would be weird. I mean what if you realize he's really disgusting and dump him. That would be really hard for him at holidays. Being alone when you were over instead of him."

She winks at me and I laugh. Maybe telling Ash would be a good thing.

"Just tell me if you decide you want to live out some teenage fantasy and make out with my brother. I'd need to prepare myself. Like maybe go into therapy or something.

I really hate surprises and may have to kick your ass if you spring it on me without warning. A year's warning, minimum."

Or not.

Ashton and I ended up staying up too late and she spent the night. Sharing a bed with Ashton Sullivan is not nearly the experience it is with Bentley Sullivan. My bed is large but Ashton has the ability to take up three quarters of it and kick a person enough to leave bruises.

After she left this morning I promised to come over early to help with dinner while the guys watched football. I'm going to use the next few hours to decide once and for all what I'm going to do about Bentley. I feel a shift in every aspect of my life today and I need to put my big girl panties on and take control of my life. There is really no room for self-doubt at this point. I need to put it all on the line and see what happens. No risk, no reward.

I decide to take a run to work off some of this tension. Instead of running in my neighborhood as usual I drive to the trails across town. I need to be in a more serene environment and this is it.

I warm up a little before I start off down the main trail. A winding three-mile path with a few hills to challenge me is exactly what I need. My running playlist is booming in my ears and my pace is quick as I make the last curve before the trail loops back around. Something to the left catches my attention and I blink a few times as the figure comes into focus. Ben.

Slowing my pace as I approach, I watch as a smile takes over his handsome face. It's been less than a week and I miss that smile. The feeling hits me hard and my already labored breath quickens under his guise.

"Hey," I say between breaths.

"Hi."

"How are you?"

"Okay, you?"

He doesn't look okay. He looks tired. Exhausted may be more accurate. Sad and maybe a little defeated.

"So, this is awkward," he comments, taking the words right out of my mouth.

"I know. I'm sorry, Ben."

"Want to walk back and talk? I have to get home to help my dad with some stuff before everyone comes over."

I nod in response and fall in step beside him. The trail is wide enough to allow us to walk side by side and not touch. I want nothing more than to reach out and grab his hand. To apologize for pushing him away. For jumping to conclusions about him and Laurel. I want to beg him to love me back. I don't.

"Piper, can you tell me what I did wrong? What changed?"

"Nothing changed. I just … I don't know. I'm so confused and my head is a mess. I am my own worst enemy and know that. I am who I am though, Ben. I just need some time to figure things out. Sort through it all and consider all possibilities."

Stopping, Ben sits on a nearby boulder and runs his hands through his hair. His beautiful dark-brown hair that is a little longer than it used to be. It's perfect. His scruff is neatly trimmed and I expect that was for his mom and today's dinner. I take this moment while he's silent to really look at him. I know under that shirt lays a set of abs to give Thor himself a run for his money. Just the thought of those abs has my breath quickening and wondering when the temperature rose.

"Are you done ogling me?"

"Whaa ... what?"

Softly laughing, Ben reaches for my hand. "It's okay. I miss you ogling me. God, Piper. How has it only been a week and I feel like it's been years? I miss you. Why are you pushing me away?"

I take his other hand in mine so we're holding hands. I take a step forward so I'm standing just before him, eye to eye.

"I'm not avoiding you, Ben. I'm avoiding us. It's all too much and overwhelming. I don't have the best track record and I'm scared."

"I know you're scared, Piper, but I promise this will all be okay. Trust me."

I let go of his hands and take a step back.

"I saw you."

I see confusion on his face.

"At the deli. With Laurel."

"Piper," he begins, but I stop him.

"It's okay. I talked to her and she explained why she's here. But I didn't like how I reacted to that. The way I felt and how upset I was. I don't want to feel like that, Ben."

"Nothing happened. Nothing *is* happening with Laurel. You have to know that, Piper." His voice is frantic and his face reflects the panic he's feeling.

"You said I should trust you. I do, Ben, and that's part of what scares me. I believe you when you promise you'll never hurt me. But the reality is you can't promise that."

I shake my head like I'm trying to clear my mind. "Not only that, we've gone about this all wrong. Lying to everyone for months, Ben. I know you kept the secret for me but I was wrong."

I feel the tears begin to form and a lump appears in my throat. Standing from his perch, he steps close to me. Putting a hand on either side of my face, his fingers in my hair, he tilts my face up to his, forcing me to look directly in his eyes. My hands go to his forearms, attempting to brace myself as a piece of my recently built wall cracks.

"Piper, I've let you use Ashton as an excuse long enough. Yes, she may be upset because we've been crap friends and lied. She may also have one of her dramatic responses and declare she's not going to speak to either of us for the rest of her life. None of that will be real, Piper. This isn't about Ashton and it hasn't been for a long time. This is about you and me. This is about you letting go."

I don't acknowledge his words as he continues.

"You're right. It is possible you'll get hurt. There's a possibility I'll get hurt. That's the risk we take. Regardless of what may happen, you have to believe. Believe in us. I can't promise things will be perfect or that there won't be some bumps in the road. I can promise that I will always be there with you and will never stop doing my best to make sure you're happy."

I swallow and will the tears to stay hidden.

"Piper, I don't want us to miss out on something that is so perfect because we are worried about what may happen or of hurting someone's feelings. At some point we have to put ourselves first. We deserve this. *You* deserve this."

I close my eyes as I absorb his words. It's quiet with the exception of the sounds of nature surrounding us and our own breathing. I take a deep breath and I open eyes to find him staring at me. A look so pure and loving my pulse speeds up.

Not allowing me to respond, he turns and takes off in a jog. No kiss, no hug, no declaration. I take the spot he vacated on the boulder and let his words settle.

Ben makes everything seem so simple and possible. I want to believe he's right, it just doesn't come natural to me. Risk for the reward, is it that simple?

Chapter 25

Ben

I'm done waiting. Although it was only a short period of time with Piper this morning, I know it's time to end this bullshit waiting game. It's grand gesture time and since we'll all be together tonight I don't think there is any reason to put it off. I'm going to need help and I know just the person to help me.

When I walk in the door from my run the kitchen is in chaos. Every year my mom goes all out for Thanksgiving dinner. Laurel and I opted to stay home the last few years so I kind of forgot the crazy that ensues.

"Hey, ladies, how's it going?" I ask as I open the refrigerator for a bottle of water.

"Save yourself, Ben! Mom's lost her mind!" Ashton responds dramatically.

"Hush up, Ashton, or I will throw this pie straight in the garbage!"

"Don't hurt the pie, Mom! It did nothing to you. I'll peel

the darn potatoes, relax!"

I catch Laurel laughing at the table, where she's snapping beans.

"Hey, Laurel, do you think you could step away from those for a few minutes? I mean if the drill sergeant here will allow it?" I ask, nodding toward my mom, who responds by throwing a piece of carrot at me.

"Bentley James, you better get out of my kitchen unless you want to start helping!"

"I'm going, I'm going. I'm stealing Laurel for a minute though."

"Fine, but not too long. We have a lot to do."

I nod and motion for Laurel to follow me. I walk up the stairs and straight to my room.

"Close the door, would you?"

"What's going on? I know you're all messed up over Piper but I'm not going to fool around with you, Ben."

"Funny. Sit. I want to talk to you about something."

She does and I spend the next twenty minutes relaying my conversation with Piper this morning and my plan for tonight.

"Wow, when you make the grand gesture you really go all out. What about your sister? Are you going to tell her? Your parents?"

"Ashton, no. My parents, yeah. I think I have to so they don't ruin the game plan."

"Agreed. I'm a little worried about Ashton's response though. She's spunky, but I can tell she's sensitive too. You know she's going to be pissed you've been keeping this from her for months, right?"

"Yeah, but this isn't about her. This is about Piper. I

need her to know I'm all in and I need her to take a leap of faith. Ashton loves us; she'll come around."

"I hope you know what you're doing. I'll help, but I'm going on the record with Ashton that I did not condone the secrecy."

"Noted. Now, go snap those beans so I can get to work."

We both leave my room and I go in search of my dad while she returns to the kitchen. It doesn't take long to hear the cursing from the back of the house. I turn the corner and find my dad with a pile of wood set to be split.

"Hey, Pops, need some help?"

"Oh thank goodness. I'm too old for this shit. Here, you split some of this wood so your mother can have her precious fire. I don't understand why she insists we do this every year."

"I don't know why you act like she won't. Why not keep a bunch of this already split? Move out of the way, I've got this. Besides, I wanted to talk to you about something."

"Sounds serious. Everything okay with Laurel?"

"Laurel's fine. I'm worried about her going home tomorrow but I know she has to. I just hope that asshole leaves her alone."

"You're a good man, Ben. Not everyone would have stepped up and invited her here. I think it's been good for her. Your mom and Ashton, too. They weren't always the warmest to her when you were together. They seem to really enjoy her now."

"I know and I'm grateful to all of you. I actually wanted to talk to you about someone else. Someone I've been seeing."

Silence develops between us as I split a few logs in quick

succession. Once I'm done I set the ax aside and turn to my dad.

"Like I said, I've been seeing someone. It's been kind of rocky the last few weeks or so but I'm ready to take it to the next level."

"The rocky part wouldn't have anything to do with Laurel coming to town, would it?"

I hadn't thought of that, though now that he mentions it, this did all start when Laurel and I first talked. I just assumed it was Piper's talk with her mom that started this, but it could be a combination. Interesting.

"I don't know exactly. We've been taking it slow and just spending time together alone. Kind of our own little world, if you will. I've been patient waiting for her make a commitment and really make a go of it. Unfortunately, I may have been too patient and she's managed to get inside her own head and now she's overanalyzed it so much she's backing away."

"Ahh, this woman wouldn't happen to be Piper, would it?"

"How did...?"

"There is only one person I know worth that kind of patience other than your sister. And, there is only person I know with the ability to get inside her own head enough to talk herself out of something like a relationship. I've known that girl most of her life and cared for as if she were my own. I knew something was going on with her when she stopped coming around as much. Now it just makes sense."

I sit down on the chopping log and take the water my dad offers me. Once I've emptied the bottle I lift my shirt to wipe the sweat from my head.

"Yeah well, that girl you mention is a frustrating woman."

My dad laughs. "I don't doubt it. All the good ones are. Your mother challenges me at every turn. I pity the man that falls in love with your sister."

I can't help but agree with that. Poor bastard. Dad and I sit in comfortable silence as I wonder if I've completely lost my mind to move forward with this plan of mine.

"I'm done waiting for her. I've agreed to take this painstakingly slow so that she warmed up to us being more than friends. Me being more than her best friend's brother. We both know Ash isn't going to take this well and wanted to make sure this was worth the drama it is about to create."

"I see. So you've been lying to your family and friends for months for Ashton's sake?"

Ouch. "When you put it like that, we sound like jerks."

"No, son, I don't think either of you are jerks. I truly believe that you both are putting Ashton's feelings ahead of your own. That's a little stupid, but it doesn't make you jerks."

"Stupid? I thought it was noble. And maybe a little selfish."

"Noble? Oh, Ben, you are grasping now. I think you're scared of your sister. Hell, she scares me sometimes and I'm her father. Look, here's how I see it. You've known Piper most of your life. She's been part of this family and like a sister to Ashton. You've been gone for years, just making the occasional appearance. We're all happy to have you home and you're afraid your sister is going to vote you off the island or something if you tell her you've fallen in love with her best friend."

"I never said I was in love."

"Are you?"

"I'll tell you what I've told Laurel and Jameson – if I am, then the first person I tell should be Piper."

"And that's the answer. Give your sister a little credit and accept that she's going to react, most likely poorly. But, she'll come around and in the end you'll have the one thing you've always wanted and deserved. True love."

"You're so certain it's true love?"

"Yes, son. I'm certain. You have your mother's and my blessing."

"Good, because I've decided I'm done waiting and there's no better time than Thanksgiving for a big declaration. I'm going to need you to help run a little interference though."

"Oh this sounds intriguing, tell me what you have planned."

I catch my dad up on my plan and let him know Laurel is in on it, too. He thinks it's brilliant and promises to clue my mom in a little so she doesn't ruin it. I'll make sure Jameson is in on the plan when he gets here. I check my watch and realize the next four hours are going to pass slower than any other time in my life.

Jameson was happy to play along with my plan and thinks the fact that everyone is in on it but Ashton is even sweeter. Those two need to get over their hatred of one another or this is going to be a long life.

Piper arrived a few hours ago. Not unlike every time I see her, she looked sexy as hell and I was instantly hard. I'm not sure how I'll get through life with a constant hard-on but I figure there are worse things in life. Once I managed to get my act together and calm down the activity in my pants, we exchanged a very awkward hello.

Now that I've managed to get her alone for a few minutes, I'm going to feel things out. Hopefully she'll give me some sort of indication of where she stands after our talk this morning.

"Hey, Princess." She startles a little.

"Oh, geez. You scared me. Hey."

"Sorry. What're you up to?" I ask as she turns her back to me again, looking in the oven. I begin walking up behind her as she responds.

"I'm just checking the rolls while your mom and Ash put the food out. You?" Her breath catches a little as I stand close to her back. I catch her reflection in the oven window and see she has her eyes closed. It's as if she's calming herself.

"Just waiting to eat. I'm starving."

"Uh, yeah, well good thing there's food. These are probably ready now."

"The timer says two minutes left."

"Oh, so it does."

"You look beautiful today, Piper. You know I love when you wear your boots," I whisper close to her ear and watch as she shivers. Good. That's the response I want.

"Ben," she sighs.

I place a kiss to her shoulder and walk away. I'm almost out of the room when I hear her groan and rest her head on her forearm against the handle of the oven. I start to whistle as I walk. That was the confirmation I needed to move forward with this plan.

Dinner is delicious as usual and the conversation is casual. Piper doesn't seem to be upset by our encounter in the kitchen earlier. She's sitting between Ashton and Jameson, which is enough to drive a person crazy, so each time she looks my way I try to reassure her it isn't forever. A few eye rolls from her confirm she is ready for us to finish up our meal.

While multiple conversations are occurring around us, Laurel catches my attention and raises her brows in question. I nod that it's time.

"So, what is the Sullivan after-Thanksgiving dinner tradition?" she inquires.

"We have pie in front of the fire," Ashton responds while reaching behind Piper to smack Jameson.

"Watch it, brat!"

"Kids, settle down. Ashton, stop being abusive," my mom says, then shrieks in horror and covers her mouth and looks at Laurel.

"Patty, it's fine. Jameson is a bit of a pest; I think Ashton should swat him."

Everyone laughs, but I can see the regret in my mom's eyes. Dad rises and walks over to her and pulls her into a hug while whispering reassurances. I glance at Piper, who has a confused look on her face. Laurel must recognize her expression, too.

"That's why I'm here, Piper. The man I was seeing recently had a bit of a violent side. The Sullivans offered me a place to regroup. I guess I didn't tell you that before, did I?"

"Oh, Laurel. I'm so sorry. That's awful. It's none of my business, please don't feel you have to explain."

"It's okay. This week has shown me what it's like to be

around a family and see true love," she says, glancing at my parents, who are holding each other now.

"Anyway, enough of that. Pie and fire? Is that it?"

"What else did you have in mind, dear?" my mom asks.

"Well, one of the things we've done after dinner the last few years with friends was play charades. Dinner is always so heavy and it's a great way to avoid the nap everyone wanted to take."

I smile at her and turn to Jameson, Piper, and Ashton across the table. Jameson is smiling like the Cheshire Cat while both Piper and Ashton look confused. Ashton speaks for both of them, "Charades? Really?"

"Yep, it's fun. We don't play the traditional version, though."

"Oh, is it strip Charades?" Jameson asks.

"Uh, no. But nice try. We don't limit the categories, anything is approved." She hesitates and looks at Jameson and clarifies, "Within reason, of course."

"What do you all say?" I ask then. "Feel like playing a little game? Oh, and there's one other rule, remember, Laurel?"

"Oh yes, we play teams of two and the teams can keep going until they have a wrong answer."

"That could take forever, why would you do that?" Ashton asks.

"You'd be surprised how entertaining it can be. Remember, there are no categories. Some answers are easy and others not so much."

"Sounds fun. Shall we move into the living room? All of this can wait until later," my mom says while looking directly at me and smiling. Now *she* looks like the Cheshire Cat.

Once we're settled in the living room, Laurel suggests the teams should be based upon the closest relationships. My parents are obviously a team and Laurel suggests since Ashton and Piper are so close they should be one too. That leaves either Laurel and me or Jameson and me. Jameson bows out and offers to be the time and score keeper, leaving Laurel and me as partners. After explaining the rules, which have never existed before this afternoon, Laurel stands and pulls out the bowl of clues she had placed on a shelf earlier.

"I guess you were prepared for us to play," Ashton jokes.

We rally back and forth between teams for the lead. After about thirty minutes everyone is having fun and laughing. I wonder if we should actually make this a tradition. Jameson announces to everyone that we are currently tied for the lead at three points each. Dad decides this is a great time for a break. His suggestion is perfect because it allows us to move our seats. I take the seat that puts me directly in Piper's sightline. As everyone returns to the room, Ashton notices everyone has moved. When she starts to take the spot that should be Piper's, my mom speaks up.

"Ash, why don't you sit next to me," she says, patting the spot next to her.

"Okay. Let's do this. Ben and Laurel, you're about to go down. Piper and I are going to wipe the floor with you."

"Ashton, hush up. It's not even your turn. Let your brother and Laurel have their turn. I swear, Paul, I don't know where she gets her sass."

Everyone laughs and I take a deep breath. Laurel steps up to me like she's giving me a pep talk.

"Ready for this?"

"As ready as I'll ever be. Did you pull the clues?" I ask.

"Yeah as soon as the girls left the room. Those are random words if I've ever seen any. I assume they are not the standard Charades list. You know, if we had ever actually played this game before," she laughs.

"They're random to you but they won't be to her."

"Alrighty, Laurel, you're up," my dad says, winking.

Chapter 26

Piper

I have to admit, when Laurel suggested Charades I was a little uncertain. I don't like being in front of a group of people acting like a fool. That's what I assumed it would be like, how I thought it would feel, but with the ability to add basic words and topics to the clues, Ashton and I have racked up a few points of our own and I'm having fun.

Now it's Ben and Laurel's turn. For people who have played this game a lot and as partners, they aren't all that great. I expected them to run away with the lead right away, but they didn't.

"Okay, Benny boy, let's do this. I feel good about this round," Laurel shouts.

Benny boy? That makes me cringe and Ashton looks at me and rolls her eyes. We both share a laugh before turning our attention back to Laurel.

Laurel stands at the front of the room and grabs a piece of paper. She holds up one finger to indicate it's one word.

Laurel begins her movements and I have no clue what she's doing. It's almost like she's tightening a rope.

"Bar!" Ben shouts and she high fives him.

I'm not sure how he got that, but whatever. This goes on for three more clues – whiskey, crying, phone. They are rolling through these clues when Ashton leans over and whispers to me. "I think they've been sandbagging; they're doing too good now."

I nod in agreement. The fact that Ben and Laurel are so in sync makes those uneasy feelings reappear. I find it difficult to look at them; jealousy is a crap feeling. Then I hear the next few words and my attention is drawn back to them. Selfie. Lake. Rocks. Running. I realize then that Ben is looking at me. He's not looking at Laurel at all.

"These are most random words ever," Ashton declares, leaning back in a huff. I do the opposite and move to the edge of my seat.

"Next word, Ben," Jameson says, handing Laurel another slip of paper.

Smiling and looking straight at me instead of at his partner, Ben says quietly, "Whiskey." Jameson hands her another paper. "Honey."

I feel the lump forming in the throat. My heart is in in my stomach, palms wet, warmth spreading through every pore of my skin. Another slip of paper.

"Heart."

I audibly take in air.

"What's happening?" Ashton asks, sitting up and realizing Ben isn't looking at Laurel but is giving answers.

Another clue.

"Forever."

The first tear falls. I look at everyone in the room. Paul and Patty are holding hands and both have tears in their eyes. Jameson has a huge smile on his face and nods in my direction. I look to Laurel, who is freely crying and smiles at me. I look up to Ben as Jameson holds up another slip of paper and lets it fall to the ground.

"Always."

I turn to Ashton, who looks confused and, for a moment, I feel horrible for what is about to happen. I may be sacrificing the single most important relationship in my life to date.

"Piper? Why are you crying? What the hell is happening around here?"

"Ashton, remember what you told me at my house the other night?"

"Uh, not really. We talk about all kinds of shit. You're freaking me out. Oh my God, is someone dying?"

"No, Ashton. I told you I would tell you before it happened. I didn't do that before and I'm sorry. But, I'm doing it now."

"Okay seriously, what are you talking about?"

"I'm going to kiss your brother," I say before I stand to walk toward Ben. I don't make it two steps before he's in front of me.

"Piper, I'm tired of being patient. I love you."

"I love you, too."

"Thank Jesus," is all I hear before he scoops me up and kisses me. This isn't a kiss with any doubt. This is a kiss of promises and forever. A kiss by the man I have loved all of my life and the only man I want to spend the rest of it with.

I hear a gasp and commotion behind me, but I'm too

wrapped up in this moment to even care. The kiss goes on for what feels like forever and equally not long enough. That's how it is with him. Everything feels like it can go on forever and yet it's never enough time.

He puts me down and does his thing with my hair. Gosh, I've missed that. I lean into his hand and he places another chaste kiss to my lips.

"Really?" he asks.

"Really. I'm sorry it took me so long to come around."

"Don't ever apologize for being true to yourself. I'm sorry I did it this way, but it was the only way I could guarantee you wouldn't shut me out again. I do love you, baby."

"I know." He raises a brow at me. "I do, Ben. I know you love me. I believe you. And I trust you." He kisses me again when we hear a throat clear and turn to see Paul standing there.

"Kids, while we couldn't be happier for you and glad you've found one another, there seems to be a little issue in the kitchen."

I turn to Ben. "I'll go. This is my mess to clean up."

"No, this isn't a mess, and we're in this together," he replies and turns to his dad. "We'll go talk to her." Before we leave the room I turn to Laurel.

"Thank you, Laurel."

She's still crying a little and nods as Paul puts his arm around her in comfort.

Ben and I enter the kitchen, where only Patty stands. She motions to the deck, and we see that Ashton is out there being consoled. By Jameson. Oh, this is worse than I thought it would be if she's letting him be her solace. We walk out the door and she turns to us, eyes red and puffy.

"Ash," I begin.

"How long?"

"It's not that simple, Ash. Please, can we go inside and talk?" Ben asks.

Ashton stubbornly holds her ground. When Jameson begins to put his arm around her, she swats him away. "I had a moment of temporary insanity. Don't get any ideas, man-whore." Jameson backs away with his hands up in defense.

"Whatever, Ashton. You don't have to be such a bitch about it."

Ignoring Jameson as he moves to the other side of Ben, she looks at Ben and then me.

"I'm fine here. Explain, if it's not that simple."

I don't even bother letting Ben attempt an explanation.

"Ashton, look, I know you're surprised and quite frankly I think we both are, too. We never meant to hurt you. If you want to be angry with someone, please be angry with me. Ben wanted to tell you and I asked him not to."

"Tell me what exactly, Piper? You've been seeing my brother long enough to make some sort of declaration in front of everyone and embarrass me. It's obvious everyone else is in on this so guess the joke's on me, isn't it?"

I begin to answer her, but she doesn't give me the chance.

"I thought we were like sisters? What changed? We tell each other everything, for shit's sake, Piper! Instead you're fooling around with my brother behind my back? That's great."

"You're right," I begin as she arches a brow at me. "We are like sisters, but nothing changed. I just … I don't even know. I was scared. This is so much more than I can explain right now. But, I want you to know that I wasn't fooling around with your brother. I love him, Ash," I say as I reach for Ben's hand, her eyes following.

"How long?"

"Actually together?" Ben asks and she nods.

"Since Halloween," I answer.

"That's not even a month! How do you fall in love in less than a month?" Ashton huffs.

"You don't," Ben answers, squeezing my hand and looking at me. "You do it in an instant."

"Jesus. You're really something, big brother," Ashton scoffs.

Huffs and scoffs, I'm sensing a pattern and quite frankly it's a little childish.

"Ashton, I'm not going to apologize for falling in love. I love your brother," I say, looking at Ben before I turn my attention back to Ash. "And crazy enough, he loves me. Did we plan this? Nope. Did I ever dream this would happen? No way. When this first started I tried to stop it. I tried to not like him or care about him. I did that because I never allowed myself to believe it would be reciprocated. There was no way in this world that Bentley Sullivan would have any kind of feelings for me. I'm Pathetic Piper, nowhere near his league."

"Baby," Ben begins to respond, but I stop him and turn back to Ashton, who is crying again.

"Why would you say that about yourself, Piper? You're perfect and my idiot brother would be lucky to have you."

"That's how I felt, I can't explain it." I release Ben's hand and take a few tentative steps toward Ashton. "Then, we started spending time together. Just as friends. When it was becoming more, he wanted to tell you and get your blessing. I wouldn't let him. I was convinced that it was short-lived and there was no need for us to create drama for something that was never going to last."

Wiping her tears, Ashton looks between us before responding. "You wanted my blessing, Ben?"

"Of course, Ash," he says, stepping up behind me and placing his hands on my shoulders. "You're important to both of us and we know this is going to change things. I wanted you to know how I felt, but I respected Piper's request to not tell you. I made her give the secrecy a deadline and everything. I knew this would be hard on you."

"You guys lied to me," she says with a small amount of acceptance in her voice.

"We did and I'm sorry for that. It was not with malice, I promise," I reply as I take the final step toward her and put my arms around her in a hug. A hug she eventually reciprocates.

"You are my very best friend in this world. I am so sorry I lied to you. I've never lied to you before. Well, not true. I did tell you that I like you in that sweater dress. I don't. It's awful. You should burn it."

Laughing a little, she sniffles and pulls away from me.

"You don't? But I love that dress."

I laugh too and hug her again, "Forgive me? Us? I really love him, Ashton. But if you can't give us your blessing, I understand."

"Oh Jesus, shut up. I'm just caught off-guard and felt stupid. I was the only person in that room that didn't know what was happening. I was just embarrassed and it's a lot to take in. I mean, I thought you only had a crush on him growing up. I didn't know you loved him."

Wiping her eyes and nose, she stands taller. "I'll get used to it. Oh my God! Are you guys going to get married? We'll be real sisters!"

I shake my head at her. That's Ashton, one extreme reaction to another. Ben walks up behind me and places his hands around my waist, resting his head on my shoulder. "Yes, you will be."

I gasp and look at him.

"My, my, it appears I'm not the only one in the dark around here. I'm going inside now; it's freezing out here."

She grabs Jameson by the arm and drags him in the house. I turn to watch them walk in, arguing the whole way, and find myself in Ben's embrace now.

"What do you mean, we will be?" I ask.

"Don't worry, I'm not proposing, too."

He must sense my relief because he laughs. "Don't be so relieved. It's going to happen, just not today."

"Oh you're so sure of that, are you?"

"Absolutely. This is it, Piper. You and me, baby. Always."

"Ben?"

"Yeah?"

"Do your thing with my hair and kiss me."

He complies and I melt into him. Thanksgiving is now my favorite holiday.

Chapter 27

Three weeks later …

Ben

"I think that's the last of the boxes," I say, standing in the doorway of the one place I know I can always find Piper. Tracing the intricate design of the stained glass on the kitchen door of the farmhouse, she turns and smiles at me. The sun casts a beam of light right on Piper in the room and falls on her perfectly. The sight never ceases to take my breath away. She's beautiful. And she's mine.

The last few weeks have been a whirlwind. Once we settled things with Ashton at Thanksgiving, we locked ourselves away for a few days before returning to work. I also managed to convince her that we could move into the main floor of the house and give up her apartment. It'll be a little longer before we can move into the master bedroom, but we have a functioning bathroom and kitchen here so it's no different than staying at her apartment.

She finally relented and, after offering to put in a good word with the landlord to transfer the lease to Ashton, who passed, she put her notice in on her apartment. The last part of business with our relationship was disclosure at work. The principal offered congratulations but did warn us that all relationship turmoil was prohibited at work.

True to my word, I found an old phonebook that Piper reads to me every night. She thinks I'm crazy but I wasn't kidding when I said I could listen to her voice every day and never tire.

I walk toward Piper and put my hands around her waist as she leans back into me.

"I love this kitchen."

"I do, too. And I love you."

"I know; I love you, too, Ben."

Piper

If anyone had told me a month ago that I'd be living with Bentley Sullivan, I would have called for the straight jacket myself. To think I'm not only in love with the man of my dreams, literally, but living with him at his farmhouse, *our farmhouse*, is even more unbelievable.

I've never been happier and am so grateful Ashton has a forgiving heart. I really messed up with my decision to keep things from her, and although it's a little awkward sometimes, everyone is adjusting and we're moving forward.

Yesterday was chaotic and stressful. We were lucky

enough to have moving day fall on the same day as the first snow of the season. Ben tried to convince me as we fell into bed exhausted that it was a positive thing. A sign of new beginnings and a clean slate.

I'm slowly waking up when I realize what has actually stirred me awake. Ben's hands are under my T-shirt and his mouth is feasting on my nipple. I sigh and my hands find the top of his head. Sex with Bentley Sullivan is nothing short of euphoric. Morning sex with Ben is my favorite way to start the day.

"Morning," he mumbles, never taking his mouth from me.

"Hmmm," I reply as the warmth takes over my body and my back arches.

He pushes my shirt up farther and I help him by taking the hem and pulling it over my head. I lay back down as he positions himself between my legs. I feel exactly how awake all of him is this morning as my knees drop open and my foot rubs the back of his shin. His lips find my neck and the sounds filling the room add to the intensity building inside me.

Each movement of his hips pushing more into me, the only barrier my panties, sends waves of pleasure through me. I reach for the sides of my panties and begin tugging them off; he helps. Before the flimsy piece of lace makes it off my leg, he thrusts into me. I'll never tire of the feeling of Ben inside me. Filling me, each movement bringing me closer to the edge, each touch of his hand on my body sending shivers through my body. I'm reminded with each movement that we're connected in a way that goes beyond physical.

"Oh God, Ben."

I sigh as my orgasm takes over. He follows right after me. We lay like that for what feels like minutes before he lifts himself up and kisses me.

"Morning, baby."

"I love morning," I reply, to which he laughs.

I begin to throw the covers back when Ben's arm snakes around my waist.

"Where are you going?"

"I was going to use the restroom. I'll be right back."

"Stay," he says as he begins nuzzling my neck.

I wiggle out from his arm and toss my T-shirt back on before heading for the restroom. I can tell from the amount of sunshine we've slept later than usual. Thankfully it's winter break and we have a few weeks off.

I return to bed, curling up beside Ben. As my hand snakes around his waist, I feel the waistband of his boxer briefs and smile. More sleep sounds great. I'm only in this position a second before my eyes close and I'm drifting to slumber. A dip of the bed jars me and I slightly open my eyes to see Ben reaching for something on the floor.

"What are you doing?" I ask while watching his back muscles move as he leans down. I am a lucky girl.

Without answering me he turns his attention toward me with a mischievous grin.

"What are you up to, Mr. Sullivan?"

"Funny you should ask, Miss Lawrence. Do you know what this week is?"

"Christmas."

"Yes, but what else?"

"Christmas Eve? I don't know, Ben. I was just falling

back to sleep."

"Don't be crabby," he replies, laying a kiss to my nose. "It is also the deadline I gave you to decide if we were going to make this relationship happen."

"Oh, it sure is. We're ahead of schedule, that's good," I say, snuggling into my pillow and closing my eyes. Then I feel something next to my face and open my eyes. Ben's up on his knees now, facing me, completely glorious in only his boxer briefs and a smile. I let out a groan.

"Ogling me, baby?"

"Hush, you like my ogling."

"I do. I left you a present, did you see?"

I look over on my pillow and gasp. Sparkling in the sunlight is an exquisite diamond ring. My hand goes to my mouth and Ben grabs my hand and tugs me so I'm mimicking his stance in front of him. Taking the ring from my pillow, he holds it between two fingers as he looks me directly in the eyes. His expression is serious and the love I see in his eyes is overwhelming. Beyond my control, the tears begin to fall.

"Piper, I tell you every single day how much I love you. How my life is complete and has meaning now that you're in it. What I don't tell you is that I never knew true happiness until I met you. *Again.* You are the single most amazing person I have ever known. Each day you tell me you love me back is a gift. A gift I will never take for granted. I want to live in this house with you. I want to build a family and have babies with you. I love you always. Will you marry me, Princess?"

"Oh, Ben. I love you so much. You have been the man in my dreams my entire life and the moment you walked back into my life you made my dreams a reality. Cowboy, it would be my dream come true to call you my husband. Yes, I will marry you."

Ben sighs in relief, as if he expected my answer would be anything other than yes. With the ring placed on my finger, I gasp at its beauty. I look up into the eyes of the man who melts my heart and fulfills my every desire. I see forever and beyond in his eyes. I believe in true love because of this man. He is my happily ever after.

The End.

From the author

Thank you for taking the time to read Ben & Piper's story. Inspiration hit me at a very strange time and by the opening lyrics of a simple country song. I knew from word one that this was a love story that I had to tell. What I didn't expect was Laurel. While Laurel makes a small appearance, her story and presence are a turning point that I felt compelled to tell.

Tackling a topic such as domestic violence is not something I take lightly. The fact that we have to talk about this topic hurts my soul to its very core. As adults in a modern society it shames me to know that women and men continue to be abused by the words and hands of those they love and share their life with.

Please, if you or someone you know is being abused please contact The National Domestic Violence Hotline / www.thehotline.org / 1-800-799-7233.

Andrea

Acknowledgments

I am destined to forget someone in this section and for that I apologize. I'm so sorry!

First, none of this is possible without you, the reader. Thank you from the bottom of my heart for taking a chance on me and my books. I never expected this to be my life and I promise to never take it for granted. Thank you.

They say it takes a village to care for a (book) baby. My village rocks!! I have the privilege to work with a talented and amazing team - my amazing editor Kristina Circelli of Red Road Editing, formatting genius Stacey Blake of Champagne Formats, the extremely talented Alyssa Garcia of Uplifting Designs, promotional powerhouse Erin Spencer of Southern Belle Promotions, and last but not least, my patient and encouraging assistant, Stacy Garcia. Ladies, thank you for taking this journey with me.

Christine – I appreciate you every single day. Thank you for supporting me and keeping me grounded when I'm headed over the ledge!

Alyssa & Stacy – Girls … I do not know that there are words for me to express my gratitude and appreciation for both of you. Each day with you in my life is a blessing. Thank you for loving Ben & Piper and encouraging me to tell their story. Amy & Kiersten - This is the hardest for me as words cannot express how very much I love you both. The day you clicked into my life (shout out to Facebook) it changed for the better. You make me laugh every day, thank you. #TeamBiper always

Kacey and Jennifer thank you for your friendship, support and eagle eyes. You are incredible and I am grateful for each of you.

Suzie - I cry as I type this because I am overwhelmed each time I realize you are in my life. You make me a better person and inspire me each day. Thank you for the endless laughs, love, and Bravo talks. You have a piece of my soul always, I love you.

Heather – I will never believe that we went decades without each other in our lives. I am in awe of your talent and creativity. I value you more than I can express. I am honored to call you my friend. Thank you for sharing this crazy world with me. Xo

Jeanne – Thank you for always answering my ridiculous questions and for supporting me. I adore and appreciate you.

Andee – My unicorn! I am forever grateful for your friendship. I am convinced we are destined for great times together. With wine, of course.

Sassy Romantics –Thank you ladies for being part of my journey. You rock my socks!

To my boys - You will always be the lights of my life. You make me proud every day.

About the Author

Andrea Johnston spent her childhood with her nose in a book and a pen to paper. An avid people watcher, her mind is full of stories that yearn to be told. A fan of angsty romance with a happy ending, super sexy erotica and a good mystery, Andrea can always be found with her Kindle nearby fully charged.

Andrea lives in Idaho with her family and two dogs. When she isn't spending time with her partner in crime aka her husband, she can be found binge watching all things Bravo and enjoying a cocktail. Nothing makes her happier than the laughter of her children, a good book, her feet in the water, and cocktail in hand all at the same time.

Connect with Andrea on

Facebook at www.facebook.com/andreajohnstonauthor

Twitter at Twitter.com/AndreaJ1313

Instagram at Andrea_Johnston15

e-mail her at andreajohnstonauthor@gmail.com.

Join Andrea's reader group
Andrea Johnston's Sassy Romantics : http://bit.ly/AJsSassy

Other Books by

andrea johnston

Life Rewritten

Spring Break (Phoebe & Madsen Part 1)

COUNTRY ROAD SERIES:

Whiskey & Honey (A Country Road Novel – Book 1)

Tequila & Tailgates (A Country Road Novel – Book 2)

Martinis & Moonlight (A Country Road Novel – Book 3)

Champagne & Forever (A Country Road Novella)